A POWER IN TH

Stuart Prebble was
English Language
of Newcastle upon Tyne, then joined the
trainee journalist and worked for several years as an on-screen reporter in the North-East and on national television news. In 1981 he joined Granada Television where he now works as a Producer/ Director in current affairs.

Stuart Prebble lives in Cheshire with his wife Marilyn and their two daughters. This is his first novel.

STUART PREBBLE

A Power in the Land

FONTANA/Collins

NOTE

This is a work of fiction. All the characters and institutions in this novel are wholly imaginary and are not intended to bear any resemblance to any real person, living or dead, or any company or government body.

First published by Fontana Paperbacks 1988

Made and printed in Great Britain by
William Collins Sons & Co. Ltd, Glasgow

for Marilyn

CHAPTER ONE

In the gloom and drizzle of an autumn afternoon the group of mourners trudged wearily towards the churchyard gate. The twelve men held their heads slightly bowed, caps or hats in their hands, exposing bare heads to the rain. A little ahead, six more men in worn and shabby black suits marched slowly along, stooping under the weight of their burden. The coffin was of dark heavy wood. Ornate brass handles reflected the distorted shapes of huge monuments which loomed up and then disappeared.

As the procession made its way steadily forward through the ancient and ramshackle churchyard, heavy shoes trampled over weeds peeping through cracks in the neglected path.

Weatherworn headstones recalled days of glorious lament and extravagant grief. 'In memory of Elizabeth Ann McBride, our beloved mother, who died aged 76, on 7 September 1896'. 'George Ernest Armstrong, who went to sleep aged 66 on 4 August 1908'. Here and there a wingless angel or decomposing cherub presided as nature won her quiet victory over the stone and beneath the earth, returning ashes to ashes and dust to dust.

At last, as if by silent consent, the group left the path and newly buffed shoes of coarse black leather squelched into the mud. Trouser turn-ups were spattered with the dew and dirty rain. One man tightened the knot of his white muffler in a vain attempt to keep out the chill. Moving between the graves, the procession crept on and turned an unmarked corner. The priest began murmuring quietly and monotonously from the text of a tiny black volume which he held cupped before him as he walked. His long black robes soaked up the damp and mud as he shuffled on with the silent group trailing close behind.

In a distant corner of the churchyard two workmen stood with elbows resting on their shovels. As the mourners approached they stopped talking and edged silently away towards a clump of trees. One man reached into his jacket pocket and offered his friend a cigarette. They leant close together to prevent the wind from extinguishing the match.

The procession came steadily on towards the mound of dark earth. Beside it was a canvas sheet, weighed down on each corner by building bricks. The priest took his place at one end of the canvas while the rest of the group held back, apparently reluctant to approach the graveside. The penetrating wind whined softly among the headstones. One of the more elderly pall-bearers let out an involuntary grunt of effort as they laid down their burden, by clumsy stages, on to the grass.

Twenty yards away Anthony Shilvers stepped a pace forward for a clearer view. He had witnessed the whole commonplace event with particular interest, but had deliberately kept himself apart from the intimacy of shared grief. Now he saw for the first time the slight figure of the only woman in the company. Dressed in a dark coat and brimless hat, her face appeared to be tortured by her grief. Her iron grey hair was scraped back with startling severity, emphasizing the sharpness of her features.

The priest embarked on the soft words of the committal, the sound muffled by the rustle of slow rain falling through the bare branches. As Shilvers moved closer to hear the words, his shoes sank into the mulch of sodden leaves. The woman's clear blue eyes stared fixedly at some invisible point above the grave. Seldom blinking, they seemed unaware of the droning monologue from the priest, who paused only to wipe away the perspiration and rain from his brow.

As he spoke, the mourners huddled together at the graveside for mutual comfort, a lonely oasis of humanity in a desolate landscape of decaying stones. Deep lines on their faces betrayed the difficulties of life in a place where survival was a bitter struggle against the elements.

Next to the woman was a tall and gaunt man with wavy grey hair, dressed in an ill-fitting black suit with unfashionably wide lapels. A waistcoat hung loosely against his spare frame. He too wore a linen scarf tied tightly around his neck. His frequent nervous and concerned glances brought no response from the stony face of his companion. The other men at the graveside shared a common dejected sadness. As they gazed steadily forward they occasionally winced away the rain which drizzled down their faces.

At last the priest was silent, and at a signal the pall-bearers stepped forward to take their places around the heavy coffin. Each picked up an end of the lengths of dirty red rope which trailed across the mud beneath it. Fixed to the lid of the coffin was a small brass plaque bearing a message for some curious grave-digger of the future: 'Alfred Norman Penshall. Born 21 March 1926. Died 16 November 198–'.

One of the bearers walked to the far side of the grave and began to roll up the wet and muddy canvas which covered the gaping hole in the earth. Shilvers could not prevent himself from leaning over to peer into the ditch. As he did so a cold blade seemed to enter his body, overlaying the chill he already felt. It had been raining steadily for days, and the hole was flooded with dirty water, which now lapped against the clay walls.

Shilvers took another step forward as if to intervene, but he flinched back as the bearers brought their load towards the grave and began, with irreverent haste, to lower it. There was a slight splash as the heavy wooden box hit the water and briefly submerged, only to float quickly up again, buffeting the sides of the ditch. The whole company stared into the hole, stunned into silence, until finally the coffin seemed to half-turn like a crippled battleship and then sank beneath the murky water.

The coffin vanished from sight, and the water closed around it and was calm again. For what seemed many moments even the rain appeared to have stopped rustling through the trees, and the group formed a grey tableau of horror. Then there came from among the mourners a cry that grew louder and became a piercing shriek which rent the silence, and went on and on, shuddering at last into a choking sob. Several of the men reached out towards the woman as she collapsed forward on her knees at the graveside. Her face was contorted into a grimace of agony and her lips quivered as her crying renewed. With arms flailing wildly she pushed against the men in what seemed an attempt to get near enough to reach down into the water.

Shilvers looked away. The tortured faces about him reflected his own heartache as the sobs gradually subsided into pathetic whimpers. The men raised the widow from her knees, mud staining their clothes and hers. At last she turned her gaze from the grave towards the face of the man beside her. They exchanged a brief and agonized look and then she threw herself into his arms, burying her head in his embrace.

The others could only stand in anguished silence. They remained still for a few moments before retracing their steps towards the row of black cars waiting beyond the cemetery gates. The only sound as they walked was the spasmodic whimpering of the woman, who was leaning on the arm of the thin old man. The rain had stopped.

As they reached the cars, Shilvers withdrew a few paces. He watched as the woman was led towards the nearest car, and the rear door was opened for her. She did not get in, but turned, apparently more in command of herself, to take her leave. One by one the men stepped forward and took her hand, muttering a few words as they did so. The woman said nothing.

It was only when the main group of mourners had spoken to her that another man, who had not been at the graveside, stepped forward. He was tall and smartly dressed in a heavy black overcoat, but his shoes were city shoes, in contrast to the rougher wear of the local men. He was in his early fifties, with carefully styled greying hair and a face which lacked the rough crags of a man who has worked on the land. He looked out of place among this gathering, and his demeanour betrayed his discomfort. Nevertheless he approached the woman, who was now preparing to get into the car. Noticing him, she stopped and turned. Her head, which had been bowed, came up to face him and Shilvers saw that the look of vulnerability was gone. Her mouth tightened.

The newcomer stood a foot away from her, his gloved hands

held behind his back. He spoke a few quiet words. Shilvers watched as he appeared to finish his remarks and tilted his head downwards in a slight bow of respect. As he did so the woman swiftly and suddenly brought up her arm and struck him a heavy blow to the side of his face. The man gasped and drew smartly back, raising his fingertips to the already reddening skin. One of the group stepped forward as if to assist him, but he stood upright, and with a stiff bow to the woman, turned abruptly away towards a dark-red limousine.

A chauffeur in brown uniform stood motionless by the car, as shocked as the rest of the group by what he had seen. As the man approached he collected himself and swung open the back door. Even as the man sank behind the tinted windows of the car, Shilvers saw him once again raise his hand to the side of his head where he had been struck. For only a moment Shilvers thought the man was looking directly back at him. A few seconds later the car had turned around, skidding on the gravel, and was speeding away into the distance.

No one spoke as the company slowly climbed into the old black cars. Shilvers looked up into the dull sky. In the distance a helicopter whirled apparently silently beneath the low clouds. It hovered motionless, and then wheeled away.

Later, as Shilvers drove his car through the drizzle of the dead end of the day, those traumatic events in a churchyard in Cumbria crowded in on his mind. The narrow and winding country lanes led him back to the tiny coastal village of Winderwath. As he recalled the haunting expression of grief and despair on the widow's face at the graveside, and then her look of hatred and horror at the outsider in the expensive car, he resolved to do whatever he could to find out, and publish, the full truth behind the death of Alfred Norman Penshall.

CHAPTER TWO

Deep deep deep below the surface of the good earth the long low vibration began like the distant menacing growl of an ill-tempered wild beast wakened prematurely from a fitful sleep.

Beneath the heavy tortoiseshell frames which were contoured to meet the flesh all around his eyes, a small nerve in the corner of Dr Smedley's left eyelid twitched invisibly behind dark shaded lenses. The rest of his distorted features remained motionless and unresponsive to the faraway but now constant pulse beneath his feet.

Smedley had to turn his head to forty-five degrees to check whether his colleagues had noticed it too. Nothing in their reactions suggested that they had. He turned once again to squint at the mass of readouts and dials in front of him, his left eye still twitching independently in what had become a familiar irritation since the accident. The extensive and permanent scarring which marked the entire left side of his face was at least no longer painful, the nerves beneath the tissue having long since been deadened in repeated surgery.

Dr Smedley placed his hands flat on the metallic surface of the console in front of him. There could be no mistake. Though remote and hard to define, the vibration now seemed to him to be almost audible. He pressed his feet hard against the tiled floor and could feel the movement travel into his legs and up through his body. A further check on the instruments indicated nothing amiss.

His mind rehearsed the personal nightmare which was his on every occasion that a warning light indicated the most trivial fault anywhere in the complex, involving anything from the air-conditioning to the core of the entire process. Like a sophisticated computer Smedley's brain scanned every formula, every joint, every reaction and every assumption in the research. For the thousandth time he reached the conclusion that logically nothing could be going wrong. Yet he knew that logic would not carry the conclusion 100 per cent of the way. His was, after all, a journey into the unknown. All he could do was to check, recheck, and check again the calculations on which the whole thing was based. Even so the inescapable fact kept recurring that nobody had ever done all this before; at the end of the day there had to be the possibility, though not a computable possibility, that two and two would make five and the whole thing could go very badly wrong.

Smedley's hands were still flat on the panel in front of him. Had the vibration gone away? He could not be sure. Once again he looked around. A dozen scientists, all men, all wearing white overalls like himself, were going about their normal business. Could he have imagined it? Now he was not even sure. The nightmare had, in recent months, come increasingly to inhabit his waking hours. Now there was no trace of the hum beneath his outstretched fingers. The twitch in his left eye had come to rest.

The left hand of Dr Smedley now withdrew from the flat smooth surface in front of him and gently probed the side of his face beneath his protective glasses. The accident had left his sight impaired, but the rest of his faculties undamaged. Only the horrific scarring was now his constant reminder of it. He thought about what the company doctors had told him. The trauma would be bound to have long-term effects. The accident was undoubtedly the explanation for his continuing unease about safety procedures. He really would have to keep coming back for regular chats to get the problem aired and eventually sorted out. He was, after all, their best man and completely indispensable to the project. They could hardly allow him to take the early retirement which had been afforded to so many others.

Smedley thought about retirement. He thought about his months away during convalescence and shuddered at the prospect.

He became aware that his fingers were still lightly probing

the crags and ridges of his scars, and his eyes turned to the photograph which was always somewhere near him, at his work or in his home. The unblemished beauty of the face which smiled at him was that of his daughter Jacqueline. She had joined the company just after his accident two years ago. Though he had argued with her and pleaded with her and even made a futile attempt to instruct her, she had insisted. Even before the accident he would have been reluctant to have her in the industry, but since it had happened he had wanted her as far away as possible.

Jacqueline had been polite but unyielding. She had a first-class honours degree in chemistry and was an ideal recruit. She wanted to enjoy the opportunities that only the company could give her. After all, he had benefited from them and had turned out to be one of the most distinguished and admired scientists in his field. Why should he try to deny them to her?

Smedley stopped short of using the accident as a weapon in his argument. It had not stopped him from going on, so why, in fairness, should it stop her? He knew that his only answer would have no effect on her. She was a woman, and to him, the most beautiful woman in the world. Her small pretty features and her blonde hair cut so short looked to him exactly as they had when she was twelve years old and they played together on the beach during the holidays. In his mind she had hardly changed at all.

The death of her mother when Jacqueline was fifteen had made her grow up very fast. She had become much more independent, much more fierce and uncompromising. He had been at first puzzled and then glad when Jacqueline told him that she was taking her mother's maiden name as her own for the sake of her future career. It was in part a tribute to her mother's efforts to encourage her education, and in part a wish not to enjoy privileges afforded to her on the strength of her father's reputation. Both were sentiments he could respect and be proud of.

Dr Graham Smedley's conversations with Jacqueline Smart were now unusual ones for father and daughter. They shared the same employer, but not the same house. They shared the same professional interests but not the same surname. They shared an enthusiasm for the benefits the research could and was bringing to the industrialized world but were not allowed, for sensible reasons of security, to discuss each other's immediate responsibilities. So he did not know for certain precisely which area his daughter worked in, and she did not know exactly what her father was involved in. Though they worked in the same plant, weeks could in fact go by without them even seeing each other.

The sudden howl of a siren on the works floor a hundred feet below made Smedley jump visibly in his seat. Instantly he realized his stupidity and took a deep breath. It was the end of the day-shift and all around him colleagues were already handing over clipboards to the night-shift. Graham Smedley decided to do just a few hours in the lab before going home to his empty house.

CHAPTER THREE

Anthony Shilvers had come to the West Cumbrian village of Winderwath six weeks earlier to work on a series of articles about that part of the world. It was a commission from the Tourist Board.

Working as a freelance journalist had its good times and it had its bad times. Working for the Tourist Board was somewhere near the latter. It was not as depressing as working night-shifts for the *Daily Sentinel*, which still called him in at times of need even though he had left the staff five years before. On the other hand it was not as attractive as a recent trip to Holland paid for by a glossy colour supplement to investigate why Dutch housewives seem to prefer to do their weekend shopping in the supermarkets of the south-east of England.

In fact the job for the Tourist Board had come at a good time for Shilvers. His name was well enough known and his reputation good enough to be sure that he would never really want for work, but this was a job which would take a few weeks or months rather than a few days and would give him a chance to blow away the city cobwebs. That, anyway, was the way it had seemed at the time.

Winderwath had been his own choice because he had visited the place more than thirty years earlier as a child on holiday with his parents. It had not changed much. He remembered it as a rugged, exposed and poor village resting precariously on the edge of the great and angry ocean. The people were polite, but in a reserved and even suspicious way. They were private people with little in common with the outside world, but bound together by a lifetime of struggle against cruel sea winds and thin poor soil. It seemed as though the pounding might of the Atlantic had extinguished whatever flame there may once have been within them, and now they were content to live their lives around the whim of the elements, turning up their collars and closing their shutters against the cold wind.

The huge bay below Winderwath brought giant waves smashing against the cliffs, which were gnarled and worn like bony fingers spread out to protect the faces of the people hiding for shelter behind them. The wind was wet and penetrating as it roared off the sea.

This was how it was for three seasons of the year, but in the short months of early summer the countryside could be as picturesque and delightful as any in that beautiful county. Then the wild daffodils would bravely pop up their heads and welcome the few tourists who ventured away from the well-worn routes which meandered through the mountains and valleys of central Cumbria. Now though, it was the closing of the year, and the shrouded figure of winter had come prowling back to his familiar haunt. Once more the faces took on the grim expression which seemed to echo and deepen the depressing shadows over the barren moorland.

Shilvers had rented a holiday cottage about half a mile above the village to the north, approachable only by a narrow footpath and facing the ocean over a huge craggy drop. The owner had been only too pleased to let the place for a nominal rent because his normal season had ended weeks earlier. When Shilvers arrived the cottage had already been boarded up for the winter. The owner told him that it had at one time been home for a shepherd who had worked the barren and exposed moors above the village. The soil was now too poor and what grass there was too coarse for more than a handful of the most hardy sheep, and the shepherd had long since retired to the village.

The cottage was a tiny building of local stone which had been roughly covered with cement and painted white. The door seemed to have been hammered together from ill-fitting planks, and the constant wind from the sea sang an unending chant through the crevices. There was just one small window on each side of the door, and an almost flat roof of rough quarry slate made the single-storey building appear even lower than it really was. A chimney at one end completed the ideal cottage which a child might have drawn.

The main door led directly into the single sitting-room. In one corner an alcove had been converted with more enthusiasm than skill into a kitchenette. Imitation tile-facing on hardboard had been nailed to the walls around an old enamel sink, and a miniature electric stove completed the landlord's interpretation of 'all mod cons' as advertised on a yellowing postcard in the window of the village post office.

One door of the living-room led to a small bedroom at the back of the cottage. A tiny window high up in the wall looked out on to the moorlands behind. A tall and lumpy bed with an accidentally beautiful brass bedhead took up most of the room, and a white laminated wardrobe and dressing-table looked out of place crowded up against it. The only other room, accessible from either the bedroom or the sitting-room, was a bathroom, also at the back of the cottage. Typically it was also cramped and cheaply fitted out, but Shilvers soon discovered that after the water had run rusty it would run muddy, and after it had run muddy it would run clear.

'Perfect,' he had told his landlord when he saw it for the first time.

'You'll find it easy to heat,' said the solicitous old man, opening the door of the iron stove with a flourish. 'Plenty of wood chopped and ready out the back, and you'll get lots of peace and quiet since that's what you're wanting. You're out of the way, see, and people round these parts keep themselves very much to themselves.'

Shilvers had started his work, studying records of the local history, but generally spending his days without exertion. He was determined to smoke less, drink less, and allow the penetrating wind to blow away the crowded city from his mind.

As far as he could see this was an area which had been totally untroubled by twentieth-century life. The same farms were often owned under the same family names for many generations. George Bowness had owned the village smithy in 1848. James

Bowness had taken it over in 1880. Another George Bowness had become owner in 1915 but had been killed in the Great War. Arthur Bowness had carried on the tradition until 1943 and there, sure enough, on the edge of the village green, was a forge belonging to Andrew Bowness. Shilvers felt enthusiastic as he scribbled down the details for inclusion under the 'industrial heritage' section of his work.

The commission had been a sensible one. Nobody wanted to portray West Cumbria as the Las Vegas of the country, nor was the idea to attract people who wanted to sit on beaches or ride donkeys and model railways between the crazy golf and the candy floss stall. There was no beach, no donkey ride, and certainly no fairground. Shilvers had advised that the appeal of this part of the world had to be the opportunity for peace and quiet in an unspoilt community of real people; the chance for an easy-going break, with perhaps a bit of folk-culture thrown in. There were not many jobs in folk-culture, and the people of West Cumbria had displayed little enthusiasm to pander to the wants of 'townies'. Indeed Shilvers wondered whether the warmth of their welcome might not be enough to freeze out even the most enthusiastic visitor. Then again, his job was to get people there. He was not responsible for the welcome they got when they arrived.

The cottage felt ideal for Shilvers to soak up a little of the feeling of the locality. Certainly he knew that the commission was only for the Tourist Board, but the pieces were going under his byline, so he wanted them to have some style. Shilvers detested the pretentious and patronizing writing which usually characterized such articles, and he was especially keen to avoid the criticism that they had been written by some outsider with no sensitivity to the unique character of the area. After two weeks he began to feel that he was becoming a part of the landscape, and as he sat day after day looking out at the ocean, it began to be easy to see how the relentless and untiring grind could eat away at the people. One morning Shilvers knocked a teacup from beside a pile of yellowing library books and swore out loud. Only then did he realize that it had been several days since he had spoken at all. He tried to remember when. It was a strange feeling, like a new taste in his mouth.

Shilvers now knew how little he had understood life in such a remote place. Far away from the busy city for even this short time he glimpsed a fragment of what it must be like to live in rural isolation for a whole life. This was a forgotten tip of the country. What went on in Manchester or London seemed as faraway and irrelevant as events in a distant land, or perhaps in another century. The world had not wanted to know Winderwath, and so this community had turned its back on the world. With the hostile ocean on one side and an indifferent world on the other, the people of Winderwath had pulled the covers over their heads, and shared only with each other the bond of their struggle. This was something unspoken: them and us. Even the young people here did not bother to leave to find fresh opportunities. It was as if what lay beyond was another planet, another species. Shilvers knew that he could never be close enough to this place to understand fully, but as he stared out over the turbulent sea, he began to get a hint, only that, of the unique character of life here.

As Shilvers gazed through the cracked window-panes he began to think, for the hundredth time in recent days, of Julia. Shilvers had been with her for seven years, since before he had given up the routine and security of the *Daily Sentinel* for freelance writing. That change had brought with it lots of uncertainty, lots of travel, lots of odd working hours, and lots of problems for their relationship. Somehow the two of them had stayed together through some difficult and testing times, and in the last eighteen months Shilvers had begun to feel that things had been better. The work had often been easier and more sociable, and things had seemed good between them. Though for most of the time Julia had stayed in his flat, she had insisted on keeping her independence. Her own flat a few miles away was kept on even when they were very short of money. For Julia, keeping the flat seemed to mean that she was with Shilvers because she wanted to be, not because she had nowhere else to go. Sometimes she would go many weeks without even calling in to it. Even some of their close friends were unaware that she had a separate address and a separate telephone number. They were regarded as a couple.

Shilvers went to his bedside and picked up the picture of Julia. It had been taken on the promenade at Brighton on what they had both been happy to describe as their first ever 'dirty weekend'. Her red hair was swept back by the breeze, and her startling green eyes set wide apart shone out in a sparkling smile. It brought a broad smile to Shilvers' face, as it always did, to look at the picture. It was crinkled and perhaps even fading a bit with age, but still her vitality reached out over time and space to warm him. At that moment he ached to have her there with him, and to his amazement his eyes were full of tears as her last words rang inside his head.

She did not know, she had said, where all this was leading. They had not been getting anywhere, had not been developing. She wanted to feel that their relationship was more than just a habit, that it all meant something beyond just more of the same.

He was alarmed and confused by the suddenness of her outburst. If only she had told him before of her dissatisfaction, then he might have had a chance to put right whatever was going wrong between them. Now, without warning, he seemed to be on the brink of losing her. He felt powerless and frustrated.

Nevertheless Shilvers had not resisted or enquired too much when she said she had been offered some work in Paris. She would take it, and would use the time to think. Everything would be all right, she was sure. She had squeezed his hand and wrinkled her nose in warm reassurance when they had parted. She had some friends in this part of the country and she would come to see them in a few weeks. He was to leave his address at the post office in Winderwath and she would find him. 'It will be O.K. I don't know how long, but it will be O.K.'

Shilvers propped the photograph on the mantelpiece above

the old stone fireplace which was the only really attractive feature of the cottage interior. It had a large open hearth with the old-fashioned wood-burning stove inside it. The collection of logs was lasting well, and the constant fire in the stove kept the whole building warm.

He sat uncomfortably in a wooden chair in front of the stove and fixed his eyes on Julia. What would he say to her, what would things be like when she returned? He had been surprised and hurt. It was true that he had accepted this job knowing that they would be separated for a while, but had imagined weeks of hard work punctuated by glorious and sensuous weekends in the company of Julia. He now realized that he was in a long-term bad temper because she had failed to fall in with his selfish little plan. That was probably why he was taking so long to unwind, and why even now he felt guilty as those vivid green eyes stared back, laughing at him from above the stove.

Shilvers reflected for the thousandth time how in his life he had never really appreciated anything while he had it, and only began to realize its worth once he had lost it. 'Ain't it the truth,' he heard himself say, and the sound of his own voice, and the longing for the sight and sound and smell of Julia, reawakened him to himself, and he wanted her desperately.

In those first days at Winderwath Shilvers had seen little of the local people. He had bought a large supply of food at the grocer's shop in the village when he had first arrived, and had been the object of a good deal of curiosity.

'Staying long with us, Mr . . . ?' enquired the little old lady who had been stacking shelves with tins of dog food and was now adding up his purchases.

'I'm not at all sure yet,' said Shilvers, deliberately avoiding both questions. 'It depends how my work goes.' He had no reason to keep any secrets but he felt mischievous and enjoyed making the woman work for her gossip.

'Oh, so you're working here then? Not here for a holiday?' she asked.

'Well, it's a little work and a little holiday as well I hope.'

'You can more or less please yourself when you work in your line then?'

'More or less. How much do I owe you?'

'Nineteen pounds twenty-three pence.' It was about five pounds more than it would have been at the corner shop at the end of his street in London. 'It must be nice to work when you want to?'

Shilvers counted the exact cash out on to the counter.

'Yes it is. Have a nice day,' and hurried off.

Since then he had lived on an unhealthy mixture of baked beans, tinned soup, dehydrated Chinese snacks and crackers. Tea-bags or instant coffee with powdered milk made him long for the disgusting taste of the machine brew from the newsroom of the *Daily Sentinel* which left dark stains on the inside of plastic cups. He shuddered to imagine what it had done to his stomach. Shilvers took some comfort from the fact that several years earlier he had adopted the habit of taking one vitamin tablet each day and that, he supposed, helped him to keep the most dreadful diseases at bay. With his ample supply of provisions and plenty of background reading to do, there had been no reason to go down to the village. Now the thoughts of Julia, and the growing boredom brought on by his diet, made him think that a trip might be worth while. There might be a message for him at the post office where he had left word of his address. Anyway, it amused Shilvers to wonder what the locals were saying about him, and what they made of their mystery visitor. Perhaps they thought he was a recluse. The way he was going they could be right.

It was late afternoon when Shilvers got out his walking shoes and prepared for the short walk down to the village. It was a raw and gusty evening, and he put on a thick roll-necked sweater and his heavy navy-blue donkey jacket, buttoned up tight to the neck. Even then he instinctively hunched his shoulders as he closed the rickety door of the cottage behind him. The wet wind penetrated any chink in even the warmest clothing.

Shilvers set off briskly down the hill, hoping to reach the post office before it closed, though he knew that all the shops in the area worked their own idiosyncratic versions of flexitime.

Hundreds of feet below as he walked, the sea lashed the shoreline, and even at that distance brought a continuous roar to his ears. The pathway was only clear where the coarse grass had been worn away, and it meandered now nearer, now further away from the edge of the cliff. From time to time great chunks had slipped away into the sea as the waves had continually pounded at the foundations of the rock. Shilvers observed that soon parts of the path he was walking on would disappear. Already in places the edge was perilously close, but there was no fence and there were no warnings. He made a mental note not to drink too much at the village pub before returning home on a dark night.

The pathway led directly into a small gravel car-park at the back of the only public house in the village. The Huntsman stood alone at the edge of the harbour, and the owner of the cottage had assured Shilvers that it too kept elastic opening hours.

It used to serve the fishermen you know,' he had said with a wink, 'and you can never tell when they're going to arrive home.'

Shilvers walked around its pebble-dashed and whitewashed walls and headed along the hundred yards or so of empty pavement before he reached the village green. All of the shops and businesses in the village were arranged neatly on three sides of the open green area, and all of the houses, mostly old stone terraces, were equally neatly set in rows in side streets off the green. There were a few old cars parked more or less at random in front of some of the shops, most of which were still open. There was a small butcher's shop, a baker, a shoe-repair service which advertised 'key-cutting' on an old wooden noticeboard that swung noisily in the wind. There were several other shops which had been boarded up and there, sure enough, in one corner of the green was a cobbled yard with an oval-shaped wooden notice over the entrance reading 'Andrew Bowness, Blacksmith'. Little do you know, thought Shilvers, you're about to become a tourist attraction.

On another side were the two shops he was interested in. The post office on one corner and next to it the grocer's, or 'Minimarket' as the inappropriately modern-looking sign announced from above the shop window.

Shilvers went into the post office. There was a loud clang over his head as an old-fashioned brass bell declared his arrival and the same two elderly sisters who had been surprised by it when he'd walked in two weeks ago were surprised as they stood behind the counter today.

'Sorry about that. I'm afraid it's a bit of a shock, but when we're in the back it's sometimes a bit difficult to hear.'

'You could hear that in Manchester.' So much for the repartee, thought Shilvers.

The two ladies were practically identical, except that one was thin and obviously the more active of the two. The other was much larger and slower on her feet. Both had pure white hair in a neat perm, and it was difficult for Shilvers to tell which was the older.

'We're twins,' said the thin sister, resolving the unasked question.

'Oh.' Shilvers realized he must have been staring rudely. 'How nice,' was all he could think of to say.

'What can we do for you?' asked the fatter, more abrupt sister.

'I was wondering whether there were any messages for me. My name is Shilvers, do you remember? I'm renting the cottage up the hill.'

'Oh yes, we know who you are, Mr Shilvers,' said the thin twin. Her tone implied more than just casual knowledge. Shilvers was about to ask, but let it go.

'Post office is closed,' said the fat twin bluntly. 'Only the sweets and tobacco counter are open at this time of night.' Shilvers looked at his watch. It was five-forty.

'Oh don't be so silly Molly,'and the thin twin started to scan a hundred tiny wooden pigeon-holes behind the post office counter to see if there were any messages. Shilvers could see at a glance that all of them were empty, but he waited patiently while the thin twin methodically walked up and down, holding her head level with each row as she examined them.

'Now who is being silly Doreen,' said Molly. 'If there had been any messages either you or I would have taken them, wouldn't we? Harry has been off all week.'

'Harry's the postman,' said Doreen, apparently oblivious to her sister's rudeness.

'So there's only us here, isn't there?' Molly continued. 'If there was any message, I would know about it, and take it from me,' she looked triumphant, 'there isn't.'

Shilvers felt like an intruder in a long-term hostility.

'Well perhaps I could just have some cigarettes then,' he said, turning to the tobacco counter. 'I'd like some Benson and Hedges please.' He waited while Molly found and reached for the packs. 'Two hundred if you have them.' Shilvers was not a heavy smoker and was trying to cut down, but he hated running out. His order sent the two sisters into a panic with fat Molly counting out gold packets on to the counter, and thin Doreen scurrying off to a store-room and returning a few seconds later brushing the dust from a large paper carton of cigarettes. It then took several minutes to work out the price, the confusion intensified by Shilvers' joking request for a discount for bulk-buying. As he opened the door to leave, Shilvers realized his little transaction had taken ten minutes.

The brass bell tolled his departure. Both sisters, thin and fat, were standing looking at him from behind the counter, nodding benignly as he left. Shilvers had expected a measure of endearing eccentricity, but thought that he probably would not include the twins in his tourist guide. It was a few steps to the village store, where he was greeted by the little old lady who had quizzed him when he first arrived.

'Evening Mr Shilvers,' she said as though expecting him. 'How's the writing going?'

'Oh, I've hardly started yet.' Shilvers immediately realized that the twins would have gossiped his name around the village, but how did she know he was a writer? He was disappointed.

He had been half looking forward to another game of cat and mouse as she tried to trap him into giving information and he tried to avoid it.

Shilvers picked up a battered wire basket and walked between the shelves. He bought nothing until he reached the canned food counter and then stacked up a can of every type of soup except oxtail and three cans of baked beans. He also chose crackers, sausages, eggs and butter, and paused before deciding not to buy any more dehydrated snacks. Shilvers was thinking about the woman's remark all the time he was filling his basket and when he reached the check-out he had made up his mind.

'How did you know I was here to do some writing?' he asked, as casually as he could.

'Oh there's not much that goes on around here that doesn't get around you know. It's a very small community.'

'But I don't think I've told anyone that I'm here to write. Not that it's a state secret, it's just that I was a bit surprised.'

The woman held a single finger straight upwards and tapped the side of her nose in a gesture which irritated Shilvers and told him absolutely nothing. He felt unable to pursue the matter further without making an issue of it, and so he had to leave it at that. The situation was ironic. Last time he was in this shop he was trying to avoid giving information, this time he was trying unsuccessfully to get it.

'Seasonal weather,' said the woman, her busy fingers punching out prices on the till.

'Very,' said Shilvers grumpily. He picked up the paper carrier bag and walked quickly to the exit.

'Good-night Mr Shilvers,' said the woman smugly.

'Good-night.' He practically slammed the door on his way out.

As he walked back towards the Huntsman, Shilvers was not sure why he felt so irritated by the woman knowing his reason for being in Winderwath. He told himself that perhaps he wanted to observe the community without them being aware that he was doing so in order to get a more accurate picture of their life. In his heart he knew it was nothing to do with that. He had enjoyed the anonymity and the little mystery he thought he was causing. He now realized he was being childish, and that only added to his irritation. Shilvers walked on, and by the time he was halfway to the pub he had calmed down. After all, he thought, no one knew what sort of writing he was doing. Perhaps he would compensate by giving the impression that he was a great novelist come to the country to look for fresh inspiration. More childish, he conceded with a smile, by the minute.

Now Shilvers was walking the last few yards towards the Huntsman. His many confused thoughts made him feel the need of human company and he decided to have a drink before heading back up the hill for his supper of baked beans, and more work. He was about to push open the door when his attention was caught by raised voices from inside. He paused and listened to what seemed like a fierce argument between three or four men with local accents.

'It's no good kicking up trouble. We won't achieve anything, and it'll just bring trouble down on us. You know what's past is past. You can't undo it, what's the point?'

'And besides,' said another angry voice, 'where the hell would we be without them? Eh, what's your answer to that? Back in the nineteen thirties, that's where we'd be. And I don't want that and neither do the rest of us. If you start making trouble you'll be responsible for the consequences, keep that in mind.'

'But we're not talking about money or jobs here, we're talking about people, quite a few of them if you care to add it up. We're talking about the lives of ordinary people.'

'And what sort of life will it be for my kids without them Alf?' It was the first voice again. 'It's all right for you, you've got no kids. If you get your way we'll have no jobs and no money neither. They'll find a way of getting back at us. No one is indispensable you know.'

'That's all too bloody obvious isn't it –'

At that moment the conversation broke off and the whole building went quiet. Shilvers was immediately aware that his eavesdropping would not be welcomed, and felt a momentary fear of being caught. He was an outsider in a community where outsiders were instinctively distrusted and kept at arm's length. Any second now one of them would come out and he would be discovered. His instant reaction was to get away, but a moment later he realized it would be foolish to try. Without hesitating any longer he straightened himself and went into the pub.

The whole room was quiet as Shilvers walked as casually as he felt able towards the bar and ordered a drink. Perhaps a dozen men from the village were grouped around the fireplace, some seated on stools. A few of them looked directly at him. Shilvers felt very uncomfortable, and was doing his best to look perfectly relaxed.

'Evening Mr Shilvers,' the harsh voice of one of the men broke the silence. 'Let me get that one for you.' An enormous man with brown curly hair and several days' growth of beard was approaching him, fingering in his jacket pocket for change. He produced a single coin and placed it on the bar.

'Cheers, that's very good of you,' said Shilvers. 'You know my name?'

'Oh there's not much goes on around here without everybody knowing it Mr Shilvers. You're a bit of a writer aren't you?' The man was dressed in the rough and well-worn clothes of a farm labourer, and heavy shoes.

Shilvers had been a journalist for more than twenty years, ten of them in Fleet Street, and had written four books on big news stories. He supposed that the description was apt. 'Yes, I suppose I am a bit of a writer. I have already gathered that this is a close-knit community.'

The rest of the men were now talking again and Shilvers felt the atmosphere begin to relax. The big man stretched out his hand. 'My name is Roache. Bernard Roache.'

'Pleased to meet you. Cheers.' Shilvers took a long drink.

'What sort of writing is it you do, Mr Shilvers?' The big man took an equally long drink.

'Oh just bits and pieces, I'm a freelance journalist.'

'Oh yes, we knew that. Alf over there recognized your name from the paper. Says he's seen it a few times.' Roache nodded his head towards the group of men but Shilvers was unable to distinguish which one was Alf.

'Observant chap.'

'Interesting line that must be, Mr Shilvers. What exactly are you writing about just now like?' The tone of voice did not convey a sense that this was a casual question. Shilvers glanced up at the big and rounded face. The enlarged features carried a hint of a genetic deformity somewhere in the man's family history. The overall effect was intimidating. Now, faced with the direct question, and given the precarious nature of his welcome, Shilvers thought he would be well advised to tell the truth.

'Oh just a few bits and pieces for the Tourist Board. They want to get a few more people visiting the area in the summer. Bring in a bit of foreign currency I suppose.'

'That's a coincidence,' Roache spoke conspicuously louder, as though to catch the attention of the other men, 'we were just having a few words about tourists when you came in. It got a bit heated as a matter of fact. Some reckon it's a good thing having them brought in here spending their money, others don't like them poking around for a few months of the year looking at us as though we're something that ought to be in a zoo. Good job you arrived when you did.'

'I'm afraid I wouldn't have much to contribute to that argument.' Shilvers thought he would continue to be diplomatic. 'I'm just paid to do a job. What the Tourist Board do with my stuff when they get it is anyone's guess.'

'Oh no doubt we can look forward to a great flood of visitors when you're finished.'

Roache gave no indication of whether he welcomed such a prospect or not. You are nowhere near as stupid as you look, thought Shilvers, but you're not clever enough to convince me with that crap about tourism being the subject of the argument.

Anyway it was enough to have apparently got away with the eavesdropping.

Shilvers bought a drink for Roache in return and talked for a few more minutes. He then told him that he had work to get on with and downed the dregs of his second pint. Once again the noise was subdued as he left, and only Roache returned his good-night.

Shilvers walked briskly away around the back to the car-park and then along the cliffside path up towards his cottage. After a short while the only sound was the crashing roar of waves on the cliff. The wind was fierce and frightening, and Shilvers had to battle his way up the hill. All the time he was thinking about the argument he had overheard in the Huntsman. Who could it be that they were afraid to upset? Not tourists certainly. What could the man have meant when he said people were not indispensable? The argument had been angry and real. Shilvers considered how nearly he had been caught listening. Obviously they still suspected him, and there was a natural hostility towards outsiders. He thought that perhaps he had acted naturally enough for them to give him the benefit of the doubt. Maybe.

Not much goes on around here without people knowing. He had been told that twice tonight. Shilvers thought how true that was. Already he knew there was something the people here wanted to keep secret. What could it be? His journalistic instincts started working. How long, he wondered, before he found out the rest of the story?

CHAPTER FOUR

The next day once again dawned grey and gloomy. A drizzle had fallen constantly through the night, and while Shilvers had been down in the village, the stove had gone out. He had dived, shivering, into a chilly bed rather than try to rekindle it and this morning the whole cottage felt cold and damp.

Shilvers had slept heavily, and now as he gradually woke up and looked about him, he wondered what on earth he was doing in this tiny ramshackle shepherd's cottage perched on a cliff-top in the middle of nowhere. He lay still, wondering whether his first priority should be to rush over and plug in the old-fashioned electric kettle on the draining board next to six cups which still exhibited traces of his last half-dozen cups of coffee, or to try to get the stove burning and come back to bed until it warmed up the house.

He could not face either, so he turned over and pulled up the bedclothes and began to think about the overheard conversation of last night. What could it have been that those men were so angry about? Such anger seemed quite out of character with the sleepy feeling of this rural community. For a reason he was unable to rationalize, it annoyed him. Perhaps it was that he had just begun to think he was getting to understand something about what made the community work. This took him quite by surprise and set him back. It proved that in fact he knew nothing of what was really in the minds of these people. For half an hour his thoughts wandered around the experience of last evening.

Eventually Shilvers resolved that it was time to press on with his work. As he got out of bed his limbs felt heavy and stiff. The results, he decided, of that brisk walk up and down the cliff, mixed with the damp atmosphere of the cottage. He ran the water for two minutes until it looked fit for human consumption, and then filled the kettle. While waiting for it to boil he raked over the ashes at the bottom of the stove. The smell as the dust spread into the air reminded him of his childhood. Wood-burning stoves. Shilvers could not recall why the smell seemed familiar. Perhaps it was from rented cottages on holiday in Winderwath. After several futile attempts to kindle a flame from the damp and yellowing pile of newspapers, eventually a thin wisp of grey smoke snaked up the chimney, and fragile flames began to lick around the logs. As much use as a candle in a storm, thought Shilvers, and went over to wash the stains from the cups and make his first cup of coffee of the day.

Several cups later Shilvers was sitting on a rough wooden chair at a rougher wooden table by the window leafing through a thick and musty volume entitled *Crafts of Ancient Cumbria* which he had borrowed from the library at the nearby coastal town of Westermouth. The howling wind still careered through the cracks in the door, and the thin branches of an invulnerable shrub beat a tapdance on the window-pane. The unending roar of breakers hundreds of feet below floated over the distance to complete the bleak cacophony.

The work was going badly. Time and time again Shilvers found his thoughts wandering away from the sentence on the page and his gaze shifting towards the window and out into the sky. Over and over again he read the same paragraph and tried to make notes in scrawled handwriting in the open shorthand pad in front of him. He could not concentrate. Shilvers felt that to write about the area, he needed to understand it. He thought he had begun to, but now? Damn it. He threw his pencil on the table, his eyes rolling to the ceiling as he saw that he had broken the point.

'Damn and blast,' he said out loud, slamming the book and sending a cloud of decaying paper over the desk. Shilvers stubbed out his third cigarette of the day and decided to let the wind blow these latest thoughts out of his head. He would have a good walk and then come back for lunch and start afresh. He reached for a pair of hiking boots which he had owned for a dozen years and buttoned his donkey jacket up to the neck. He had not yet explored the moorland area further up the hill away from the village, but a local Ordnance Survey map he had borrowed from the library showed a small lake not very far away. Shilvers decided to take a look at it, and instinctively picked up his battered old Pentax and slung it over his shoulder.

The camera felt like a friend to him. Together they had travelled to some strange and troubled parts of the world. To Cyprus when he had covered the outbreak of troubles between Greeks and Turks in 1974. To Hong Kong where he had done a series of pieces for the *Sentinel* about the opium trade. To Paris in 1968 when it looked as though the whole of Europe would rise up, and the enthusiasm for revolutionary ideals which had crept into his copy had led to a sharp lecture from a crusty old night editor called George Ffitch. The pictures had never been part of his professional duties, but he found as he flicked through the old scrapbooks which he had always kept that the photographs were a much more potent reminder of distant events than the faded and yellowing cuttings from foreign or British newspapers which were clipped in beside them, sometimes with his byline, sometimes without.

Once or twice being at the right spot had earned him a few bonus points. There was the time when he had snapped a French riot-policeman slipping a baseball bat from inside his tunic during student demonstrations on the Champs-Élysées. The picture went on the front page of the *Sentinel*, which syndicated it across the world and even paid him a small proportion of the profits. In his mind Shilvers always retained the thought that one day he would snap the jumbo jet pirouetting out of the sky, or the landing of the Martians. More likely though he would see his big scoop on a day when he had left the camera behind. That uncomfortable fear encouraged the discipline of taking the camera with him as much as possible.

Shilvers set off up the hill, the cold wind immediately bringing streams of tears to his eyes as he hunched his shoulders and braced himself against it. The ground levelled out after a few hundred yards and the thin trail through the grass grew thinner until he was walking on unmarked and apparently unending moorland.

Shilvers pressed on through the slight stitch and shortage of breath. As the cool air stung his lungs he promised himself for the ten thousandth time that he would give up smoking. After a mile the moor was quite level and the cliff less steep as it trailed away to his left down towards the sea. Far out through the mist on the horizon he could faintly make out a small island which appeared from the map to be level with the lake he was aiming for. Shilvers turned inland on to the thicker grass. Here and there large boulders stuck out of the earth, and as he passed one particularly huge rock three scraggy sheep which had been sheltering on the other side took fright and darted away bleating their displeasure.

Shilvers laughed aloud and strode on, now thoroughly warmed up and enjoying the freshness of the bleak open moor. Another group of sheep were eyeing him suspiciously, and he deliberately headed towards them. They stood their ground until he let out a roar which made them leap away in panic. Shilvers laughed again and then shouted at the top of his voice, confident that no human ears could hear him.

He had walked perhaps another mile inland when the land began to be more hilly. At the top of each of a series of peaks Shilvers expected to be able to see his lake. Every time there was a taller summit to his left or right, and he would ascend it to try to get a better vantage point. Several times he was quite sure that the lake would be visible, but there was no sign. After three-quarters of an hour Shilvers began to think that his navigation must be at fault, and he was on the point of giving up and returning to the cottage. It was now after one o'clock and he had not yet had his first meal of the day. An unusually tall and isolated peak stood a little way over to his left, and Shilvers made up his mind that this would be the last one he would climb before giving up and going home.

By now his enthusiasm was beginning to be overtaken by his fatigue, and the last few yards leading to the top of the peak became increasingly difficult to negotiate. Twenty yards from the summit Shilvers stopped for a short rest to regain his breath. He felt a sudden weakness in his calves and knees, and seemed to hear a deep rumble beneath his feet as his legs threatened to give way beneath him. He looked around. Had he imagined it? He felt that if he allowed himself to sink down, he would be sucked into the soft ground beneath him, and become part of the enormous vibration he could still feel. He concentrated. Was it still there? He could no longer hear or feel anything. He looked around again and a blur across his vision began to clear. He reckoned that he must be at least three miles from home now, and a six mile round trip was far more than he had planned.

After a few minutes Shilvers decided he was ready for the final assault. His eyes scanned the horizon as more of the countryside beyond the peak came into view. All that could be seen, as a wider and wider area was revealed to him, was more of the same moorland, punctuated with craggy rocks. Here and there were occasional dry-stone walls forming no recognizable pattern and small groups of sheep.

Shilvers had resigned himself to failure and was on the point of retracing his steps when his eye flashed on to and then quickly away from a glint of what seemed like metal over the horizon. He craned his head while still walking, sooner to discover what it could be. As he came nearer to the summit something which looked like an enormous distorted circle came into view. Shilvers registered confusion and displeasure at one moment. Seconds later it looked as though it might be the top rim of a cooling tower. He kept walking and saw the top of another tower next to it. Then there was a third. Shilvers' mind raced for an explanation and produced nothing.

Now Shilvers could see the tops of three enormous towers, and beside them a series of narrow metallic chimneys supported by ropes. He was confused and astonished. What could this be? It seemed surreal to discover an industrial installation in such an unlikely location. As Shilvers' mind turned somersaults to take in what he was seeing, he already felt that something about it seemed quietly threatening.

Now Shilvers approached the top of the peak, and still more of the complex came into view. Next to the towers there was a maze of concrete blocks, some without windows and resembling gigantic surf-breakers on a beach. Then there seemed to be dozens of small office-buildings, up to five or six storeys high. The whole site was enormous, covering perhaps a couple of square miles. His eyes followed the tall wire fence around the perimeter, towards what looked in the distance to be the way in. Then he saw it, away to the north and crisply silhouetted against the billowing sky: a massive metallic dome of steel perched on a concrete plinth.

That sight immediately solved the mystery for Shilvers. This was Dounscraig, the nuclear reprocessing plant. The dome was familiar to all those who had taken any interest in the national debate surrounding the investment in this and other parts of the nuclear programme. The characteristic silhouette had been the logo which drew the eye to newspaper coverage of public enquiries into expansion and development of facilities here. Shilvers searched his memory for what little he knew about Dounscraig. It was run by Imperial Nuclear Industries on behalf of the government. It had been a military station in the frontier days of developing nuclear weapons, but had been handed over to civilian use in the Sixties. It was feeding into the national grid, and was said to be entirely devoted to experimenting in applications of nuclear technology for peaceful use. Still, the whole place remained subject to rigorous official secrecy, something which by definition made it an object of curiosity for people like Shilvers.

Though no sun pierced the dense swirling clouds which covered the moorland, Shilvers brought his hand across his brow to focus on the spectacle before him. He felt the cold sweat on his body beneath his heavy clothing. His eyes registered the information and his memory supplied the context.

The only aspect of the work here which did receive publicity was the foreign currency and profit-making potential of reprocessing spent nuclear fuel from overseas and domestic power stations. This was one of only a handful of such sites in the world, where the dangerous by-products of making electricity from nuclear fission were made slightly less dangerous and stored until someone could think of something better to do with them.

Shilvers knew a little about Dounscraig and he now remembered that of course he had known it was in this county. Until now though he had had no clue that it was in this area, and just up the road from the sleepy village of Winderwath which he was just getting ready to write about as though the entire twentieth century had passed it by.

His eyes once again scanned the site as he tried to absorb its scale. His view was of the back of the complex, and as he shielded his eyes from the sky Shilvers could make out, far into the distance on the other side, a network of access roads which wove into the hills. There must be little development of any sort for several miles, he thought, making this one of the most isolated spots in England. He was still contemplating the maze of concrete buildings, internal roads, towers and fences which made up the largest industrial site he had ever seen, when he remembered his camera and decided to take some pictures. Shilvers regretted that he had not brought his wide-angle lens to capture some of the scale of the site, but his eye patrolled the horizon through his telephoto lens, picking out dramatic contrasts between glinting metallic towers and barren pale-green moors.

Shilvers snapped the reverse side of the familiar dome and the twin towers on either side, then took another shot of the three giant cooling towers at the other end of the complex. He was panning slowly across the many rooftops looking for another interesting skyline when he spotted something flashing at him from inside the site. Shilvers steadied the camera and focused on what seemed to be a lookout tower. He looked hard to make sure what it was. After a few seconds he realized that it *was* a lookout, and that at the top of it was a man with a lens of some kind looking back at him.

For a moment Shilvers wanted to look over his shoulder to see what the man could be interested in, but there was no mistake. There was one man looking at him through a telescope, and another standing next to him and pointing in his direction. Shilvers snapped a couple of pictures and then felt an urgent need to get away. Turning quickly, he began to make his way back down the hill. For the second time in two days he had been made to feel like a spy. He did not like it, but almost in spite of himself he broke into a run as he reached the bottom of the valley.

As he scuttled away Shilvers considered his surprising discovery. Now he wondered why he had failed to realize that Dounscraig was so close to the spot he had chosen as the base for his project. It was simply that the sleepy life of Winderwath had seemed so rural and apparently unspoiled by modern society. It felt unexpected and therefore disturbing that such a huge twentieth-century monster should be sitting just over the horizon.

Shilvers knew that the nuclear industry was proud of its safety record. There had never been any leak which had extended beyond the perimeter fence; that was the frequent boast from I.N.I. There was however a comprehensive plan to evacuate the entire area in case such an eventuality did occur, and Shilvers now speculated that Winderwath must be included in it. How would he handle this in his piece for the Tourist Board? Could be get away with not mentioning it at all? It certainly was not a tourist attraction, and anyway he felt sure the Dounscraig security men would far from welcome snap-happy foreigners sending home pictures of a still secret nuclear establishment.

Shilvers recalled his discomfort at having been spotted by whoever was on the lookout tower and now wondered about the status of the plant as far as security was concerned. He had been startled that the site should have such a tower and to realize that he had been observed taking photographs. After all, though, it was not a military site, and there were no warning signs. He must be within his rights. He felt at the same moment indignant and yet disturbed and fearful.

Now Shilvers was within sight of his cottage and was glad to see a thin curl of smoke coming out of the chimney, even though the still strong wind was immediately gusting it into oblivion. The sight of the tiny shepherd's cottage clinging on to the edge of the moors seemed a million miles from the concrete and metal mass of Dounscraig.

CHAPTER FIVE

Four hours later Shilvers was still sitting on the upright wooden chair with his feet on the desk and staring out into the mist which blurred the edges between sea and sky. From time to time a screeching seagull would rise up on a gust of wind above the cliff-edge and hover unsteadily level with the cottage. Then with a piercing shrill it would dive, only to be caught once again as the wind battered the cliff-face and drove itself and everything in its path onwards and upwards.

Shilvers was not focusing on the gulls, but far out towards the distant horizon where no fixed point interrupted his gaze. So many diverse thoughts crowded his head. The surreal sight of Dounscraig looming up out of the rocky moorland landscape. The only just discernible hum of power which penetrated the earth, the stones, the rocks and the air. It seemed to defy nature and assert an almost divine right to be where it stood.

Why had the discovery made such an impression on him? He was puzzled. He knew of the existence of I.N.I. and Dounscraig, it was merely that he had not known the precise location. It was, he now understood, the complete unexpectedness of the discovery which so unsettled him. When he analysed it Shilvers realized that the sinister connotations he attached to Dounscraig were ridiculous. The spot was remote, but that of course was sensible in case of an accident. It was surrounded by barbed wire, but that too was wise to prevent entry by unauthorized people, perhaps crazy protesters, or even terrorists. The lookout tower? Maybe that was just a realistic precaution.

Shilvers had nothing against the nuclear industry. The nuclear power establishment was constantly assuring the public that theirs was the safest form of energy production. No one had ever been killed making nuclear energy. Could coal mining say that? Of course not. Mining had a grisly history of appalling underground disasters.

It was nothing to do with the industry that made him feel hostile, it was much more the people who ran it. When he had encountered them in his journalistic life they had always seemed somehow smug and self-satisfied. Obviously nuclear energy production was far too complicated for mere laymen to understand. So, they seemed to say, just take it from us that everything is under control. We are the professionals. Just leave it all in our capable hands. Much of what they said was clearly right, but it was frustrating for a journalist to tackle a subject in which he did not even know the right questions to ask to get the interesting answers. How could a layman make sensible criticisms about the frontiers of nuclear technology? The long-haired and duffel-coated brigade made a pretty poor showing and Shilvers had little in common with them. Still, he knew that he preferred their earnestness to the condescending attitudes of the men from the nuclear industry.

His eyes looked long and hard into the distance. He thought about nothing for a while, and then about Julia and of how much he missed her. The days were long and lonely and seemed empty without her, and from deep within himself he felt something like a sob rising. The only picture he could summon into his mind and superimpose on the mist far away was that laughing expression on the photograph from Brighton. That had been a glorious weekend. He recalled the hesitation and the discovery and the excitement and the ecstasy and then the sadness that it all had to end so soon. Where was she now? Who was she with? Had she made up her mind to finish with him? Had she wanted to be on her own to gain the strength to go through with it? Why had he not known that she was unhappy and in turmoil before it had reached this crisis? Shilvers ached to have Julia with him and wondered how long it would be before he saw her again.

Now dusk had fallen and Shilvers began once again to feel stiff and cold. The isolation from human warmth made him vulnerable to emotion. He gazed into nothingness. Then, with no warning, a shadow seemed to pass in front of the window. The glass itself was quite out of focus for a few seconds as he collected his thoughts and wondered whether he had imagined it. Had someone passed in front of the cottage?

Shilvers heard a shuffle outside and an unexpected fear gripped him. He thought of the security guards at Dounscraig. In the distance Shilvers thought he could hear something like a whirling engine. It felt like a fragmentary echo of the distant but immense power he had felt in the shadow of Dounscraig. Then perhaps it sounded more like the far off turning blades of a helicopter, mixing with the gusting wind and surf. He spotted his camera thrown casually on to an armchair and without thinking he leapt across the room to put a cushion over it. As he did so there was a loud hammering on the door. Whoever had passed the window would have seen him sitting at the table, so there was little point in pretending not to be at home. Shilvers could not have explained why he would even want to. Nevertheless he felt apprehensive about his uninvited visitor.

Once again there was a knock at the door. Shilvers tried to control himself. He opened it to reveal a small and stout man in his late fifties with untidy greying hair and a deeply lined face. The man removed his cloth cap and when he spoke his accent was local.

'Good evening Mr Shilvers. Could you spare a minute or two for a word?'

The shock of the unexpected visitor had dulled Shilvers' hospitality.

'What is it that you want?'

'Just a few minutes of your time sir, that's all.' The man brought up his hand to touch a long since vanished forelock. The unexpected deference made Shilvers realize that he had been abrupt. Now he began to think from something about the man that he had seen him before.

'I'm very sorry.' Shilvers stepped back and opened the door wider. 'It's only that I don't get many visitors up here. In fact,' he paused to consider whether it could be right, 'you're the first. Do come in.'

'Oh I know that sir,' said the man, shuffling across the threshold. 'Word would have gone round the village if anyone had been up here. We're a close community in Winderwath.'

'Oh yes, I've discovered that already,' said Shilvers. 'Anyway, what is it that I can do for you, Mr . . .?'

'Penshall. Alf Penshall is my name. I hope you don't mind me bothering you like this, only I saw you in the Huntsman the other night.' *That's* where I've seen you before, thought Shilvers. 'I gather you are a bit of a writer or journalist like. Would that be right?'

A bit of a writer. Shilvers smiled. 'Yes, I suppose I am.'

Penshall had shuffled over to the upright wooden chair on the other side of the table from the one Shilvers had been using, and slowly sat down. His shabby grey overcoat was now unbuttoned, revealing a blue boilersuit underneath. Penshall's shoes were stout and made for working outdoors. Like some others in this community, Shilvers noted, this man was using elaborate courtesy to keep at arm's length anyone regarded as an outsider.

'Can I get you some coffee or a beer, Mr Penshall?'

Penshall's eyes went to an iron bucket full of water in which were floating half a dozen bottles of Newcastle Brown Ale.

'It keeps them cool,' Shilvers explained.

'Not much need for that in here I shouldn't think.' Penshall had not removed his coat, and sat hunched up with his cap in both hands. 'But I wouldn't say no if you're having one.'

Shilvers first opened the lid of the stove and gave the contents a prod with a heavy iron poker which had lain in the hearth.

'Sorry it's so cold in here. This is quite effective when it gets going but unfortunately I keep neglecting it. Too spoiled by central heating I suppose,' said Shilvers, and immediately regretted it. He put another log in the stove and replaced the lid. Before he opened a bottle of beer he had to wash two thick glass tumblers. The two men sat in silence for a moment.

'Cheers,' said Shilvers, raising his glass.

'Oh, right you are,' said Penshall, putting the glass to his lips.

As he watched Penshall drink, Shilvers wondered whether this would be a tip-off about some local sheep-rustling or embezzlement of the local jumble-sale funds. Perhaps it might even be a suspect choirmaster. In the awkward silence he even had time to start wondering what local press agencies or newspaper he could sell it to.

'Anyway, as you were saying Mr Penshall, I am indeed a bit of a journalist.'

Penshall put his glass down and leaned forward in a far more earnest manner. His brown eyes seemed to penetrate Shilvers for a few seconds as though he was making a last effort to assess his character. Then he began to speak.

'Mr Shilvers.' His voice was a whisper and Shilvers had to lean towards him. Perhaps this was something better than fiddling the local fête. 'I believe you heard raised voices when you visited the Huntsman the other night.'

'Oh I hardly –' Shilvers began to interrupt but Penshall had not stopped talking.

'. . . and we aren't a community to feel very much anger with each other, only at the outside world.' Now he paused. 'And not very much of that either if the truth be known.' Penshall took a swallow of his beer. 'But just lately there's been a lot of anger in this village, a real lot of anger. To speak the truth some folks' tempers are running high. Very high indeed. There are some who would be very unhappy if they knew I was up here talking to you tonight. Very unhappy.' Penshall was looking directly at Shilvers. 'That's why I came here a roundabout route.'

Penshall paused again, as though waiting for some response.

'Do go on, Mr Penshall.' Shilvers was still not quite taking the visit seriously, but now his curiosity was rising to know what it could be about.

'I've lived all my life in this village, Mr Shilvers, and I know just about each and every person living hereabouts near as well as I know myself. We don't have much to do with outsiders, and mostly they don't want much to do with us. So we keep ourselves to ourselves very nicely if you understand me. They're a good sort of people round here, Mr Shilvers, damned good people though they may not seem that way to you.'

Penshall had paused again as if for acknowledgement. Shilvers swallowed his mouthful of beer.

'Oh I'm sure they are –'

'It don't really matter much anyway, but all I'm saying to you is that they take a bit of getting to know. Anyway, we've had our troubles round here. It's cold and it's bleak and the soil is thin and the sea is unfriendly and it hasn't always been easy to make a living. But whatever problems we've had, we've all had them. You probably won't know what I mean being an outsider. We're all in the same boat as you might say. Problems affected all of us and all of us have faced up to them together. Until now.'

The gravity in Penshall's voice now made Shilvers desperate for him to come to the point, but he was reluctant to appear too anxious in case it should put him off continuing. He need not have worried.

'I've thought long and hard about whether to bring you in on this, Mr Shilvers. I'm taking a big chance. I don't know you and I don't know what sort of a man you are, and like I say, there's some round here who think we should sort out our own problems the way we've always sorted them out in the past, together and on our own.'

'And you?' asked Shilvers.

'I think this has got past anything we know how to handle. We're used to working hard and for some of us that believe, praying on a Sunday when things go wrong. But this isn't like that. This won't just go away. God help us I wish it would.'

'Why don't you tell me about it?' Shilvers tried to sound reassuring.

Penshall took a deep breath, another swallow of his beer, and put the glass gently down on the table between them.

'Like most people round here, I work at Dounscraig. Have done for twelve years, ever since the military moved out. Before that, again like most, I worked on the land, and a damned hard living it was too.' Penshall held out his hands for Shilvers to inspect. There was no doubt they were the hands of a manual labourer.

'What we do up there is supposed to be secret like, and I've always respected that. I've even kept the missus in the dark about most of it, though that's got well up her nose to be sure.' Penshall seemed momentarily amused. 'But the less you know, the less you've got to repeat all over the place if you take my meaning.' Shilvers nodded that he did.

'Not everyone is as careful as me in that respect, more's the pity. Anyway, I suppose a thing like this couldn't stay secret for ever. I don't know why they thought it could. But lately,' Penshall paused, 'well over the last few years really, things have been happening up there that shouldn't be happening. I'm a bloke who likes to do his job, mind his own business, collect what I've earned, and go home at night. But what's going on up there shouldn't be going on, and someone has got to do something about it. But . . .' he paused and took a sip from his beer glass and replaced it on the table, '. . . but it's not that simple.'

Shilvers had to prevent himself from forcing the man to hurry on with the story. He waited quietly while Penshall stared for a few seconds out into the darkness.

'What isn't so simple, Mr Penshall?'

'Accidents that's what.' The man was obviously struggling with himself, even now unsure of whether he was doing the right thing. 'Bad accidents sometimes, where people have been getting hurt. People have been getting very badly hurt.'

'Accidents involving nuclear fuels? Leaks, that sort of thing?'

'There've been many of them. Different problems. There've been leaks, fires, and even a couple of small explosions. Lots of people have been hurt, very badly hurt indeed.' Penshall was now looking down at the table. Clearly keeping this information locked within him had been a habit, and disclosing it to an outsider was painful.

'But I.N.I. have to inform the authorities about accidents on the site. They have to tell the Department of Energy, don't they, and the facts are made public?'

Penshall shook his head. 'Sometimes they tell the government there's been a little problem and sometimes they say nothing at all. They never say what really goes on up there. They couldn't, or else . . .' He shrugged his shoulders and his voice trailed away.

'How many accidents have there been, Mr Penshall? How many people have been hurt by them?'

'Dozens in recent years. Dozens of accidents. Dozens of people hurt. The alarm goes off, the whole place is evacuated, the workers are told to come back after a few days. Then when you get back, nothing is ever said about the accident or the people that have been hurt.'

'Well what happens to them?' There was a long silence. Penshall looked away from Shilvers and out into the blackness. Shilvers glanced at the moonless sky, and saw reflected in the glass the outline of Penshall's face. He thought he had never seen a man so deeply troubled. Then Penshall turned back to him.

'They disappear.'

There was again a silence as Shilvers waited for some clarification. Penshall was gazing out into the darkness and saying nothing.

'I'm sorry, Mr Penshall, I don't think I've understood you properly,' said Shilvers. 'How do you mean they disappear? What happens to them?'

'Just exactly what I'm saying to you, Mr Shilvers.' Having once wrenched the information out of himself, Penshall now seemed impatient. 'They disappear. At the time of the accident the site medical team moves in and evacuates the area of everyone affected. There's a proper medical centre at the site and the workers are taken there, but after they've gone you just don't ever see them again.'

'Well what happens to them?' Shilvers was exasperated.

'I don't know, that's the whole point.' Now Penshall's voice seemed to be filling every corner of the cottage. '*No one* sees them any more. They may be hurt, badly hurt sometimes, but you don't get any news of how badly they're hurt, you don't hear any news about anything, and you're not encouraged to ask.'

Shilvers flopped back in his chair, looking at his beer, then at his visitor. He did not know how to cope with what this man was saying to him. Obviously the story was insane. Workers at a government-backed nuclear reprocessing plant could not just disappear without anyone knowing anything. But why was Penshall telling him this? Was the man mad? It even occurred to him momentarily that friends might be playing a joke on him – setting him up. He dismissed the thought as soon as he had it. Aside from anything else, none of his friends knew exactly where he was. Shilvers got up and walked around the room in silence before sitting down again opposite Penshall.

'Look Mr Penshall, let me see if I understand this properly. You are trying to tell me that ordinary workers at a government research establishment are being injured while they are doing their jobs – men from this village?' Penshall nodded. 'And they are being taken away for medical treatment somewhere else on the site and are never seen again.'

'Exactly.'

There was another pause.

'How many?'

'How many what?'

'How many people have vanished in this way?' Shilvers felt he would explode with frustration. 'How many people from the village have disappeared?'

'They're not all from our village. Some are from outlying farms roundabout, others from other villages not far away. But I would say thirty in all.'

'Thirty?' Shilvers involuntarily shouted in his astonishment and disbelief. Now his voice echoed around the building and he realized he was showing his incredulity far more than was sensible. After all, part of this man's story might be of use to him. Accidents at a nuclear station were very good copy. All he would have to do was to sort out the confusion about the missing men, and he could get back to more detail about the accidents. 'You'll have to forgive me, Mr Penshall, but you'll appreciate I'm sure that this is very hard to understand.' He hesitated. 'Perhaps you could tell me the whole story. Tell me everything that happens when there is one of these accidents.'

Shilvers got up and fished another bottle out of the bucket and pushed it across the table to Penshall. Penshall, now very calm and resigned, half-filled his glass and placed the bottle back on the table. He looked directly into Shilvers' face.

'Most of the men from the village just do the manual work at Dounscraig. It's pushing trolleys around really, driving transports, fork-lift trucks and that sort of thing. But everything that goes on there is dangerous and the work often takes you into the areas where the most difficult work is being done. When you go into those areas you're supposed to take precautions. You wear these plastic overshoes for example, and every pair is supposed to be worn just once then thrown away. They can't be taken away from the restricted area. But they're pretty careless and most of it is a lot of nonsense. It's for the tourists really.'

'What do you mean by that? Surely those areas aren't open to the public?'

'I mean the visitors. It's all to impress the visiting politicians, diplomats, overseas governments who they're trying to persuade to send their nuclear rubbish to Dounscraig for reprocessing. Most of them are only too glad to get rid of it it seems to me. There's a V.I.P. trip which goes around the perimeter of the area where all the really dangerous stuff gets done. It's just close enough to the real thing to give them a sense of adventure and impress them with the science fiction, without getting close enough to have a chance of seeing any of the problems.'

'What sort of problems?'

'The same problems any thirty-year-old plant in constant use would have. Old and outdated equipment, leaking pressure pipes and concrete storage tanks, holes in underground reservoirs so that if one of them geiger-counters goes by it goes off like an earthquake. It's a bloody shambles in there, and all they're doing is putting their fingers in the dyke. It's too dangerous to do most of the repairs, and in some cases they don't even know how to. And there's the new research too. Half the time even the top boffins don't know much about what they're doing.'

Shilvers watched Penshall closely as he talked. The way he described the processes and the plant he was obviously familiar with it, without perhaps fully understanding the complexities of the procedures. He could tell that Penshall had not spoken much of this before, and was still having difficulty in breaching the personal code which had prevented him from doing so. But now having started, Penshall talked more and more freely. Shilvers concentrated once again on what he was saying.

'. . . and that's the real problem. They've got these contracts to take nuclear waste from all over the world, and it's all coming in faster than they know what to do with it. What they have got in store already is leaking all over the place, and they have so many accidents in the decanning that there's a stockpile they don't know how to get rid of. That's the reason, if you ask me, that folk have got careless and there've been so many accidents.'

Shilvers now knew that he had a story and a damned good one, once the business about the disappearances had been explained away. He wondered if he dare risk taking a few notes, but decided not to in case it gave Penshall second thoughts about continuing.

'Anyway, there's been quite a few leaks and accidents with this stuff recently and when that happens all hell is let loose. There are different procedures for different levels of emergency, but mostly you just have to clear out of the central area as fast as possible and assemble at a specific point to be checked and counted. When an accident like that happens we're always sent home for the rest of the day, sometimes longer.'

'How serious can these accidents get?' asked Shilvers.

'I was coming to that.' Shilvers wished he had not spoken, and reminded himself not to try to hurry Penshall along.

'Very occasionally there's a big one and we have to evacuate the whole plant. We then have to go directly to our homes and wait there until we are told to come back to work. Sometimes it can be several days.'

'But how come these accidents aren't known about? Why aren't they reported in the papers? Things like this can't go on without some word of it getting out.'

'You forget, Mr Shilvers, everyone around here either works directly for Dounscraig, or someone in the family does. And I.N.I. takes great care that not much is obvious to outsiders. If we do have to evacuate, everyone has instructions to spread themselves out among the various exits so it doesn't look as though we're all pouring out at once. We're told to appear casual as we leave, and to say nothing to anyone about it, including family. We're always told that the future of the industry depends on public confidence, so if we spread alarm, we're endangering our own livelihoods.'

'Are any of these instructions written down?' asked Shilvers.

'How do you mean?'

'Are workers given any written instructions, any pieces of paper, telling them about these rules in case of emergency? Things like appearing casual and so on.'

Penshall looked at Shilvers almost as though he pitied him.

'Mr Shilvers, I.N.I. have been getting away with this for years. They may not do a very good job of running a nuclear plant, but they aren't entirely stupid either.'

Shilvers felt duly reprimanded and nodded understanding. Penshall continued.

'Anyway, in some of these accidents people have been very badly hurt.' He stopped speaking for a moment and once again his eyes turned to stare into the pitch-black sky. 'I've seen them, and I know. Sometimes it will be radiation poisoning, sometimes the effects of burns to the skin or lungs.' He stopped again. Shilvers could see that his mind was wandering over some particular incident. 'When this happens,' he spoke slowly, measuring every word, 'the people concerned are taken to the medical centre and are never heard of again.'

Once again Shilvers wondered how to deal with the situation.

He needed to ask questions without giving the impression that he thought Penshall was mad.

'But what about their families? They must live in the village. They must be told what has happened. What do they say?'

'You don't understand, Mr Shilvers. It isn't just the workers who go.' Shilvers could now see there was a tear forming in the corner of Penshall's eye as he spoke. 'It's the whole families. The wives, the kids, furniture, even the household pets belonging to these blokes up and vanish. Off the face of the earth. Like they never existed.'

Shilvers could only gaze into the face of this peculiar man who had turned up from nowhere in the middle of the night and was telling him the most unlikely story he had ever heard in his life, but in so down to earth a fashion that it seemed unnatural to disbelieve or doubt him. Several times Shilvers began a sentence with further questioning, and each time he had to draw himself up as he remembered that Penshall had already answered. A couple of minutes passed.

'I think we need a stronger drink.'

Shilvers had finished two large whiskys and Penshall was still sipping his first and neither men had spoken again. Shilvers had been keeping the whisky for emergencies or for a celebration if and when Julia turned up. He had not intended to touch it otherwise, but this situation definitely counted as an emergency.

What was he to make of it? The man was clearly sane but was talking like a madman. Everything he said sounded plausible until he got to the part about the disappearances, then it became incredible. It had been bad enough when Penshall seemed to be saying that just the workers disappeared. Now he said their entire households went with them.

At one moment Shilvers was angry with himself for even considering the possibility that what was being said to him could be true. At the next he was searching his mind for some explanation that did not insult this man's obvious intelligence. He dare not even suggest that the company might provide long-term convalescence for the victims of accidents and their families, in case he irritated Penshall more than his scepticism had already done.

At last Shilvers drew a deep breath. 'If all this is true, Mr Penshall, and you'll forgive me if I say that some of it sounds a bit far-fetched, why have you come to me? Why not go directly to the police?'

'I came to speak to you because you are a journalist.' Penshall was speaking more quietly again and with apparently inexhaustible patience. 'The police around here are like that,' he indicated two fingers close together, 'with the security people at Dounscraig, and even if my complaint forced them to do something they would get to hear who had made it. Like I say, most of the people round here rely for their livelihoods on Dounscraig. They don't want to go back to scratching a living off the land. Few of them could anyway. That's what the row was about in the Huntsman the other night. I, and one or two others, think things have gone far too far. Others want to say nothing. While they feel like that I'm taking a big chance even being here, and whatever happens my name must not be mentioned.'

Shilvers gave him the necessary reassurance. He had to admit that what Penshall had said did fit in with the fragment he had heard in the pub the previous night. He was wondering what to do next when Penshall spoke.

'I know what you're thinking, Mr Shilvers.'

Shilvers hoped he did not.

'You're thinking that there is a simple explanation, and that I'm a simple country fellow who can't see it. Well you are wrong, Mr Shilvers, dead wrong, and I can see I had better tell you why.' Penshall sat up straight in his chair and put his glass to one side, looking directly at Shilvers. 'My own brother, Mr Shilvers, my brother George. He went to work up at Dounscraig at the same time that I did. We gave up farming the same miserable plot at the same time and chucked it in to get an inside job. We've both been well thought of because we were both brought up to do a fair day's work for a fair day's pay. One day George was getting rid of some harmless rubbish from one of the research labs run by a bloke called Smedley. A canister was dropped, all hell broke loose and the area was evacuated. Everyone near the accident was taken to the medical centre and nothing was heard of any of them. I eventually asked at the centre and they said he had been discharged so I went to his home. It was empty. His wife Gloria, the two kids, George and Annie and all their things gone. Not a trace. Not a damned thing left. Everything was gone. Then four months later Smedley turned up again, his face very badly scarred. There was no sign of George. No sign of the family.'

Penshall's voice had grown fainter as he related the story, and as he came to the end of it Penshall put his head in his hands and sat silently. Shilvers had no idea what to say.

'I'll do my best to help you, Mr Penshall,' he said finally. 'I don't know what the answer is, but I'm sure there is one and your brother and his family are safe and sound somewhere. I.N.I. wouldn't dare do anything silly, and they'll turn up in good time. I'm sure they will.'

Penshall was still sitting silently, his head resting in his hands. Shilvers watched and saw a single tear fall on to the table in front of him.

CHAPTER SIX

Penshall wrote a list of six names and addresses, with approximate dates next to them, before setting off down the cliff path to go on the night-shift at Dounscraig. These were men who, he said, had vanished after accidents at the plant. Shilvers noticed that he had chosen to go back towards the village. Obviously his own route across country towards Dounscraig was not the accepted one.

Penshall also left his own address, but begged Shilvers not to contact him in case it became known that the two men had talked. Shilvers decided to be particularly careful to protect Penshall as his informant. Whatever the truth of this story, the angry voices he had overheard in the Huntsman were real. He did not want to put his only source, a man who had put trust in him, in jeopardy.

Shilvers sat down at the table, looked out across the nothingness and listened to the crashing waves beating against the rocks. If he concentrated hard on the noise it seemed deafening, as the great might of the ocean battered itself relentlessly against the ungiving cliff. Yet the face of the cliff did give way. As it rolled on and on, back and forth, year in and year out for decades and centuries, the untiring sea appeared to have no effect on the land, the immovable object. Yet almost imperceptibly, little by little, inch by inch, it nibbled away at the solid rock barrier. Now the cliff edge was only a few yards away from the front door of this cottage. Thirty years ago the cottage probably had a front garden. One hundred years ago sheep probably grazed between the cottage and the edge. One thousand years? Ten thousand years ago? What about a thousand years from now? Ten thousand? The cottage would certainly be long gone and so, perhaps, would Dounscraig too. The boundless energy of the ocean, which never gave up when pushed back time and time again without number, would eventually claim its reward. The apparently firm obstacle would give way after all.

Shilvers slept uneasily. The story and the whisky and the thoughts of Julia intermingled in his brain. Penshall must be mad. It was the most insane story he had ever heard. Why had he even bothered to sit there politely while someone who had appeared from nowhere told him the most outrageous story he had ever heard in his life? He thrashed back and forth in bed, trying to relax. And yet. And yet if it was true. If there was even a single element of truth in it. If. If. If. If that were so this was the biggest and most important story he would ever get near. At the moment it was his story. He was determined that it should remain so until he discovered whether it had any element of truth whatever.

In the twilight world between fitful sleep and disturbed consciousness, Shilvers' mind wandered through fantastic thoughts and dreams. Extravagant and eccentric possibilities and ideas crowded in and mingled with the distant unending roar of waves lashing a shoreline a million miles away.

Certainly he was prepared to believe that there were many accidents that the public never got to hear of. Certainly it made sense that Dounscraig would not want the world to see what could happen when a man came too close to a radioactive cocktail. But to lift people out of the world as though they had never existed? To remove their entire families? How much would Dounscraig have to pay to guarantee absolute silence? What about their friends, distant relatives? The whole thing was mad, absolutely stark raving mad. He must put it out of his mind. He must. In his dream he heard an enormous thunderstorm, trees crashing to the ground, brought down by the force of the sea-gales. He heard a man screaming a long slow scream, then it stopped. He saw lights and heard voices, men crouching low as an enormous bird hovered in the air and threatened to grab them with its talons. Then there was silence.

As another damp dawn broke Shilvers was still thinking about Alf Penshall. He looked around the room and examined the peeling whitewash which seemed to be holding the ceiling together. Eventually the stale taste of too many cigarettes and whisky forced him to get up. The living room was full of the same dull fog which clogged in his mouth. Two unwashed glasses on the table by the window reassured him that the conversation which now seemed part of the bad dream had been real. Without enthusiasm Shilvers went about getting the place warm and habitable, preoccupied all the time by the extraordinary information he had been given.

Once or twice he caught Julia laughing at him from the mantelpiece where her picture was an echo of a sunny carefree day in another life on another planet. Was she laughing at him now, obsessed as he was by this ridiculous notion, or was her smile encouraging him to get involved in a damned good story? If only she were here to tell him. She always had a good perspective on whatever he was involved with at the time. When he was too close to something to be able to see it for what it really was. When he was cursing several Fleet Street newspapers for being too crass to see the point of what he was offering them. When he railed against the editors for not allowing him to stick his neck out for one inch in case the proprietors' axe came down. Then Julia was always able to remind him of what he had overlooked. The basics of the story. Who did it hurt? Who did not want it known? What influence did those people have on the newspaper? If only Julia were here now.

Shilvers sat where he could not see her picture and winced at the strength of the black coffee. What did he know about Dounscraig? Not very much. He began to wonder who might. Whose patch was this overlooked part of the world? Then he remembered George Ffitch. George Ffitch had been the Night Editor on the *Sentinel* when Shilvers had first arrived in Fleet Street from his regional newspaper in Bradford. Ffitch had been a damned good reporter in his day, moving all over the world, filing despatches from war-zones and trouble-spots and riot areas and royal tours, and floods and droughts and famines. Ffitch had been one of the best firemen in the business. His job was to go wherever there was trouble, where nobody in their right mind wanted to go, where bombs were falling and landmines were blowing people's feet off.

'You always know you're in the right place laddie,' he would say in his strong Glaswegian drawl, 'when the planes going in are empty and the planes going out are full.'

Eventually Ffitch, like all the others with any sense, had come in from the cold, but his animated and anecdotal style still entertained younger colleagues like Shilvers. They had become friends, the older jibing the younger about the toughness of the old days, the younger ribbing the older about romanticizing the reality, but secretly knowing that most of it was true. Ffitch had quit the *Sentinel* shortly after Shilvers himself had left to go freelance. Shilvers remembered that Ffitch's wife had come from this part of the country and he now recalled that he had set up a news agency in the area. In any case Dounscraig would almost certainly be a part of Ffitch's patch, and if there was anything unusual going on there, he would be sure to know about it.

Shilvers went to his jacket and pulled out a scruffy little red contacts book which went everywhere with him. He looked up Ffitch. It was a Westermouth number, and that was only twenty miles down the coast. He decided to call him straight away.

Having dressed quickly in the same clothes he had worn yesterday and splashed cold water over his face, he examined his reflection in the tiny and slightly distorted shaving mirror which stuck out on an extending steel arm above the bathroom sink. He was immediately struck by the dark shadows under his eyes. He raised his eyebrows to study the ever-deepening lines burrowing into his forehead. He wrinkled up his face to inspect the lines around his eyes and in his cheeks. He had to accept that he looked older than his forty-two years. He had not shaved or brushed his hair for four days, which added five years to his appearance. Even so time, he knew, had not been a friend. Twenty cigarettes a day and two bottles of Scotch a week had not been any help. So much for the healthy seaside life, he thought, and buried his face in a towel which was still damp from yesterday.

Shilvers put on his donkey jacket and opened the door. As he did so it occurred to him for the first time to lock it behind him. Recent events had had a profound effect.

Once in the village Shivers made straight for the telephone-box which stood on a corner of the green in front of the post office. As he swung open the door he caught a glimpse of one of the twins peering through the rows of boiled sweets which seemed to have faded with many generations of feeble sunlight. She disappeared behind the board which displayed the postcards where Shilvers had first seen the advertisement for the cottage.

He was enormously relieved to use a telephone box which did not have all the windows smashed or smell of stale urine. There were after all some advantages to village life. The code-book was in pristine condition, and attached to the handset by a piece of string. He flicked through to find the code for Westermouth. Shilvers carefully dialled the number from his contacts book. He heard it ring three times before there was a click and he struggled clumsily to press his 10p coin into the slot.

'George!' For some reason he was shouting, but the mechanical voice on the other end took no offence and continued to drone out a familiar message.

'This is the West of Britain News Service. There is no one here at the moment, but if you have routine copy you can dictate it on to this answering machine, which does accept transfer charge calls. Or leave your name and number and Mr Ffitch or his staff will get back to you. Start speaking after the tone.'

Shilvers had coped with these machines for years, and even had one in his own flat, but his mind still went blank when faced with the challenge of composing a single sentence which summed up everything he wanted to say. When the urgent tone finished he prepared himself.

'George? It's me, Tony Shilvers. I'm up here on business for a while. I'm not on the telephone, and don't have a car, so I wonder if you feel like driving down to Winderwath where I'm staying? I'll be in the Huntsman tonight if you can make it. Hope to see you later, you old bastard.'

Shilvers immediately regretted the closing remark, but the machine had clicked off anyway. He stepped out of the telephone box and found himself ankle deep in damp autumn leaves. It was still overcast and the ugly dark clouds were being swept across the sky, pursued by an apparently unending series of even darker ones. Shilvers put up the collar of his donkey jacket and wondered what to do next. In his pocket he could feel a piece of paper. It was the list of names and addresses Penshall had given him. For one brief moment he toyed with the idea of simply walking into the post office and asking the twins where these people were. He dismissed the thought immediately. If anything Penshall had said was correct, then the dates of the disappearances might match the dates of the few accidents at the Dounscraig site which were notified to the Department of Energy and published. He went back into the telephone box and dialled a number which was permanently filed in his head. A few seconds later the call was answered.

'Daily Sentinel.' Shilvers asked for the newsdesk, and as he heard it ring he wondered whether any of his old friends would be on duty. Moments later a tired and familiar voice barked into the telephone.

'Newsdesk.'

'Hello Frank, don't they ever give you a day off?'

'Who the hell is that?' Shilvers then heard a muffled voice call across the desk, 'Hey you, shut the hell up a minute will you, I'm trying to talk here.'

'It's me. Tony Shilvers. You've got a short memory.'

The two former colleagues chatted until Shilvers' money ran out and he put the receiver down to wait for a return call. Frank Chaplin had occupied the desk next to him during freelance shifts over two years, and had been a well-known character in Fleet Street for many years before that. Every experienced newsman had some moment of good or bad luck or glory on which he dined out for decades. Frank's had been that he had been on the London Underground train which had crashed at Moorgate killing dozens of people. He had escaped with minor injuries himself, but his eye-witness account had been carried on every front page. He had never travelled on the tube since. As he waited for the phone to ring, Shilvers visualized the cluttered desks, the full ashtrays and nicotine-stained walls and was glad he had left that behind him. The telephone rang.

'Frank? I'll come clean. I want a favour.'

'Oh really, and here's me thinking you had a sudden urge to enquire about the welfare of Betty and the kids. They're fine, thank you for asking.'

'Touché. This will be one I owe you. Could you send me the cuttings on the Dounscraig nuclear reprocessing plant in West Cumbria? I want anything we've got on history, finance, expansions, accidents,' Shilvers included the latter as casually as he could, 'anything of interest. Maybe you could copy it for me and send it care of the post office at Winderwath which is a village nearby.'

'I can do that.' Chaplin was scribbling in a notebook. Then his instincts got working. 'Why, is there something up?'

Shilvers assured him that there was not. He was doing some pieces for the Tourist Board and wanted to be able to reassure holidaymakers that they were not likely to go home with radioactive sunburn and lungs full of fallout. Chaplin did not sound as though he believed it, but agreed to send the material.

'I'll remember you are in that area and if anything else comes up of interest I'll call on you. And remember, we get first look at anything you dig up, right?'

Shilvers smiled. The *Sentinel* probably would not touch this unless the entire board of I.N.I. management reported personally to the editor with signed confessions in triplicate. Even then they would want a doctor's certificate testifying to their sanity.

'O.K., Frank, I'll remember, but there's nothing. Really.'

Once again Shilvers was out in the chill air. He wondered about the list. The obvious first call was the electoral register which was usually kept in the public library, but in this case that was twenty miles away. He walked over to the post office and as he did so he noticed that he was whistling. Maybe, just maybe, he was on to something.

The sisters told him the electoral register was kept at the police station which was at the edge of the village. It took Shilvers ten minutes to find it, only to discover that it was not a police station but a police house, exactly like all the other houses in the street except that an outhouse was the local police office. Shilvers walked up the garden path and examined a notice in the window. It gave a long list of telephone numbers to be called in case of emergency, and the office opening hours as between one and two o'clock weekday afternoons. Shilvers looked at his watch. Eleven-thirty.

There was no sign of life at the house, but Shilvers rang the bell and waited. There was no answer. He walked a few steps to the office window which was divided into tiny diamond-shaped panes by thin strips of lead stuck on as an afterthought. Shilvers peered in to try to detect any sign of life. Nothing moved. Now he looked for the familiar thick volume which would be the electoral register. As he shielded his eyes and distorted his face to cut out the reflection he heard a loud and deliberate cough behind him.

'Good morning Mr Shilvers, something we can do for you?'

Shilvers wheeled round to see a large man wearing enormous blue trousers held up by both belt and braces, and a pale-blue shirt with no collar. He had a large head with bright red hair and a thick beard which accentuated his brilliantly ruddy complexion. The mass of untidy hair and great bulk gave the impression that the man was in his fifties, but the unlined face told Shilvers he was more probably around thirty-five. In his hand he held a half-eaten piece of toast which he waved around as he spoke.

'The office isn't open until after dinner. Is it an emergency?' The accent was unfamiliar.

Once again Shilvers felt he had been caught in the act of doing something suspicious. So much for the investigative reporter, he thought. He apologized for interrupting breakfast and asked how the man knew his name. The bushy red eyebrows knitted together.

'It's my business to know what goes on around here, Mr Shilvers. When you appeared up here I asked old Mr Shaw who owns your cottage who you were and what you were up to.' That answers quite a few questions, thought Shilvers. 'Anyway, the dear old ladies in the post office regard it as their civic duty to keep me informed. You'd be amazed how easy they make my job.' Shilvers was past being amazed at anything that went on in Winderwath but resisted the temptation to say so. He was relieved that the policeman seemed to be in a good mood.

'I am looking for the electoral register. Do you keep it here or is it in the library at Westermouth?'

'Oh yes, we're just about trustworthy enough to look after a volume of the electoral list. That's about all like, most things have to be referred upwards you know.' The policeman spoke as though he was repeating the maxim which governed his existence, and Shilvers thought the resentment had probably long since turned to resignation. 'I'll have it for you in a moment.' He crammed the last corner of toast into his mouth and approached the door, feeling in his pocket for the keys. As he reached it he turned round.

'But I'm sure I can help you with whatever you want to know about people round here. What is it that you're after?'

Shilvers was taken by surprise. Once again the policeman's enquiry had made his bushy eyebrows knit together in a tangled and continuous mass in the middle. Shilvers had not had time to invent a credible story. His mind performed a somersault.

'I'm checking on a few local family names. As you already know so much about me you no doubt know that I'm writing some articles for the Tourist Board. I'm interested in long-standing local families who may be able to trace their roots back into history. What's your surname for example?'

'Charlton. Constable Charlton.' Shilvers gathered that the man had little idea what he was talking about.

'Well that might well be a traditional name in this area and

I might well be looking up your ancestors. Anyway, can I take a look at the register?'

The officer turned back to open the door and rustled the large bunch of keys until he found the correct one. Before he opened the door he turned back again to face Shilvers.

'My family comes from Jarrow.' He pushed open the door. 'The office isn't really supposed to be open until this afternoon. The sign says it clear enough. Not until this afternoon.'

Both men went in and the policeman jerked his head to an old-fashioned lecturing plinth with a red leather-bound volume on it.

'Help yourself,' said the policeman.

'I'll be quite a time if you want to finish your breakfast,' said Shilvers. Charlton hung around at the door awkwardly, apparently reluctant to leave.

'The office isn't supposed to be open until this afternoon. But when it is open, I'm supposed to be here.'

'This'll be a favour I owe you then. I'll give you a shout when I'm through.'

The policeman grunted again and shuffled awkwardly out of the door, his hulking frame blocking the light temporarily as he retreated. Shilvers waited for the crunch of heavy footsteps on the path to recede before reaching into his pocket for Penshall's list.

The register was compiled under addresses, but it was not difficult for Shilvers to run his finger down the surnames on the right-hand side of the page. Two of the people on the list, Thomkins and Parsons, appeared to live next door to each other. Shilvers wrote down the addresses. According to Penshall those were the most recent victims of accidents. Two pages on Shilvers found Erly and Aldwich and wrote down their addresses. There was no sign of the last two, Alf's brother George and a man called Morrison.

Shilvers looked around for an earlier copy of the register and saw it on the window-ledge. He quickly looked up the names and found all six. For some reason the last two, Penshall and

Morrison, had failed to register last time round. Shilvers looked at the dates on the paper in his hand. Sure enough, according to Penshall's list, his brother and Morrison had had accidents before this latest list was compiled. So far so good.

Now Shilvers would need the register of births, marriages and deaths. Once again he looked around, but could see nothing that looked likely. He closed the volume in front of him and went towards the door. As he did so he heard a distinct crunch on the gravel outside. He walked directly to it and immediately pulled it open. The policeman was standing a few feet away.

'I just came back to see if you wanted anything?' Charlton was trying to behave casually but both men knew he had been caught. Shilvers looked at the policeman's feet. The heavy shoes were gone and now he was wearing slippers. 'Did you find what you were after?'

'Not entirely,' said Shilvers. 'I was wondering about the register of births, marriages and deaths. Is that here?'

'No, no. Much too important to be kept down here, that's up at Westermouth. Anything else I can do for you?' He stepped forward and past Shilvers to pull the office door closed behind him. Shilvers glanced back in time to make sure he had not left the two volumes open.

'No, not just now thank you.' As Shilvers set off down the path he turned around to see Charlton standing at the door, feet wide apart and hands pushed deep into his pockets. Now the policeman had a smug smile on his face.

'This is a very small community, Mr Shilvers. Not much happens round here without people knowing about it. You might do well to remember that.'

'I've had that advice already, but thanks anyway.'

Shilvers walked quickly away, wondering what Charlton had meant. His repetition of the cliché Shilvers had heard so often in recent days carried an unmistakable warning. Was it known that he had overheard the angry exchanges at the Huntsman, or even that Penshall had visited him? Whatever was going on, the local policeman was part of it. Penshall had said something like it. The uncertainty meant that Shilvers would have to tread still more carefully.

'Gently does it,' Shilvers whispered to himself. 'Not too soon. Not too soon.'

CHAPTER SEVEN

Dr Graham Smedley took advantage of his isolation at the end of his normal working day to dim the lights in the laboratory and remove his shaded glasses. The heavy spectacles served the dual purpose of shielding his sensitive eyes from what was for him the glaring brightness of ordinary light, and of protecting others from the sight of the hideous damage done to his eyes by his accident. Now, in the dimness of his own room, Dr Smedley held his head only inches away from the page in front of him and peered through the gloom at his work, occasionally cross-checking his calculations on the visual display unit at his side.

Graham Smedley's official working day had ended at three o'clock that afternoon, and as usual since the death of his wife and his own accident fifteen months before, he was in his private laboratory putting in extra hours. On the desk in front of him was a large sheet of white paper with an elaborate drawing in fine lines, and at his side a sophisticated computer cabled into an enormous mainframe which served the entire complex. After years of using it continually, Smedley felt totally at home with the computer, but still his slide rule remained at his side and was consulted almost as often.

The computer screen had become for him the embodiment of the research project which had its real existence hundreds of feet below him in a sealed chamber set apart from the many other functions of the plant. It was as though the diagrams, blueprints, formulae and molecular structures detailed on the strobing display in front of him were in themselves the subject and the object of the exercise. Without actually admitting it to himself, Smedley knew that it helped him to think of the work in such terms. It was clean, clinical, remote and controllable, and the worst possible consequence of an error was a bleep and a user-friendly phrase discouraging further programming.

Only very occasionally was it necessary for him to visit the specially adapted laboratory in which the work was housed. Smedley's calculations and instructions were fed constantly via the terminal to expert operatives within the project, and the results and readings fed back to him to be checked by his squinting eyes direct from the screen.

This afternoon, for perhaps the fiftieth time, Dr Smedley was rechecking the calculations for the most critical and pioneering part of the experiment. This was the part which, if successful, would revolutionize the reprocessing of irradiated nuclear fuel, doubling its potential value for recycling into the fast-breeder reactor, and rendering it infinitely less dangerous and more manageable than was presently the case. Success would mean an incalculable world lead for his company and his country in a competitive international field, and would probably win him a Nobel Prize as well.

Such thoughts, however, were very far away as Dr Smedley went over the same areas of his work again and again, because nagging in the recesses of his mind, with an insistence he had never experienced in the thirty-year span of his scientific career, was a lingering doubt about the safety of the project. It was that doubt which brought him to the laboratory so frequently after everyone else on his work pattern had long since gone home.

Smedley looked at his watch. Six forty-five. An empty feeling in his stomach reminded him that he had not eaten since breakfast, and the staff canteen would be closing in fifteen minutes. The food here was unappetizing, but nowadays he hardly ever shopped, and still less often felt interested enough to prepare and cook food for himself. Only occasionally, when Jacqueline was coming to stay, would he go to any trouble to make sure there was a proper meal in the house. Otherwise he would make do with whatever was available.

The scientist picked up his tinted spectacles and put them on, at the same time standing up and heading towards the light-switch a few feet away from his work-bench. In the few seconds between those two actions he was looking with poor eyesight through darkened lenses in a gloomy room, and it was just at that moment that he felt the movement below his feet. From deep in solid rock, in what could have been the very core of the earth itself, came a long low growl, and with it a perceptible low-frequency vibration which spread through the cushioned floor of the laboratory and into his shoes, there to be sensed in his feet and ankles, and up through his legs to his entire body. Dr Smedley was for a moment a part, himself, of the rumble deep below the earth.

The monochrome world which he constantly inhabited settled around him and he turned to the keyboard of the computer and tapped out the menu for monitoring checks. Beneath his feet the movement was already settling and subsiding. The snarl had reached a quick climax and was fading. Within moments a mass of green print reviewed a checklist of vital monitors, and an automatic program was ticking off each element to confirm that it was within critical limits. Smedley's eyes avidly read off the screen, his face turning to follow the cursor from side to side of the screen as it wrote. His hands gripped the edges of his bench.

One by one the readouts came up and one by one the computer checked them off as positive and within safety limits. Smedley had never counted them. Perhaps there were a hundred separate readings to be checked and co-ordinated. Each readout was of course automatically monitored all the time, and an alarm was programmed to sound should any of them even edge towards the critical. No such alarm had sounded. None of the readings was in any way odd. Smedley took his eyes from the screen and looked around him. He looked at his hands gripping the bench and noticed that they were shaking. The ends of his knuckles were white. Unable to make sense of messages from his hands, Smedley pressed his feet harder against the floor to see whether the vibration was still detectable. He concentrated hard. He thought that it was not. Then he reached for a telephone with no dial. Second later there was a click.

'Project Nine Hundred.'

'Smedley. Is everything all right?'

'Yes, I think so sir. Why?' The voice was calm and relaxed. 'Have you got a problem?'

Smedley's anger was about to splutter into the mouthpiece when he checked himself.

'No, I have no problem.' Smedley made sure he was under control. 'Has anyone down there reported anything out of the ordinary?'

'No sir. Is there any reason to think they should have done?'

'No no. None whatever.' Smedley suddenly felt completely exhausted and had to support his head on his hand. 'I was just double-checking before knocking off for the night.'

'No. Everything's O.K. Good-night Dr Smedley.'

'Good-night.' The receiver clicked dead. Smedley's elbow was pressed hard against the desk and his brow was pressed into his hand. There was no vibration and no sound. Despite himself Dr Smedley's contorted face contorted still further into a long yawn. His right hand pressed his glasses up to his forehead to rub his eyes. Wearily he looked about him and at the computer screen, still running through constant readings and checks. He turned heavily in his seat and began to tap the keyboard. Once again he was going to check and recheck his calculations.

Three hours later, with the vast silence that inhabits an enormous empty space crowding in all around him, Dr Graham Smedley was focusing on a small area of his calculations. As he worked with slide rule and pencil and calculator and computer, Smedley became aware that the ache he could feel entering his head from the left side was partly caused by pressure from his left hand. The stress he was under had caused his entire body to lock up, so that every molecule of him was dedicated to the problem in front of him. He felt that he had never concentrated so hard as at this moment, never been so obsessed with solving a problem. And now he was in the area of the error, and was hunting it down. There was something wrong, of that he was now quite sure, but what it was still eluded him. In his pool of light in the centre of darkness, Dr Graham Smedley struggled in silence. The whispered interruption had the impact of a thunderbolt.

'Hi Pop. Working late again?'

Smedley wheeled around to see his daughter Jacqueline standing over him with a half-eaten bran roll in her hand and her raincoat thrown over her shoulder.

'Good God girl. You could have killed me.' His surprise was expressing itself in anger and the words had no sooner left his mouth than he regretted them. He struggled to regain composure. 'You can talk. If you're here checking on me you must be late too.' He had retrieved the situation before the offence had made full impact.

'Well it sounds as though we've both earned a break.' She perched herself on the corner of his desk and threw the remnants of the bread roll into his waste paper basket. 'How about buying your favourite daughter some dinner?' She smiled a beautiful smile.

Smedley was about to make an excuse. He glanced down at the V.D.U. and the notepad in front of him. The error he was searching for was somewhere in there and he had to find it. On the other hand he had not seen or spoken to Jacqueline for a fortnight and he disliked passing up an opportunity to do so. He looked at his watch. It was ten o'clock.

'O.K., you're on. Where's open?'

Forty-five minutes later father and daughter were sitting on either side of a small table covered in a red gingham cloth in the only restaurant in Westermouth which opened late. It was an unpretentious establishment and Smedley was a sufficiently regular customer for the waiters to have become used to his disfigurement and show no reaction to it. It was one of the reasons why Smedley liked coming here. Now he looked at his only daughter as she chatted about nothing in particular and thought how small and fragile she looked, and reflected that he had thought the same about her when she started school twenty-five years ago and that he had been worried about her ever since. Now she was a fully grown, well educated, independent and very attractive young woman, and for him nothing had changed. He still felt overwhelmingly and insanely protective towards her, and quite impotent since he knew that nothing he could do could ever make her change her mind once it was made up. He was still looking at her, immersed in his own thoughts, when he became aware that her tone of voice had changed.

'Are you going to tell me about it?'

He was jolted into a response. 'Sorry? I'm not with you.'

There was not a trace of reproach in her voice. 'You haven't listened to a word I've said since we got in the car, and you aren't registering a thing I'm saying even now. You've got a problem, and I'm asking you if you're going to share it with me, or whether we are going to have a one-way conversation all night?'

Graham Smedley peered through the dark shades at his daughter and if she had been able to see through the tinted glass she would have noticed a small tear forming in the corner of his contorted left eye. In that moment she had reminded him as so often before of her mother, dead ten years earlier from leukaemia. The special bond he shared with Jacqueline was partly born from the fact that they had endured the tragedy together. He looked down at the table and blinked away the tear before replying.

'O.K., Sherlock Holmes, I'll come clean. I have a problem, and I am a lucky man because I have a daughter who can understand what I'm talking about when I describe it.'

It was late, and the last customers were saying noisy farewells to the waiter, who then immersed himself in drying an apparently endless series of wine glasses. Smedley spoke in low whispers and Jacqueline had to lean across the table to pick up all his words. He gave a general description of the project he was working on, leaving out precise details of the means or the end. He described the two small incidents which he seemed to be the only one to have sensed, but omitted his concern that perhaps he had hallucinated them. He revealed that he thought he had found an area of the calculations in which there could be a fundamental and potentially dangerous error, but said that he could not be sure and had not isolated any specific problem. All the while Jacqueline listened intently, giving her undivided attention, and asked only occasional questions. When he had finished talking she remained silent for a few moments. Then she put down her fork and pushed her plate away.

'What is the bottom line? How dangerous could it be?'

Now it was Smedley's turn to face the question he had been trying to avoid. His mind raced through the computable factors which contributed to an answer to her question.

'Apocalyptic.'

CHAPTER EIGHT

Shilvers was now totally preoccupied with the question of how to pursue the story. Time and again he turned things over in his mind, and every time he reached some tentative conclusion he felt an overwhelming need to discuss it with Julia. He found himself searching the cupboards to see if he needed anything which would justify the walk to the village so that he could enquire at the post office while he was there. He felt unwilling to go solely to make the enquiry, and then wondered why he was reluctant. Perhaps if he allowed himself to acknowledge his dependence on her it would hurt too much to discover that he had lost her. He felt it was all too complicated for him. He was trying to protect himself from the pain that was inevitable.

At last he made up his mind that he was being foolish. He would go.

'I could do with the walk.' He knew he was still deceiving himself and yet went ahead anyway. An hour later he was at the post office.

'Were you expecting something important?' asked the thin twin. His disappointment must have been obvious. He shrugged his shoulders and set off back up the cliff path to the cottage. He was puzzled to have heard nothing from Julia. It was true that she had said it could be several weeks, but he had been sure that there would have been a note, or something, before this. He stopped to regain his breath and looked out over the ocean.

Julia had been a fashion photographer when Shilvers had first arrived at the *Sentinel*. She had done bits and pieces for most of the popular women's magazines, and did occasional freelance work for the women's pages of the *Sentinel*. The paths through news and women's features seldom crossed, but Shilvers had noticed her the very first time she walked through the newsroom. She was tall and slim and her auburn and slightly wavy hair had bounced on her shoulders as she walked. From behind the safety of his typewriter and across the distance, Shilvers watched her chatting to some of the women in the newsroom. Her eyes sparkled and she laughed infectiously.

One day he asked about her and was told that her work was very well thought of. The only reason that she worked irregularly was that she preferred designing clothes to photographing them. The photography paid the rent while she made a series of efforts to break into the tight circle of successful fashion design.

Shilvers had already been aware that Julia was a very stylish dresser. One day she bubbled through the office wearing an impeccably cut black velvet suit and a black beret, her camera bouncing on her slim hip as she walked. He had manoeuvred so that it looked as though their meeting in the lift was an accident. He started some banal conversation which had led in just four floors to an invitation to dinner. To his amazement and delight she had accepted.

They had gone to a French restaurant where she was known by her first name. Shilvers looked across the table into her smiling eyes and wondered how many other men had brought her to the same place, the same table. He could not take his eyes from her as she voraciously ate avocado followed by seafood and washed it all down with chilled Chablis. Her hair had been tied back, and in the occasional silences she smiled across the table at him, her vivid green eyes sparkling in the candlelight. He had been mesmerized.

Later that night as they had made love in her tiny apartment above an aromatic Jewish delicatessen in Earls Court, Shilvers thought he had never been as happy with a woman before. He was thirty-five, had never been married, and was content for it always to be so. She was ten years younger, beautiful, and very independent. Their romance was ecstatic and quite unlike anything either of them had known previously, and that weekend in Brighton had ended with her moving more or less permanently into his flat. She kept on her place in Earls Court for her own peace of mind, she said. He had not argued.

As Shilvers started up the hill he realized that once again he was blinking through a mist of tears. It alarmed him that he felt so vulnerable without her. He could scarcely bring himself to believe that this would be the end of things between them. It had been seven years, much of that time very good indeed. Had he taken her for granted? Neither of them had discussed the subject of marriage or children, but it was just something that had never arisen. Both of them were very much aware that the failure rate of marriages in their business was enormously high. So many of his colleagues were living in squalid bedsitters and paying the mortgage on houses which they only ever visited as guests, watching their children go on holiday with the new man in the life of their wives. He had witnessed the agony of colleagues who knew that the problems had been created by themselves.

It was the job, they all said, the long hours. Shilvers always nodded sympathetically, but knew that this was only a part of the problem. It was not just long hours, it was the obsession with the story. It was always just one more phone-call and just one more meeting in a dingy pub for that extra elusive piece of information. Then with the climax of getting the story on to the presses, the need to wind down with the colleagues who had shared it. Meanwhile wives or husbands or boyfriends or girlfriends waited at home, and waited and waited until they got tired of waiting and waited no longer. They got tired of being second to the story, and of being told that things would be easier when this particular enquiry was over.

With Julia things had been different. She was not one to wait at home. She had worked hard to get on in her own career, and was doing well. Gradually more and more of her drawings were accepted at reputable fashion houses and her name began to be mentioned in magazines read by people she referred to with some contempt as the 'in-crowd'. Increasingly the photography took second place, but the same contacts were more and more useful. Then, just occasionally, Julia would call him and cancel a meeting because she had to see an important person in the fashion world. Sometimes it would be a buyer in town from abroad who would want to take her to dinner. She could not refuse, she said.

The first time it happened Shilvers felt a jolt. He realized that he resented coming second to her work and it pulled him up sharply. Then one day she had come home full of joy and told him that a fashion house wanted her to go to Rome for a week to look at some ideas and adapt them for the home market. A week in Rome, surrounded by the pretty young men of the fashion world. Shilvers had reacted irrationally. He did not want her to go. He extracted fulsome promises of faithfulness from her. He felt in agony at being on the receiving end of treatment which he had so often before thought nothing of giving out.

While she was away she had telephoned him each night and he had sulked and brooded. By day he was quietly proud of her independence and excellence in a fiercely competitive world. By night he was tortured by images of extravagant parties, agonies he tried to drown through immersion in his own work and, when that failed, in drink.

When Julia returned things had been different. He was distinctly more attentive, more appreciative. She saw it and enjoyed it. He had always treated her well as a woman, now he treated her well as a successful person. She liked it a lot.

For her the trip to Rome meeting beautiful people had underlined the glamour of the world she had chosen to work in. It had also underlined for her its shallowness. Bright young men and dizzy young girls, obsessed only with their own appearance, their vivacity excusing their lack of personality. The only meaningful relationship was the one between the model and the camera lens. The puckering and pouting and manipulation and miaowing were all aimed at the market, and that was the front cover of one of a small number of exclusive magazines. Today's one-off idea was tomorrow's rack full of clothes with fancy labels and fancier prices.

When Julia returned to Shilvers she knew she was returning to the world of real people. She knew that he felt insecure and she did her best to reassure him, but she also knew that the separation had done them both good. It was a renewal of their romance, because the flash of joy she felt in her career brought the unexpected bonus of his new appreciation of her. She felt happy.

Then, as weeks and months went by and both were busy in their jobs, imperceptibly, inevitably, they slipped into a routine. More and more her work took her away and his took him away. They would meet on the stairs, a piece of toast in hand, and kiss each other fleetingly on the cheek as they hurried for this train or that plane or another meeting. They were both successful and took passing pleasure in each other's success, but became increasingly wrapped up in their separate lives.

When Shilvers returned from a trip to Sicily where he had been enquiring into the most recent Mafia killings he left a suitcase of dirty clothes in the hall and went straight into the office. The candles on the dinner table she had prepared had waxed and her feelings of welcome had waned, until both were eventually extinguished. When Shilvers had returned at 1.30 in the morning carrying a copy of the *Sunday Times* with his article splashed all across the front page he was exhausted but exhilarated with achievement. Julia was curled up in bed, her pillow wet with tears, and unable to explain why she was so distressed.

One day, after an especially frantic struggle to meet a design deadline, Julia had come home and spent the entire weekend looking out of the window of Shilvers' flat. It was a view she had not looked at for more than a few seconds in the entire six years she had lived there. She was rushing from job to job, he was away more than he was at home. Nothing was happening in their relationship except more of the same.

She had found a note telling her that he had been given a job which would take him up to the north-west for a few weeks. Would she try to arrange to join him at weekends? She picked up the phone and accepted the design project she had been asked to undertake in Paris. When he came home, she told him she was going away, and would use the time to think about separating.

'Think about separating?' Shilvers had been confused and hurt by what seemed the suddenness of it all.

'About everything. Us. Me. You. Where we're going together, or where we're going apart. I don't know.' There were tears in her eyes which she fought to control.

'Going apart?' Shilvers had been aghast. At a loss.

'I don't know. Nothing is happening between us. We share a flat, you put my clothes in the launderette, I do your ironing, we occasionally eat together and even less often we make love. I just don't know what it's all about.'

Shilvers had acquiesced. He had no choice. In a final and desperate effort he had asked her to marry him. She had laughed and cried all at once. That was not what she meant. She yelled 'not' at him, frustrated that he appeared to think the problem so predictable and the answer so simple. But she warmed to him before they parted and assured him that things would be all right. She would just use the time to clear her head. He should do the same, and if he left his address at the post office at Winderwath she would find him.

'It will be O.K. I don't know how long, but it will be O.K.'

Julia's words echoed around his head as he reached the summit of the cliffside climb towards the shepherd's cottage which he recently called home. It felt a long way from home just now. Shilvers stopped and peered over the precarious edge down to the grey and white patterns in the surf all that way below. He thought about how those same waves crashed against those same rocks with the same endurance and the same violence when we were watching, or when we were sleeping, or when we were going about our business hundreds of miles away, and long before any of us were born and long after all of us have died. They were the nearest thing to eternity we could understand, and yet even here the rocks were being pushed gradually back, gradually back.

After lunch of soup, beans, crackers and coffee Shilvers once again tried hard to make progress on the business he had come here for. The Tourist Board wanted ten thousand words for a comprehensive guide to the area, and several shorter pieces on different aspects of the local attractions for everything from holiday brochures to the backs of postcards. The work, which had been going so well, was now going very badly. What would the Tourist Board say when they realized that he was taking the time they were paying him to write copy to make people visit the area, actually to write a story which would keep everyone away? He would worry about that when he had to.

Half-past three. Four hours before he would go down to the Huntsman and wait for George. Try as he would to concentrate on the attractions of rural Cumbria, the same thoughts kept filling his head. Was Alf Penshall mad? Did he just have a vivid imagination, or was he simply mistaken? At last Shilvers conceded defeat and decided to go for another walk to look at the Dounscraig plant. Once again he put on his donkey jacket and hiking boots and locked the door behind him. As the thunderous roar of the waves crashing ashore receded into the howling wind, Shilvers' thoughts scurried around Penshall, Julia, Dounscraig, the Tourist Board and the Huntsman. As he strode along he felt the need to exert himself physically up to, and beyond, the limit of his endurance. Perhaps then he could flush these thoughts out of his head. He quickened his pace as the wind beat ceaselessly into his face and through his hair. Even at this height the air was so wet it was as though the sea-spray was mingling with the wind to send shivers through his body and into his bones. His face was damp with the air and perspiration. His breathing was heavy and his fingers maliciously crushed a pack of cigarettes in his pocket as he quickened his pace again. Jumping over small rocks and puddles of water he scuttled on.

After the crisis of crippling pain under his ribs and alarming breathlessness Shilvers at last started to feel a little more comfortable. The light-headed feeling that at any moment he might trip and collapse in a heap had now passed and he began to feel happier that although he was a physical wreck, he might not be totally beyond repair.

Now he was beginning to look out for the metallic domes of Dounscraig, and listen for the dull moan of power. Any sound was drowned out by the howling wind gusting now from in front, now from behind.

At last Shilvers recognized the hill which had hidden the plant on his first visit, and peeled off left towards it. As he crossed a valley before the ascent he was running, determined to reach the top without a pause. Halfway up, he felt certain that he would die before he reached it. His knees ached, his chest heaved with exertion, his legs mutinied at the command to go forwards and upwards. He tucked his head into his chest for a last effort and surged on, ever nearer the top.

Then, as he was a few feet away, Shilvers once again lifted his head to take in the sight which had so astonished him a few days earlier. This time he was ready for what he saw. First the massive rim of the cooling tower, then a second nearby. Each step brought more chimneys and roofs of more buildings into view. He felt like a visitor from another planet, quite unable in his mind to establish a relationship with the metal and concrete edifice before him. There was hardly a window or opening in some of the massive concrete blocks, which could only be offices. Perhaps a quarter of a mile away from the nearest building, the forbidding barbed-wire fence which stretched as far as the brows of hills in the distance on both directions.

As Shilvers scanned the scores of structures of every shape, he tried to sort out in his mind the sounds that crowded into his ears. The wind seemed to whistle around the blocks below, and mingled with the potent dull growl of power which filled the air. It vibrated through the wind and through the ground. Shilvers realized that the sound did not appear to be coming from the direction of Dounscraig, but rather it was all around him, in the air above, and in the rocks and earth below, and for a few moments it almost seemed as though it was the sound of the ocean on the rocks now miles away. Shilvers wheeled around as if to catch the direction and lost his balance. He missed his footing and fell heavily on to one knee. Stumbling to regain himself he discovered that the sound seemed louder nearer the ground. Now his head was full of the sounds from the cottage, the huge seas battering the headland, mingling with the sound of immense power from the nuclear plant.

Shilvers leaned down to put his head still nearer to the ground. The sound was louder yet. He put his ear to the rock below him and heard the rumble deep in the earth. It sounded clearer now, more like a regular, mechanical throb. It seemed like a vast engine throbbing deep within the ground. As Shilvers listened it was as though his own heart was beating simultaneously with the underground pulse. His body was part of the massive machine. As he pressed his head hard against the ground it seemed to Shilvers that he could feel his heart pumping blood around his body and into his head, until he felt that the total noise was within him and his ears were ready to split from the pulsating blood and thumping beat. In the deep background of the din, a thin, repeated sound wailed through the rest. It was a claxon, an alarm, a warning of escaping vapour deep in the heart of the nuclear plant.

With his head still spinning Shilvers tried to right himself and had to crouch to regain his direction and balance. As his head began to clear he blinked in what felt like bright sunlight. When he did manage to stand, the sound seemed to have once again receded into the background. All he could decipher was the distant low hum from the power plant and the swirling and moaning wind.

A few moments later Shilvers was retracing his own footsteps down the hill. As he headed back towards the coast he wondered about the power of Dounscraig. Was it so strong that nothing could dent it, or might he be able to push it back just a few inches?

CHAPTER NINE

Walking down the hill towards Winderwath, the darkness had closed all around and only the light from a full moon illuminated the winding path in front of him. Shilvers looked up at the stars, pinpricks in the sky his mother had told him, but in reality lights leaving their sources thousands of years ago. Those stars which twinkled above might have been destroyed when this cliff was being trampled over by Roman legions wondering why they had come so far from home to this inhospitable country. A thought for his piece for the Tourist Board; the first Shilvers had had for several days. Now that he considered it and looked around him into the heavens, the scientific theory of the stars seemed far less likely than the explanation given by his mother all those years ago.

Shilvers began to think about the man he hoped he was on his way to meet. George Ffitch was the journalist who had seen it all and done it all and whom nothing could surprise. Shilvers recalled those early days when he was frequently given jobs which never really stood a chance of getting in the paper. He remembered the occasional word of encouragement from Ffitch when the latest story hit the spike. The hard man on the newsdesk turned out to be someone who could remember his own time running around the newsroom exchanging copy for coffee on the desks of rude and debauched-looking reporters. Don't be too impatient, he had told Shilvers in his soft Glaswegian voice, your time will come.

Ffitch had his hard side too. He could stand no hint of a lack of professionalism. Shilvers remembered the occasion when he had uncovered a story about a local councillor who had a swimming-pool in his garden installed by the same builder who had just won a contract to build the municipal baths. Lorries would drop off workers at the council site, then trundle on to drop off more workers at the councillor's house. The tiles lining the councillor's pool were even the same as those lining the municipal pool. Shilvers had written up the facts, alongside the councillor's 'no comment' and presented it to Ffitch.

'Rubbish rubbish rubbish,' Ffitch had yelled around the newsroom. 'Where's your proof, eh laddie? You've got none, have you. Not a receipt, not a cheque-stub, not a bloody thing. What's more you've blown your chance of getting it because that lying bastard will be covering his tracks so fast you won't see him move. You went in too soon, laddie . . .' The words had echoed around the newsroom and echoed around Shilvers' head. 'Too soon.' With the pompous brand of indignation that only journalists possess, Ffitch was most angry that this so-called public servant had wriggled off the hook. Shilvers had learned his lesson and never made the same mistake again. He thought how appropriate the advice was to his present investigation.

Now the man who had guided so much of his career might be able to help him again. He would have to handle Ffitch carefully. Ffitch had a nose for a story like nobody else he had ever met. If he got even a hint of what Shilvers had been told, he would be unable to resist making enquiries among his own contacts. Then it would take no time at all for Shilvers to be left behind. Shilvers would not be able to blame Ffitch; any reporter would do the same.

There were half a dozen locals in the Huntsman when Shilvers arrived, but no sign of George. He took his pint of beer to a corner table and considered how to handle the conversation. George would be furious when he eventually read the story and realized that he could have been in at the beginning, but Shilvers knew though that in the end he would understand. No journalist ever shared a scoop if he could help it, and so far he had no reason to do so. Shilvers realized he was running ahead of himself. At the moment he had no story, only one lead, and not a single attributable source. He would have to tread carefully. Don't go in too soon.

Shilvers sat silently for fifteen minutes, occasionally glancing at the group of locals who were huddled in a far corner of the bar talking in muted voices. The man Roache was among them, but none acknowledged his presence. He noticed worried glances exchanged between them, as if their conversation was a serious one. Shilvers would have given much to eavesdrop, but after his recent experience he dare not even try.

Through the frosted-glass window the twin beams of powerful headlights illuminated the inside of the bar and Shilvers heard the clunk of a car door. Seconds later an elderly man in a camel coat with a dark collar walked in. It was not George after all. Shilvers returned to his thoughts as the man went to the bar and ordered a drink. Moments later he was aware of a bulky figure standing at his shoulder.

'Anthony,' the gravelly voice was familiar, 'still not buying your turn I see.'

Shilvers looked up and recognized the gnarled face of George Ffitch, except that he looked totally altered. As he stretched out his hand in greeting, Shilvers took in the face of a man who had grown dramatically older. He had put on weight but had deep lines on his face, which seemed hollow and haggard. He stood with a slight stoop.

'George.' Shilvers was on his feet and trying to disguise his dismay. 'Do forgive me, I was miles away.'

'Well this is a pleasant surprise.' Ffitch sat heavily, opposite Shilvers. 'I instantly recognized that horrible cockney strain on my answering machine. What brings you to this godforsaken armpit?'

Shilvers glanced across to the group of local men in the corner, anxious that they might hear and be offended. He saw that they were now more animated but still immersed in their whispered conversation. There was no danger that they had overheard.

'Now then, George, I'm surprised you call it that. After all this is your adopted home isn't it?'

'Not here, this is wild country. Westermouth is like New York in comparison to this dump.'

Shilvers glanced up anxiously again. The intense conversation at the other side of the bar was continuing. He could see that Roache was leaning across the table and gesticulating at the others, obviously dominating the discussion.

Shilvers told him of the commission for the Tourist Board and his little cottage up the hill. Then Ffitch recounted the story of the West of Britain News Service and of the five promising young lads who were working for him for next to nothing in pay, and the two part-time secretaries whose typing was not too good but whom he found extremely attractive.

Half of Shilvers' attention was on the group at the other side of the bar. He was looking in their direction as he continued his casual chat.

'And how is that wife of yours and your two delightful daughters?'

There was a silence which drew Shilvers' attention back to his companion. Ffitch was looking into his drink and moving the glass from one hand to the next. In that moment his already haggard face looked about one hundred and fifty years old. After a long moment he spoke.

'Margaret and I split up. She's living in Scotland I believe. The girls have grown up and married. I don't see much of any of them these days.'

Shilvers was embarrassed and apologetic. He broke the awkward moment by taking their empty glasses to the bar for a refill.

'Anyway, you haven't brought me out here for a walk down memory lane,' Ffitch said when Shilvers returned to the table. 'What exactly are you up to?'

The emphasis was on 'exactly' and Shilvers recognized the suspicious glint in his old mentor's eye. He momentarily reconsidered the possibility of including him in the story, but a few seconds' further thought banished the idea from his mind.

'Well I was out for a walk the other day, George,' Shilvers took a swallow of his beer and spoke as casually as he could, 'when I came across the Dounscraig plant. That's about as welcome there as a french kiss at a family reunion isn't it?'

Ffitch laughed. The awkward moment had vanished.

'You'd better not let the locals hear you say that. It may not be a wonderful addition to the scenery but if you speak out against it round here you'll get a thick ear. There was a public enquiry here a few years ago when there was talk of expansion and a load of long-haired weirdos turned up to demonstrate. Half an hour later a group of locals turned up and gave them pretty short shrift. It was all right for them, they said, turning up once a year to go into a poetic trance about the beauty of the landscape, they had to live here all the time, and they needed the jobs Dounscraig provided. "You can't eat scenery" was our headline for the story. We made a fortune out of that one, selling it to the nationals.'

'But what about safety? Aren't the locals worried about that?'

'There's certainly been nothing spectacular,' said Ffitch without hesitation. Then there was a pause. 'Unless, of course, you know different?'

Shilvers shrugged his shoulders. 'No, I've heard nothing. I was just wanting to be sure that all the herds of people who come here after I write my stuff won't be roasted by gamma rays or whatever the hell it is these places give off.'

Ffitch looked at him carefully and Shilvers thought he could see that familiar glint in his eye. The old swine had changed enormously in his appearance, but the instincts were as sharp as ever.

'Well I.N.I. who run the plant are required to tell the Department of Energy of any accidents, and from time to time they do so.' The strong Glaswegian voice sounded cynical even without meaning to. But now Shilvers could detect no real trace of scepticism. 'There's never been anything involving casualties, and none of the stuff has ever leaked out of the site. If it had I would know about it. There's not much happens around here –'

Shilvers interrupted him. 'I know that already.'

As the evening wore on the two old friends moved on to talk of other things. From time to time Shilvers would raise the matter of Dounscraig, trying to catch Ffitch out. In the end he felt sure that Ffitch knew nothing more than he was saying. After several hours and a great deal of drink Shilvers and Ffitch shouted good-night to the barman and to the same group of men who were still engaged in their earnest conversation at the corner table. There was no answer. Outside, Ffitch returned to the subject of Dounscraig.

'Since you're so interested I'll turn out our cuttings on I.N.I. and send them over to you. So long laddie. Be seeing you soon.'

Seconds later the sound of crunching gears and squealing tyres confirmed for Shilvers his fear that Ffitch was in no fit condition to drive home. He wished out loud that Constable Charlton was safely tucked up in his bed, and set off up the hill.

Next morning Shilvers woke up suddenly to hear the sound of footsteps on the light shale outside the cottage door. A soft whistle told him that his immediate jumpiness was misplaced, and a second later there was a loud knock on the door and a cheerful voice calling out in a local accent.

'Postman Mr Shilvers.' Still reacting spontaneously Shilvers leapt out of bed and flung on a dressing-gown, tiptoeing with bare feet across the icy stone floor. An enormous blast of cold air whistled past as he opened the front door and the postman walked in as though invited. The man was stout, middle-aged, and looked as if he had been squeezed into a uniform which had been made for someone several sizes smaller.

'Registered letter Mr Shilvers.'

'You must be Harry,' said Shilvers, glad to have remembered that the twins had mentioned him. 'I didn't know you call up here though. I had my mail addressed to the post office.'

The man's face screwed up into a weather-worn smile. 'Well in the ordinary way I wouldn't come up here, but the ladies at the post office said you was expecting something and thought this might be urgent. They asked me if I wouldn't mind taking the trouble . . .' There was an unnatural emphasis on the last word, which brought Shilvers back to his senses. He glanced at the envelope and saw the address was typed, and so must be from the *Sentinel*. He tried to disguise his disappointment.

'I must give you something for your trouble.'

'Oh no, I couldn't let you do that sir,' said Harry slowly, 't'would be more than my job's worth that would.'

'Well,' said Shilvers, reaching for his wallet from the mantelpiece and taking out a five pound note, 'I won't be saying anything about it, and I daresay you won't either, so . . . '

Harry took the money. 'Well if you insist, I'm sure that's right kind of you.'

A moment later the postman's footsteps receded across the gravel and his thin whistle was lost in the wind.

Shilvers put the letter along with his wallet on the mantelpiece. It could wait until after his first cup of coffee. Five pounds was more than the service deserved, but it would be worth five pounds to him to get a letter from Julia promptly, so if it encouraged Harry to repeat the trip he reckoned it was money well spent. He put on the kettle and put a couple of logs on the pathetic embers in the stove. In a cupboard he found two cooked sausages which had been left over from a meal several days earlier. After sniffing them, he decided they would do for breakfast. As they warmed under the grill, Shilvers sat down over his coffee.

He had felt a slight boost yesterday when the names Penshall had given him had matched with names in the electoral register, and what was more two of them had failed to register on the latest list. That boost had dwindled away with the knowledge that Ffitch had heard nothing suspicious about the Dounscraig plant. A series of such big events, involving so many people, would be bound to reach the ears of the local freelance somehow, especially when that freelance was George Ffitch. How on earth could I.N.I. do it? With this question, Shilvers once again had to face the possibility that Penshall had just made some dreadful, or silly, mistake. The whole thing was a misunderstanding and he, Shilvers, was wasting time he should be devoting to profitable work.

He was shaken out of his thoughts by the smell of burning

fat coming from the grill, and he got up to scoop two blackening sausages on to a plate. As he dipped them into a jar of french mustard and took large mouthfuls, Shilvers wondered whether to give the whole thing up and concentrate on what he had come here for.

Then he remembered the bulky envelope on the mantelpiece. It was postmarked London and so he was sure it was the cuttings he had asked for from the *Sentinel*. Unusually efficient, thought Shilvers. He slit open the envelope with a greasy knife, and out fell a score or so of photocopies, stapled together with a compliments slip signed by Frank Chaplin. Shilvers tried to decipher the scrawl. 'Don't forget who gets first refusal.' He smiled and started sorting, with greasy fingers, through the cuttings. They were mostly snippets about small industrial disputes and various enquiries into the developments which had taken place over the years. Half a dozen were short pieces about announcements from the Department of Energy of small leaks of radioactivity. On each occasion the incident seemed to be minor, and it was emphasized that nobody on the site or off it was hurt in any way. One of the most recent clips was pinned to a leading article from the *Sentinel* which said that the industry should be required to give more details of such leaks. Unusually radical for the *Sentinel*, thought Shilvers.

Shilvers reached over for his notebook and the piece of paper on which Penshall had written names and dates. He compared Penshall's dates with the dates of articles reporting small leaks at the plant. Sure enough, in each case the month Penshall remembered coincided with an incident reported to the Department of Energy. The only difference was the scale of the incident and the report that nobody had been hurt. Again, it was promising, but only circumstantial.

As he turned over the cuttings, Shilvers noticed more of Frank Chaplin's handwriting on the back of the compliments slip. Something had been added as an afterthought. 'Hope this is what you wanted. There are lots more minor bits and pieces but I thought this would be enough to go on with. Hope you're not getting too stale up there. If you get a moment you could send us a few lines on what looks like a suspicious death up your way. Police are playing it down. I enclose the P.A. copy.'

A piece of telex paper from the Press Association fell on to the floor and Shilvers leant over to pick it up. His eyes ran along the lines of capital letters. 'POLICE INVESTIGATE MYSTERY DEATH'. Shilvers took another bite of his sausage and read on. 'Police in Cumbria admit they are baffled by the death of a man found on the outskirts of the village of Winderwath early today. Children playing discovered the body on the side of the road, later identified as sixty-year-old Alfred Penshall who lived in the village. Police say it appeared that every bone in his body had been broken. There is no sign of a robbery. Mr Penshall's wife was too shocked to comment last night. Ends.'

CHAPTER TEN

It was raining heavily as Shilvers pulled his hire car to a halt at the bottom of the lane leading up the cliffside to the cottage. The village had seemed even quieter than usual as he had driven through, and the pervasive misery of the weather seemed to have joined earth and sky together in a muddy grey. Shilvers turned off the engine and stared through the windscreen. The constant rainwater gradually blurred his view, allowing the images he had just witnessed at Alfred Penshall's graveside to fill his head.

The local police had made no progress whatsoever in the enquiries into the death of Mr Penshall. The post mortem showed that he had died from 'multiple injuries' and in adjourning the inquest the coroner had already hinted that he was likely to record an open verdict. There was no specific evidence of a hit and run, but that was the theory being worked on by the police. There was no expectation, it was said, of an early arrest.

Now, twelve days after the death and several hours after the funeral, Alfred Penshall was well on his way to being forgotten. But not by Anthony Shilvers. Penshall had chosen to confide in him. Aware of the dangers that he exposed himself to, Penshall had thought it worth while to take the risk. Shilvers was in no doubt that he had paid for that decision with his life. Now, as the trauma at the graveside came back to him again, he wondered whether Penshall's widow knew it too. He had tried to keep her in the dark about what went on at Dounscraig, Penshall had told him. Was it true? Her behaviour at the cemetery suggested otherwise. Maybe he was trying to keep her out of things and thereby protect her.

Shilvers felt the chill crawl across his skin, and focused on the clock. He had been sitting staring into nothingness for twenty minutes and was cold. Outside the rain lashed the windscreen, completely obscuring the view. He turned up the collar of his raincoat and resigned himself to the thought of getting soaking wet on the walk up the hill. The stove would have gone out hours before, and the prospect of arriving to a cold damp house, soaked to the skin, added to his gloom. He set off up the hill, feet squelching in the mud.

Before he was half-way home he gave up any attempt to hurry through the downpour. The sweat from exertion stuck his collar to his neck. The low heavy clouds blotted out any view of the ocean, and he could hardly even see the path as the mist swirled in ghostly trails around his feet. The roar of the rain on the ground blended with the roar of the sea below. Shilvers squinted into the mist to catch the first glimpse of the cottage.

At last he could make out the vague silhouette of the roof and chimney. He lowered his head and pushed on for the last leg. Then something he had seen made him look up again. He wiped the rain away from his brow. Could he be mistaken? No. Smoke was billowing out of the chimney. Shilvers stopped, the rain running down his face, to be certain. When he had left the cottage this morning it had not been worth putting another log on the stove because it was burning too low to have taken the flame. He had been resigned to lighting it afresh. Now the healthy trail of smoke indicated that it was well alight.

Shilvers hurried on towards the cottage. Could he have left the front door unlocked? He was sure he had not. Recent events had made him far more careful. He stepped quietly around the fragile wooden porch and approached the window. Very slowly he put his head round the corner so that he could peer through one of the dirty panes. There was condensation on the glass, and Shilvers had to squint through for several moments before he could make out the shape of a person standing at the sink. He blinked again before feeling sure that the shape was familiar, then raced round the porch and burst through the door.

'Julia!' As she wheeled round in surprise, her face crinkled into the smile he knew so well and it penetrated his chill bones to warm his insides. He went to her and they embraced for a long time without speaking. When Shilvers tried to look at her, Julia kept her face pressed hard against his wet shoulder.

'Julia, it's bloody marvellous to see you. Where the hell have you been, it's been weeks.' Suddenly his fear of having lost her and the terrible isolation of recent days crowded in on him and his voice cracked as he spoke. 'I thought I'd never see you again.'

Julia said nothing but he felt her arms around him squeeze still more tightly. Eventually she looked up at him and Shilvers could see that her eyes were smudged with the rain from his coat and perhaps her own tears.

'How long have you been here? Have you had some coffee?'

'Bloody hours,' she said, trying to compose herself. 'And there are no clean cups, you filthy degenerate.'

'And how did you get in?' said Shilvers. 'So much for an Englishman's country home being his castle.'

'You left the key where you always leave it, you idiot,' she dangled the key from her finger and wiped her eyes, 'under the mat where no one would think of looking for it. But this time it's a damn good job you did, otherwise I would have died of exposure in this wasteland.' Julia pushed her fingers through her mass of red hair, and her beautiful green eyes flashed at him. It made him ache inside. 'Anyway, where the hell have you been. You look as though you've been to a funeral.'

Shilvers was stunned into silence. So much had happened to him since he had last seen her that she knew nothing whatever about. He had just returned from one of the most disturbing experiences he had ever witnessed, and here was this vivacious woman, full of life and thoughts a million miles away from the things which were preoccupying him. How could he begin to tell her?

'I know you didn't know when I was coming,' she went on, 'but I didn't expect you to go around in your Sunday best the whole time. Or are you courting a young lady down in the village?' Her eyes sparked again as she teased him.

'Not on your life.'

Julia looked at him, and then up at the crumpled photograph of herself on the mantelpiece. She smiled and hugged him again.

'Anyway,' he said at last, 'what have you been doing while I've been stuck here in this godforsaken garret miles from civilization with only sheep for company?'

Julia told him of her design project. She had stayed with a friend from college who had become the fashion editor of a magazine in Paris. She had seen the sights, visited the museums, the galleries, taken a boat down the Seine. It had been a tremendous success and, she told him, she felt much better. She said nothing of their relationship or of other company and Shilvers did not ask.

When he said nothing she persisted, 'Why the Sunday best?'

Shilvers sat down opposite her at the table and took her hands in his. First, he told her about the funeral, then about Alf Penshall, then he told her everything. Now and again she frowned and started to ask a question, then did not do so. When he had finished speaking there was a long silence. Then she spoke.

'Are you afraid?'

Shilvers thought for a moment.

'Yes I am.'

That night the two huddled close together for warmth. After making love urgently, and then tenderly, they lay and looked out of the window into the mist of the moorland. In the stillness within, Shilvers wondered whether Julia was back with him to stay. In their love-making she had said 'I love you' many times. He believed it, and told her the same. Was that expression a commitment? He knew that it was not. She had not committed herself tonight. He had not asked her to. Perhaps she needed more time. For him, the separation had made him realize her value. He wanted her as he had never wanted anything. He needed her.

Much later, when Julia had fallen asleep, Shilvers lay beside her and watched as the moonlight painted pale streaks across her hair. The wind howled and the rain still beat in endless rhythm on the roof, and he felt resigned to the task he had set himself. They were alone on an exposed and vulnerable cliff-edge with all the elements battering at their door. Against the might of an organization which could successfully cover up scores of dreadful accidents, and could apparently murder a man who had been guilty only of expressing concern, he felt small and alone. As Shilvers looked at Julia he realized that he did not feel nearly as alone as at this time on the day before. He hoped he would never feel so alone again.

Next morning Shilvers awoke to find Julia lying curled up beside him still sound asleep, her face half-submerged in his slightly grubby pillow. He felt embarrassed about his appalling bachelor existence. It was not that he failed to do his share of their domestic chores when they were together, but it was her presence which persuaded him to action. Left to himself he would simply do dishes when he ran out of clean plates, and allow dust to settle on more dust. Shilvers reflected that for her to wake up to a roomful of odd grey woollen socks strewn untidily over the floor would be a very long way from what she had recently been used to in Paris.

Shilvers lay still and looked into Julia's face. She was thirty-two and to him she looked exactly as she had when they had met seven years before. He guessed she would look little different in another seven years. She had high cheekbones and that slightly haughty look of the well-bred English, something he teased her with from time to time and which never failed to have the desired effect. Her nostrils would flare in her temper, only adding to the effect he was describing, which would anger her even more. Eventually she would playfully attack him and they would collapse into hysterical laughter on the floor.

Shilvers smiled as he remembered those times. Her vivid red hair was strewn lazily across the pillow, and beneath her eyelids her pupils raced as she dreamed. The rain had stopped and only an occasional heavy drop hit the window-ledge, or fell from the trees on to the roof. In the far distance the ocean still raged.

Julia half-turned and snuggled back down into the pillow.

Shilvers gently lifted himself over her to get out of bed. Naked, he darted around clearing up the most obvious debris from the floor, and then picking up his dressing-gown from the chair, slipped quietly out of the room.

Having stoked up the stove and washed some dishes while the kettle boiled, he sat down in his chair by the window. Immediately his mind returned to the subject which had haunted him for the last fortnight.

Whoever had killed Penshall, it must certainly be related to his visit to the cottage, of that much Shilvers felt sure. The absence of any realistic attempt to make the death look like an accident may even have been meant as a warning to others who, like Penshall, were getting cold feet. It would be well-known in Winderwath that Penshall was a leading dissident about Dounscraig. Penshall himself had said that there were others.

How, though, did anyone know of Penshall's visit? He was a cautious man and said he had taken care to conceal his walk up to the cottage. Surely I.N.I. could not follow everyone who ever exhibited any dissatisfaction about what was going on? Neither was Penshall likely to have told anyone else about the visit. He had been in earnest in his request to Shilvers to keep his identity secret. The only person Penshall would be likely to confide in was his wife. The decision to come to see Shilvers must have been a big one. Perhaps he talked it over with her? Shilvers thought again about the scene at the funeral the day before. He remembered the sudden and dramatic change in her expression when approached by the man in the smart clothes and chauffeur-driven car. He took it for granted that the man was from I.N.I. He wished now that he had taken the number. If Mrs Penshall was feeling as bitter as all that, she might well be prepared to go on the record about what she knew. Shilvers realized that he was counting on his hunch that Penshall had been lying when he had said that he kept her in the dark about events at the plant. Perhaps he had told the truth and she knew nothing. In that case, why had she lashed out at the man from I.N.I. at the funeral? He must surely be right. The trouble was that her knowledge was second-hand, and she was obviously under stress after Alf's death. Even if she was prepared to go on the record, would anything she said be taken seriously?

What about feeling in the village since Alf's death? Shilvers guessed that the serious conversation in the Huntsman on the night he had met Ffitch must have been about Penshall. They had already known what he was still to learn from the news agency copy. So much for the journalist on the spot, he thought bitterly.

The thought brought another into his head. What about Ffitch? Ffitch was the local stringer. He must have known about the discovery of Penshall's body on the evening of their meeting. It would have turned up in routine calls to the police. Why on earth had Ffitch not mentioned it? It surely was not every day that dead bodies were found in unexplained circumstances just a few hundred yards from where you were sitting. Shilvers considered the question and it troubled him.

How would he now proceed? He had no source within the plant, and access to no other information beyond a scrap of paper with half a dozen names and approximate dates next to them. There were apparently other people in the village with the same doubts as Penshall had, but Shilvers had no idea who they were. If they had been thinking of coming forward and speaking out, Penshall's death would certainly have made them think again.

The thought that Shilvers had been trying for nearly two weeks to keep out of his mind kept coming back until he could avoid it no longer. The arrival of Julia meant he had to confront it. If Penshall died because someone knew he had spoken to Shilvers, then that person had to presume that Shilvers was following the story. They had killed Penshall because he had leaked the information to one other person. Here was Shilvers probably planning to pass it on to millions. Now the situation was even more complicated because Julia was here. It was clear that she was in danger all the time she was here and with him. He would have to persuade her to go.

'Penny for your thoughts.'

Shilvers jumped visibly in surprise. Julia was standing in the bedroom doorway wearing his enormous white polo-neck sweater and a pair of his jeans which were so big that she had tied them up at the waist with a piece of string.

'How long have you been sneaking about?' she asked as she went to the kettle to pour hot water into the cup he had prepared for her.

'I don't know, I've just been sitting here day-dreaming.'

'No prizes for guessing the subject.' She sat in the wooden chair opposite him and pushed her hand through her hair. 'I've been thinking about it too, and what is glaringly obvious is that there's one aspect of what happened two weeks ago that you've neglected to mention.'

'And what's that?'

'You know bloody well what.' Her tone reflected real anxiety. 'If your theory about all this is right, why was Penshall killed? Because he had spilled the beans to you, that's why. If they were prepared to kill him to keep him quiet, you have got to be next. The only surprising thing is that they haven't come for you already.'

'Hold on just a minute.' Shilvers put down the now cold coffee cup and sat up straight at the table. 'There's no reason whatever to think that he was killed for that reason. None whatever. What we do know is that he left no doubt in his conversations with the other workers that he wanted to do something about the situation. One of them probably tipped off I.N.I. and they decided to shut him up before he could say anything, and as an example to the others.'

'But that's nonsense Tony, and you know it is.' Julia's concern was now giving way to distress. 'Even these guys can't go round bumping off anyone who just expresses concern about it, otherwise the graveyards would be piled up six deep. Penshall was killed just one day after coming to see you. You must see that's no coincidence. It's just common sense.'

Shilvers sat back in his chair, deflated by her logic.

'I'm not necessarily buying that. If they were certain Penshall had been to see me and told me everything, they wouldn't have hung around these last twelve days. They've had every opportunity, but they've done nothing.'

'Maybe they're just watching for something suspicious, some indication that you're making enquiries about them.'

'If that's the case, they've got nothing to go on yet. My excuse to the village bobby was a bit thin, but at least he didn't get to know the names I was interested in.'

'It's just a question of time,' said Julia. 'One slip, and you'll be where Penshall is now.'

Shilvers stared into his empty cup, running his forefinger round the cold rim. They sat in silence for a few moments.

'There is however another question.'

'And that is?'

'Well, there's your safety to think about – ' Shilvers did not get the chance to finish his sentence.

'Forget it Tony.' Julia stood up, walked briskly over to the sink and turned to face him. 'Put that idea right out of your head. If you're staying, I'm staying and that's final. No arguments.' Shilvers opened his mouth to speak, then immediately realized it was pointless. He had learned enough in seven years to recognize a closed door when he saw it.

'You make breakfast,' he said, and headed for the shower.

Five miles away, on the first floor of a three-tier prefabricated building surrounded by barbed wire, a dim red light glowed in an otherwise darkened room. The only sound was the faint splash of water spurting into a sink from the thin nozzle of a laboratory tap. In the eerie light a dark figure used a short wooden spatula to nudge back and forth a ten inch by twelve inch piece of stiff white paper in the liquid. The photographer squinted in anticipation of the image which was beginning to form.

Suspended on a piece of thin green wire hung like a washing-line across the room were half a dozen more ten by twelve inch pieces of paper. At haphazard angles and in the murky red light, it was difficult to distinguish the grey figures on the crowded landscape.

At last a faint shape began to appear on the paper in the tray. The small figure standing looking into it held the paper still for several moments as the image formed. It was the back of a man, half turned away from the camera, standing in front of some rectangular shape. Now the rectangular shape was a door, and the shape of another person could be seen peering around it. The spatula was discarded and with plastic tongs the paper was whisked out of the tray and flushed under the running tap. Water gushed off the now sharp image of a man in his forties, with a full head of hair creeping over his ears and collar, wearing a soft shirt. He was answering the door to a caller. It did not matter that the caller was unidentifiable. That much was already known.

Seconds later the dark figure reached for a string hanging above the sink, and had to squint in the now glaring white light. Not bad, considering the evening had been overcast and the distance was several hundred yards. Now it was possible to examine the face peering round the door. It was even possible to make out the features and expression. The face was handsome, but to the photographer it was not familiar.

With the surface dampness shaken off, the picture was hung alongside the others on the green wire. The photographer looked again at the row. Once again there was reason to be proud of the work. From a distance, hand-held on a grey day, a small group of people were clearly distinguishable at the graveside. The photographer smiled again. How clever to have caught the exact moment when the woman's hand came up to slap the man from the chauffeur-driven car.

Now a face in the crowd looked familiar. The photographer returned to the picture which was still dripping water on to the lino floor. Yes, it was the same man. The man answering the door was at the funeral. Not on file. The face was not on file. A note must be made.

On the bench was a red folder. The photographer reached over and put it in a drawer and locked it. As she closed the darkroom door behind her, Jacqueline Smart knew that she had done an excellent day's work.

CHAPTER ELEVEN

Shilvers and Julia sat at the table reading the cuttings which had come from the *Sentinel* and wondered what to do next. Shilvers talked about his enquiries in the electoral register and the need now to cross-check the names in the register of births, marriages and deaths which would be in the public library at Westermouth. If the men concerned had been hurt as badly as Penshall claimed, then some of them must have died. If that were the case, even I.N.I. would have difficulty falsifying the records. And if the men had not been killed in the accident, it was possible their deaths had been faked in order to forestall enquiries from the taxman or other parts of government bureaucracy. Either way, the register needed to be checked. Shilvers told Julia the cover-story he had used to look up the names in the electoral register. She was not impressed, but agreed to go to Westermouth to do the checking. Shilvers was relieved.

'What will you do while I'm doing the painstaking donkey-work?'

Shilvers knew it was true so did not argue. 'I think I'll pay a visit to Mrs Penshall. She's bound to be still distressed after yesterday, but this might be exactly the time to talk to her. She might well be in a mood to tell all.'

Julia thought it would be better to wait a few days until she was less upset, but Shilvers was sure this was the right time. He had to return the hire car to Westermouth, so Julia could drive it there for him and get the bus back. They would meet at the cottage this afternoon. The constant rain over several days had left the air fresh and clear, and the sun was bright. The turbulent wind had turned into a gentle breeze off the sea, and for the first time in many days Shilvers felt relaxed as they set off down the cliffside path. He peered over the edge to the waves below. Perhaps they were gathering their strength, poised for a new assault on the cliff-face. The mountains of water had subsided, and now whirled around submerged rocks. As they walked, the couple spoke about Mrs Penshall, Julia performing her most useful role of devil's advocate. It was one for which she had developed considerable talent over the years with Shilvers.

'You're assuming a lot,' she warned. 'For all you know the man in the car could be a long-lost brother who got rich and never called to see them when Penshall was alive. She resented him turning up when her husband had died.'

'Could be,' said Shilvers. He heard her words but not for a moment did he imagine that his hunch was wrong.

'She might not know much about the accidents,' Julia continued, 'and it's easily possible that Penshall didn't tell her about visiting you. He told you that he didn't like worrying her unnecessarily. In which case you turning up out of the blue will send her into a further trauma.'

Shilvers considered her words. To an extent she was right, he had been taking too much for granted. He had no certain way of knowing yet he felt sure. Her perspective on it was valuable, though, and he was grateful she was there with him and told her so.

Now they were approaching the car-park at the back of the Huntsman where Shilvers had left the hire car the previous day. It was a battered and rusting Ford which the hire company must either have had for many years, or perhaps even bought second-hand. At first sight of the car he had been wary, but the rates were less than half the usual price. Now, as he looked at it, Shilvers thought it seemed to be sitting very low in the mud.

As they approached the car from the driver's side they realized that both tyres were completely flat. Julia walked round to the other side, and a glance at her face confirmed for Shilvers that the other side was exactly the same.

'And I thought all the vandals came from the deprived inner cities,' said Julia with pronounced irony.

Shilvers bent down to examine the valves. Close up, he could see straight away that several strips of rubber were protruding from the walls of the tyres. They had been conscientiously slashed.

'Holy shit.' Shilvers walked around the car to join Julia. 'I've lived in central London for thirty years and never had a car damaged. I come to the country to get away from the cares of urban life and –'

'Something wrong, Mr Shilvers?'

The top-heavy shape of the village constable wiggling along on an old iron bicycle looked like a scene from forty years ago.

'I should think there bloody well is something wrong.' Shilvers could feel the anger building in him. 'I thought you were round here to stop this sort of thing. Look at these damned tyres.' His voice was rising in volume.

'Now then, Mr Shilvers, don't get excited.' Constable Charlton was casually dismounting in a manner calculated to annoy Shilvers still more. 'No one round here would do this. They're not that stupid.' He propped his bicycle up against a brick wall and ambled towards them, pulling a notebook from his pocket. 'You must have some enemies, Mr Shilvers, that's all I can say.'

Shilvers had been about to embark on a further tirade, but Charlton's remark stopped him flat. 'I've got no enemies,' he said lamely.

There was a pause.

'Do you have a spare, Mr Shilvers?'

The stupidity of the remark renewed Shilvers' anger. 'What possible use would it be if I had? There are four tyres slashed. All four. If you've got no better suggestions maybe you can let me know who around here is handy with a knife so I can call and thank them.'

Julia walked towards him and gently took his arm, but the outburst had already taken effect.

'I can well understand why you're cross, Mr Shilvers,' the policeman said, also trying to control his anger, 'but I'll thank you not to raise your voice to me. And another thing,' now he was putting his notebook back into his pocket, 'if I were you

I'd be very careful before you go around making wild and unsubstantiated accusations against people in this village where you're a visitor. There's all sorts of people pass through this way at night, and no doubt a few of them have had too much to drink.'

The force of Charlton's reply once again made Shilvers reflect. Perhaps he was jumping to conclusions too quickly. He was about to ask who on earth passed through Winderwath, since it was on the back road to nowhere. He decided to defuse the situation and keep quiet.

'Well then, perhaps you'll begin your enquiries at the local pub.' Julia was much more in control.

'And who might you be, Miss?' Charlton was reaching for his notebook again.

'She's a friend of mine, nothing to do with this.' Shilvers did not want any more attention drawn to Julia than was unavoidable. 'Anyway, I'd better call the hire company to see if they have four spares. You'll make a note of this will you?' He had taken Julia by the arm and was edging away. 'Only I daresay the hire company will want to claim on their insurance.'

'Hire company?' said Charlton. He seemed surprised, and for a moment it seemed to Shilvers that perhaps he was almost disappointed.

'Yes, it's a hire car,' said Shilvers. 'Did you think it was mine?'

'No no.' Charlton was clearly quite nonplussed. 'No, I hadn't thought, I just assumed . . .'

There was a silence, as both Julia and Shilvers looked directly at Charlton. Then Shilvers said, 'So, apparently, did someone else.' The couple turned abruptly and walked briskly away.

Julia waited until they were out of his hearing. 'What did you make of that?'

'What did you make of it? It's as clear as day. Either he did it himself; or he's got a bloody good idea who did.'

'Or it could be what he said,' said Julia. 'Only five minutes ago you were acknowledging that you might be jumping to too many conclusions. It could easily be local vandals and nothing to do with all this.'

Shilvers stopped and turned on her. 'Nothing to do with this? Listen Julia,' he put both arms out straight and held her in front of him, 'a man comes to see me and says he thinks people are disappearing from his workplace, and a few hours later he's smashed to pulp and left dead on a roadside. The information he gave me checks out so far and even local experts know next to nothing about what goes on inside Dounscraig. Now my car tyres are slashed the day after I've been to Penshall's funeral, and you're accusing me of being paranoid. I think if anything I'm insanely trusting!'

Julia said nothing. She was taken aback by his vehemence. He too was even now embarrassed at having shouted at her. He put his arm around her and they walked on.

'I'm sorry. That was the nervous reaction of a paranoiac,' he said.

'No. It was the nervous reaction of a man who's just had his tyres slashed.'

He held her a little more tightly as they walked to the phone-box on the village green.

Shilvers told the manager of the local car hire firm about the incident. He was distraught. At the third repetition of 'I've never had anything like this happen in fifteen years', Shilvers hung up.

Julia suggested they continue with the plan as before and they walked along to the bus-stop at the corner of the green. The single-deck green jalopy was revving noisily.

As she went to get on Julia turned around and squeezed Shilvers' hand, brushing her lips very lightly across his cheek. 'Be very careful,' she whispered.

'Now who's being paranoid?'

She squeezed his hand still tighter. 'Just once in your life do as you are bloody well told without arguing,' she said, and climbed on to the bus.

CHAPTER TWELVE

'Who the hell is he?'

The man wearing black woollen jacket and trousers, with heavy walking shoes, paced up and down the office. He had been studying the picture for several minutes before speaking. When he did so his voice was staccato.

'Anthony Shilvers. Aged forty-two. Profession . . .' Jacqueline paused. She knew the next piece of information would be greeted by even more irritation.

'Yes. Profession what?' said the man in black.

'Journalist. In the area to write a piece for the Tourist Board. We've checked it out. It's genuine.'

'Then what the bloody hell is he doing meeting Penshall?' The question was addressed as much to himself as to the girl. James Gold continued to pace, then returned to the table to study the pictures further. 'Had they met before?'

'No information on that.' Now Jacqueline Smart was reading from a file on the desk in front of her. 'As you see, he went to Penshall's funeral, but he didn't mix with the other guests.' She waited while Gold examined the rest of the photographs. 'He didn't even speak to the widow after the service, just drove back to the cottage.'

'Well,' said Gold eventually, 'did he tell him, or didn't he tell him?' Once again it was a question he did not expect to have answered. 'We have to know. Is he still under surveillance?'

Jacqueline had been watching last night and again this morning. Dark shadows under her eyes betrayed the long hours she had worked on getting the photographs and then on surveillance. Gold had not commented on the high quality of the work. She realized she had been foolish even to hope that he would.

'Yes. He's still being watched.'

'Good. It must remain so until everything is complete.' Gold closed the file in front of him and looked at Jacqueline. She was as good at this work as any of them, perhaps better because she was a woman. Her youth and her innocent look: the shaggy blonde hair cut short across her collar and naïve blue eyes. Who would have thought that she was the best photographer and investigator the organization had. It did not occur to him to tell her his opinion. She did the job without questions. It was enough.

'There is one more thing.' Jacqueline looked at the floor, again aware that the news would be unwelcome.

'What is it?'

'He's been joined by a woman. Yesterday, when he returned from the funeral, there was a woman at the cottage waiting. She spent the night.'

'Worse and goddamned worse,' snapped Gold, slamming his hand down flat on the file of pictures. 'Who is she? Have we got her picture? Where is it?'

'Not yet,' said Jacqueline quietly. 'We have someone on it. We'll know by tonight.'

'By which time, for all we know, this whole thing could be all over every newspaper in Fleet Street. We have to know what the hell is going on.' Gold was shouting. There was a trace of an American accent, hardly noticeable when he spoke quietly and kept himself under control. Now it was increasingly evident. 'We can't allow these people to screw up work we've taken years to organize. And,' now his voice went quiet again, 'we don't want another death. Not, at least, if it can be avoided.'

CHAPTER THIRTEEN

Shilvers had little trouble finding the Penshall cottage. It was among a tiny group which once belonged to farm labourers just on the outskirts of the village, halfway up the hillside at the opposite end of the green to Shilvers' own. As he walked up the hill, he felt apprehensive, recalling the face of the woman at the funeral. The despair, and then the horror. Perhaps Julia had been right. Shilvers acknowledged the possibility but kept on walking. He seemed to be drawn on, almost without choice.

With the row of cottages in sight, Shilvers stopped for a moment and stood still. In the distance he could hear the muted sounds of the sea. He considered how this now faint whisper had filled the air around this spot for thousands upon thousands of years. The rocks jutting out of the thin marshy soil, if they could tell the difference, would not know what silence was. The sheep grazing on this side of the dry-stone wall would have spent their entire lives within the sound of the ocean lashing the cliffs. If, suddenly, that noise vanished, the sheep would probably look up in surprise. The silence would be so different and disturbing.

Shilvers thought again about Mrs Penshall. It was the same for her. When you get used to something or someone being around for year after year, part of every moment of your life, you just assume it will always be so. You might think about it from time to time, but generally you will go about daily life, expecting tomorrow to be more or less the same as today. Perhaps Mr and Mrs Penshall had made plans for retirement, not far away. Maybe they had plans to move away from Winderwath, near children and grandchildren perhaps. Mrs Penshall had assumed that this was the way it would be. Now it was not so. The familiar had departed suddenly, and she had looked up in surprise.

Shilvers stood there a little longer, looking towards the

empty sound of the surf. He thought about Julia. They were not even married and there had certainly been no discussion of children. Even now, though, there were times when he took her for granted. He had begun to assume that tomorrow would be like today. Recently there had been an interruption in the continuity he had become used to. He had looked up in surprise, and had not at all liked the life he had seen around him without her.

Viewed from a vantage point half a mile out to sea it was impossible to guess why the man in the donkey jacket stood alone for so long, looking into the distance. At first it seemed possible that he had caught sight of a reflection from the glass in the powerful lens which was pointed directly at him. No. It could not be. The sun was masked by a cloud. Besides, his gaze did not follow the helicopter as it cruised at slow speed along a course parallel with the coast. After several minutes the man set off again, continuing his journey towards the row of cottages. Click click click click click. Drowned out by the whirling blades above, the motorized camera body was audible only to the photographer, and still she checked the readout to make sure the film had passed behind the lens.

There was no bell or knocker at the plain green timber door which was neither front nor back but rather a side entrance to the Penshall house. Shilvers rapped hard with his knuckles but the sound deadened against the solid wood. He waited. After several moments he banged again, this time with the side of his fist. Now he could see a curtain moving at a window to his left. He walked towards it and called out.

'Mrs Penshall? Can you hear me?' There was no sound. 'My name is Anthony Shilvers. Could I have a brief word with you? I am . . . I was a friend of your husband.'

There was a long silence, then a thin voice was just audible through the door. 'What do you want?'

'I just want a chat for a few minutes. I know this is a difficult time for you, but it won't take very long. Please let me in, Mrs Penshall.'

There was another long pause, broken this time by the sound of a heavy bolt being drawn back. A chain rattled and a key turned and Shilvers wondered what the woman was so afraid of. The door opened a few inches and the same face he had seen at the funeral peeped cautiously through the gap. Even that glimpse reminded Shilvers of the burgeoning grief which weighed so heavily on the frail old shoulders of Mrs Penshall.

'What do you want?' the thin voice repeated, this time still more quiet than before.

Shilvers edged towards the door and spoke softly. 'Mrs Penshall, I would like to come in for a moment to talk about your husband. He was a friend of mine,' Shilvers paused, 'briefly a friend of mine, and I would very much like to clear up a couple of things which have been puzzling me.'

'You were a friend of his?' Her voice was full of suspicion. 'I knew all Alf's friends and I never set eyes on you until yesterday.' Shilvers was surprised that she had noticed him at the funeral. 'What do you want from me?'

'I'm staying in the old shepherd's cottage up the hill on the other side of the village. I haven't been there long. A fortnight ago your husband came to call on me. We had a chat. He asked me to find out a few things for him.'

'A chat?' She seemed genuinely puzzled. 'What about?'

Shilvers was getting nowhere. For a moment it crossed his mind to pretend it had all been a mistake and go. He decided to play his only card.

'It was about his work, Mrs Penshall. About Dounscraig.'

She did not react at all, only continued to stare at him, her frown emphasizing the furrows in her face.

'I'm a journalist, Mrs Penshall, that's why Alf came to see me. But I don't want to talk about what he had to say here on the doorstep, if you understand me.'

Still the woman did not change her expression. For a moment Shilvers thought she was going to close the door on him, but then she opened it a few inches and stepped back to let him in. She said nothing but gestured him toward the front of the small house. Shilvers stepped into the living-room. This was the moment Shilvers hated most of all. It seemed to him that every time his job had taken him to the scene of a private tragedy, the room looked just like this one. It was haunted by the presence of the recently departed. The bereaved were surrounded by souvenirs of the dead.

Shilvers' eyes went to a worn pair of men's slippers in the tiled hearth which surrounded the small one-bar electric fire. A two-seat settee was matched by two armchairs, one of them distinctly more worn. Loose covers in floral pattern had separate pieces of the same material over the arms. Next to the armchair, on the mantelpiece, a pipe-rack with four well-used pipes in a row.

On the small colour television in the corner was the inevitable picture. Alf Penshall, and a woman whom Shilvers could only just recognize as his wife, standing in front of an enormous rhododendron bush, a scene from some recent holiday. Shilvers was glad that for once in this situation he was not here to ask for the photograph. He was glad to have put all that behind him years before.

Mrs Penshall waved him towards a chair. Shilvers paused before sitting down on the edge of the settee. She too quietly avoided the armchair and perched uncomfortably on the end of the other chair facing it. Shilvers was wondering how to begin when she spoke.

'He was always very careful on the roads. Didn't like cars himself and would never have one. They brought noise and exhaust fumes and tourists, he used to say, and he didn't like any of them.' Mrs Penshall seemed to be talking to nobody in particular, just talking. 'He was always wary of them, careful you know. He didn't like them, see. In the end, though,' she looked to the ground, 'they brought him much worse than all that, didn't they?'

Shilvers waited for a few moments before speaking. He had

to clear his throat to do so. 'So your husband was run over accidentally was he, Mrs Penshall? You've been told it was by a car?'

She looked up at him and blinked. Her eyes went to the photograph on the television and she spoke softly. 'He wasn't young you know. Probably he couldn't get out of the way.' She was simply articulating thoughts as they came into her head. 'Police say the car may have dragged him along quite a distance. He was out of town you know. He never would have walked that way on his own. Nowhere to go that way, you see? Maybe they were young drunks. The policeman said it wouldn't have been anybody local. Young drunks, just passing through.'

Shilvers reflected that Constable Charlton had the same explanation for every incident in the recent local crime wave.

'But there was no sign was there, no evidence that he had been dragged?' Shilvers got no reply, and thought he would not push the point any further. She had apparently reconciled herself to a version of events which would be less troubling for her than what he believed to be the truth. But if that were so, why had she lashed out at the man from I.N.I. at the funeral?

'How long had Alf worked at Dounscraig, Mrs Penshall?'

'How long?' Shilvers could see that she had been lost in her own thoughts. Now she focused her mind on his question. 'Oh I don't know, practically since it's been there, since the army moved out. It must be a dozen years. He came off the land you know.' For the first time Mrs Penshall seemed to be emerging from her trance, and her speech sounded more like ordinary conversation. Shilvers was encouraged. 'Like lots of the men around here. I told him. I told him to get himself a job inside. The land around here is no good. Soil's too poor. He wasn't sure at first. He'd been an outside man all his life. He wasn't sure he could cope with it. But then I.N.I. bought our house along with the rest of them. Tied it was, and that did it. He reckoned he had little choice, but it didn't work out too badly. He quite liked it you know.' She paused. 'Off and on, like everything I suppose.'

'What aspects of it didn't he like, Mrs Penshall?' Shilvers was pleased. She was becoming more animated with every moment. He wanted her to be completely at her ease with him.

'This last year, that's all it's been really. Maybe the last two. In the early days he'd come home and say what a good firm they were and how they had managed to negotiate this or that for the workers. He wasn't used to all that. You couldn't negotiate much out of the land round here. He went on two or three training courses. He was well thought of. Conscientious you see, not like some. They were the days before they did this recent big building nonsense.'

'What was that?' asked Shilvers.

'Oh I don't know. They nicknamed it the laundry, but it was to do with these nuclear fuel rods or something. Making them safe. Alf didn't like all that. He used to be carting some of this stuff around, and he didn't much like it.' Her voice trailed away and then came back again. 'Alf didn't much like it.'

Shilvers thought about the cuttings from the *Sentinel*. This would be the reprocessing plant which had been the subject of the public enquiry six years earlier. Mrs Penshall was still talking.

'Sometimes they'd have these alerts. Special alerts. They were just drills mostly. Sometimes they were drills. I don't think Alf or the others knew the difference most of the time, but whichever it was he didn't used to like it.'

'What happened during these alerts, Mrs Penshall?' Shilvers tried to sound as casual as he could. He knew this was the most sensitive area, and was surprised and glad that she seemed to be talking so freely.

'Well, I believe there would be a siren and all sorts of pandemonium and people from each department would have to collect at a certain point and then they would all leave by different exits. Most often they'd come home and they would be told later on when they were to go back. One time he was off for three weeks.'

'Three weeks?' Shilvers could not help himself. His surprise was obvious.

'I don't know if I should be telling you this. I don't know what Alf would say. He didn't like to talk about this, not to me or anyone. Maybe I've said too much already. I don't know what he'd say if he heard me . . .'

Her voice broke off into a slight sob as she lowered her eyes to the carpet and began to stare once again at the invisible spot which had preoccupied her before. Shilvers damned his own stupidity. There was a long silence.

As she lost herself in her grief, Shilvers studied Mrs Penshall's face, certain that for now she was unconscious of his presence. Though at the moment her shoulders were hunched under the weight of her sorrow, Shilvers could imagine that in other circumstances she could be bright and upright. She looked thin and pale, and the grey shadows of despair emphasized the contours of her face and chin. In other circumstances, thought Shilvers, she might look smart and dignified. He tried to imagine those deep-set and faraway eyes twinkling with laughter. For the moment they could not, but in other times? Shilvers wondered how long it would be before she would again feel carefree.

'I would like to be perfectly frank with you, Mrs Penshall, because your husband was perfectly frank with me.' She did not look up but Shilvers felt that she was listening. 'Your husband trusted me at first sight with a story which he knew might prove dangerous for him to tell. At the time, I'm ashamed to admit, I was sceptical of what he told me, but now I believe him. Mrs Penshall . . .' Shilvers took a deep breath before continuing. 'I don't believe your husband was run down by drunks. I think his death could very easily have been deliberate. I think he was worried by something that was going on at Dounscraig and that he may have been killed to prevent him from saying anything more about it. The only problem is that he had already told me most of what he knew.'

Shilvers did not know what reaction to expect. Now he

immediately wondered whether he had been right. As he had spoken, she had slowly turned her gaze upwards, and now continued to look fixedly at him. In an instant Shilvers realized that he must have been wrong. This woman had persuaded herself to be content with the implausible explanation of her husband's death provided by the police. Now he had come blundering in and thrown her self-delusion out of the window and faced her with a desperate reality. And yet how could he reconcile that explanation with her reaction at yesterday's funeral? Now Shilvers unambiguously regretted his outburst and was beginning to search his brain for some explanation of his behaviour which would get him off the hook and out of the house. He was about to attempt one when she preempted him.

'Mr Shilvers.' Her gaze had not shifted away from him for a moment. 'I think I would like to tell you everything I know.'

CHAPTER FOURTEEN

Over the next hour and a half Mrs Penshall scarcely stopped talking for a moment. It was as though she had stored everything up inside herself. There had been worries and fears, times when everything seemed as though it would be fine and times when she wondered whether her husband would get through the day.

Nearly everyone in the village of Winderwath depended for their livelihood, in whole or in part, on Dounscraig. Just about every family had a husband or wife, son or daughter working there. Sometimes it was several members of the family. There were a few people, like the publican and the sisters in the post office, who had nobody working at Dounscraig, but they knew that they relied on it just as surely as everyone else. Without the plant there would be no work. Without the work there would be no money, and no customers.

To begin with she had learned most of what she knew from neighbours and friends rather than from her husband. Alf, she explained, had always taken seriously the document he had signed when he started work at Dounscraig which forebade discussion of anything that went on inside the company with outsiders. Over the years she had picked up rumours about mishaps at the plant from the wives of other Dounscraig workers. She had worried about them, but Alf had refused to discuss these things in any detail.

Eventually she had noticed that he too was worrying, but was trying to prevent her from doing so by keeping her out of what was going on. Often he would come home depressed or agitated, and it was only later, when she had spoken to friends, that she discovered that there had been another evacuation from the plant. Alf had told her not to bother about these things. They were none of her concern, and the less she knew the better it would be in the long run. She had resented it, but in her heart she knew that it was her own interests he was thinking of.

'How often would these alerts happen?' asked Shilvers. Mrs Penshall had offered him tea and they now talked in the small kitchen at the back of the cottage while waiting for the kettle to boil. She seemed composed and glad to be talking.

'Sometimes it would go weeks or even months without any problems. Other times it could happen twice in a fortnight. But the worst of it was I never knew, and I don't think he always did, whether it was a drill or whether it was for real.'

Shilvers carried the tray through to the living-room. They resumed the same seats, leaving Alf's chair empty.

'Your husband told me that there was one particular incident which was especially bad. He didn't tell me what it was, but I gathered he was directly involved?'

Mrs Penshall put down her cup and sat silently for a few moments, collecting her thoughts. She sighed, as if having made up her mind, and began to speak.

'It was about two years since, around about spring-time. There was going to be one of the regular safety drills that day, and Alf said he might be back early. Sometimes if everything went all right in these drills and it was near to knocking-off time they could come home early. But when he did get home, about half-past three, he was out of breath and shocked.

'At first he didn't say anything about what had happened, but he was sick in the kitchen, and then sat in here, in that chair, just staring into space. He said nothing for several hours, and looked right past me when I asked him what on earth was wrong. I'd never seen him anything like it. Eventually I worked myself up into a terrible state. I imagined that hundreds might be dead up there. I couldn't think what it could be. I started to cry, Mr Shilvers, and that was when he told me.'

Mrs Penshall talked steadily, without apparent emotion, but looking straight past Shilvers as she did so, out of the window over his shoulder. There was no other sound except the wind buffeting down the chimney and rattling the back of the small electric fire in the grate. Shilvers did not even murmur as she continued.

'He was working in one of the most sensitive areas, moving around some flasks or other, when the alarm sounded. At first they all thought it was the drill they'd been expecting, but it was a bit early Alf said. They took the drill quite seriously and everyone headed toward their exit. But then the voice came over the loudspeakers, saying "This is not a drill. Repeat, this is not a drill." He sat in that chair, Mr Shilvers and he kept on repeating it just like they did. "This is not a drill." He said it over and over and over again and it worried me.

'When they had these drills, Mr Shilvers, Alf told me they used to call out the names of groups of workers, and the exit they had to go to. "Section 9 technicians go to safety area B. Section 10 technicians go to safety area G", and so on.' Her voice mimicked the strident orders she had heard her husband imitate. 'But he said this time the voice was urgent and panicky, and it made the men panic a bit too. He had thought it was getting hotter inside, and men were rushing in all directions. Alf had stowed the trolley he was pushing into a harness at the side of the corridor as he was supposed to, but on his way to his safety area he passed the glass observation window into one the laboratories.'

Here Mrs Penshall stopped speaking, and continued to look out and into the sky. Shilvers remained silent. He had the urge to take some notes but resisted it. Eventually he leant forward and picked up her tea to hand to her. She took the cup and began again.

'I'd never seen Alf like he was when he told me this story. He was a strong man and a courageous man too in his way. But that day he was terrified. He told me that he had seen at least half a dozen men lying on the floor of the laboratory, arms and legs spreadeagled in all directions. Some of them were wearing the same technicians' clothes that he had been wearing. There was a steel-reinforced door in a wall opposite the observation window, which was open, and he could see blobs of hot metal and sparks flying out from behind this door all over the room. Bright blobs of this hot liquid fell on to the laboratory floor, and Alf could see, directly under the flow, the leg of one of the technicians twitching and disintegrating in front of his eyes.'

Shilvers could tell that she was now repeating her husband's description as she remembered it. There was little emotion in her voice. The faraway look had returned to her eyes.

'Alf told me that he stood and stared until one of his friends came past and got hold of him and dragged him to the exit. Once they had left the main corridor there was pandemonium as people tried to get out and the siren continued to wail and the voice droned on telling them that it was not a drill and which exit to make for. Even the management were panicking he said. Then, as he was running towards his own exit, another door blew open with a great bang and several men came spilling out into the corridor. One of them, Alf said, was clutching his face and screaming. He just hopped over them and made for the way out. That's what they were all instructed to do. Outside it was raining, and Alf said there were safety officers all over the place, counting people and ticking them off on their clipboards. But he said he saw several of them talking together and shaking their heads. That's when he found out who the man who had been screaming was.'

'And who was it?' asked Shilvers.

There was a long pause. Mrs Penshall was still holding her teacup with two hands in front of her.

'It was George. Alf's brother.'

Shilvers said nothing, but reminded himself of Alf's manner at their meeting. He had refused to talk about individual incidents. If only he had been willing to do so Shilvers might have taken him more seriously.

'Was Alf hurt himself in all this?'

'No, not hurt. They all had to go along to a special unit and have samples done. Nose blows, that sort of thing, but they never said he'd been exposed to anything. It was just the shock, that was all. When he was in the unit, though, the management came round and spoke to all of them personally, telling them not to talk about this outside, not even to their families, they said. Reminded them that the plant would have to close down if their safety record was called into question.

'Anyway on the bus home he spoke to some of the men in other parts of the plant. They'd been told it was a small fire that had caused the evacuation. Nothing to do with radiation they said. But Alf scanned the newspapers to look for some report, or some word about funerals or something, but there wasn't anything anywhere.'

'What did he reckon had happened to the men he saw in the laboratory?'

'He had no idea. He was sure they must have died, a couple of them at least. But when he got back to work, nobody would talk about it. They all pretended it hadn't happened.'

'What about George?'

Mrs Penshall looked again at the photograph on the television. Without speaking she got up and walked over to it and picked it up. She looked at it for several moments. Then she turned to a sideboard and opened a drawer to pull out a small photo album. She opened it to the first page, and pointed to a group of two adults and two youngsters in their early teens.

'That's George, and his wife and young'uns. Thirteen and fifteen. Alf went up to see Gloria directly, and when he got to the house there was no sign of life. There was no one about. We've never seen any of them from that day until this. The whole lot vanished on the day of the accident, and we've never heard a word.'

'But didn't Alf enquire at Dounscraig? Surely he must have asked? It was his own brother.'

'He asked all right. He went to the health centre they have there and he went to the management. They told him George had gone away. Been specially selected for outstanding work for secondment, they called it, to another I.N.I. plant in Australia they said. The management had sent him to work in an I.N.I. plant there and the decision had to be taken immediately. They said Alf would hear from him eventually.'

'But surely they didn't expect Alf to believe that, not about his own brother?'

'No, I don't think they did. They reminded him that he had signed the undertaking, and how important it was to the community that people kept their faith in the industry. They gave him a couple of weeks off work, and when he got back they gave him a promotion. More money too.'

'They didn't know that Alf had actually seen George in the accident?'

'No, but they must have realized that Alf didn't believe their story.' Mrs Penshall now paused again and looked directly at Shilvers. 'They must have, mustn't they, Mr Shilvers. Because that's why he's dead.'

She did not break down. Shilvers returned her gaze until at last she resumed her long stare past him and out of the window. Once again she appeared to become oblivious to his presence, and as he watched in enduring silence he felt that he could read a million memories behind the opaque pale-blue eyes. In that tiny room, indistinguishable from so many others where widows sat surrounded by the photographs of dead men, not a sound disturbed the stillness. Where there had been the rustling of Alf's newspaper, or the rasp of matches as he puffed away on his pipe, or the commentary on the horse racing on television in the afternoon, now the house was packed to every corner with silence. It was sudden and it was unfamiliar. For Mrs Penshall it was frightening and enduring and for ever.

Shilvers' own gaze lost focus as his eyes filled and he imagined that the two of them were alone in the world, isolated for a moment in this room on a hilltop resting on the edge of the ocean. Shilvers thought of Julia, then of Mrs Penshall. It was after all she who was alone, not him, and despite himself he was glad. Recent experience had confirmed for him that he had no wish to be alone.

'May 17th two years ago it was. That was when Alf really knew what was going on. That was the date of the accident.'

Shilvers blinked and wiped his eyes. 'He wanted to do something about it, and he would have but for the others. The men it was, not the women. They weren't so worried about the money. It was the men. All they knew before was farming and fishing you see, scrimping and scraping a living off this rotten land. They didn't want to know when he talked about doing something. There were arguments and Alf made no secret of how he felt. But he wouldn't do anything on his own, not without the other men. Then you turned up.' She brought her gaze from the window and looked at Shilvers. 'It was a way of doing something about it without getting involved himself. It would look as though it had come from the outside and Dounscraig wouldn't lay people off in the village. That's what he would have thought.' She paused. 'But they were right, weren't they? He should have left things be. Should have minded his own business. They said he'd be sorry and they were right. Except he's not sorry is he? He's dead. It's me that's sorry.'

Shilvers waited for several moments before asking his final question.

'Mrs Penshall, there is just one more thing that's on my mind.' She did not respond. 'The man in the expensive car at the funeral yesterday. The man you . . . the man in the smart suit. Who is he?'

'Roger Thornton. General Manager. Imperial Nuclear Industries.' She said no more. It was what Shilvers had expected. It was all he needed to know.

On his way to the door he turned. 'What will you do now?'

'Don't worry about me, Mr Shilvers. Worry about yourself, and your loved ones.'

Her final words remained with him as Shilvers set off down the hill toward the coast lane back into the village. As he walked, the roar of the sea crept back into his head, and had his thoughts not been so far away, he might have been able to disentangle it from the distant roar of rotor blades as the helicopter swirled around in the billow and headed out above the bay. As he passed the Huntsman at the other side of the village Shilvers wondered whether Julia had returned. The hire car had vanished, leaving only deep gouges in the mud where the uncushioned wheels had been dragged out by a breakdown truck.

A key was on the outside of the door when Shilvers reached the cottage and he pushed the door open. Inside there was no sign of life. Shilvers felt edgy and was being careful. He listened and after a few seconds could hear the sound of water running in the bathroom. Without a sound he tiptoed towards the bathroom door and opened it. He smiled to himself as he recognized the silhouette of Julia through the shower curtain and heard her soft humming. Shilvers thought how cold the water was and admired her bravery. She had her back turned towards him as he stepped closer and measured his angle. Then he whisked back the plastic curtain and brought down his hand in a resounding smack on her backside. She let out a scream and threw back the curtain. A split second later she reached up and directed the shower nozzle straight at Shilvers. The full flow hit him in the face. His amusement froze.

'For Christ's sake, Julia!' He spluttered back towards the door and she shrieked with delight.

'Serves you right you lecherous bastard.'

Shilvers was still pathetically mopping his face and hair with a damp tea-towel when Julia emerged in a crisp white dressing-gown with a blue towel wrapped like a turban on her head.

'That's what you get for being a smart-arse. And by the way my arse is still smarting.'

Shilvers knew his grouchiness was absurd and half turned away as a smile took over his face.

'How did you get on today?' he asked.

'O.K. But you tell me first. How was the not very merry widow?'

They both sat on the bed drying their hair, as Shilvers described his visit. He was half-way through the story when she remembered something.

'This was pinned to the door when I got back.' She handed

him a crumpled letter. The scrawled handwriting had been smudged in the rain.

'That's odd, the postman doesn't usually come up here. He's only called once.' Shilvers' voice trailed away as he puzzled over why the handwriting looked familiar. It was a local postmark. Winderwath, 16th November.

'This was posted two weeks ago, down in the village. How can it have taken so long to get here?' Shilvers was uneasy. 'And why didn't they just hand it to me in the post office?' He opened the soggy envelope and pulled out a neatly folded piece of paper. The note was in the same scrawled handwriting. He read it aloud.

'Dear Mr Shilvers. Just a note to say that something funny is going on since we met. I think I may be being watched, and it could be I.N.I. Please don't contact me. Good luck. Alfred Penshall.'

Shilvers dropped the note on his lap. November 16th had been the day that Penshall had died.

CHAPTER FIFTEEN

Even though she knew very well what was on them, Jacqueline was in a rush to develop the photographs. The news cuttings agency with which she had dealt over many years had been able to produce a list of Anthony Shilvers' work with little difficulty, and she now had a fat file. The articles covered an enormous range of subjects, giving no indication of what, if anything, he specialized in. They stretched back for more than ten years. There was occasionally a series of pieces on a particular theme. One of them concerned the remarkable and sometimes suspect methods used by pharmaceutical companies to persuade G.P.s to prescribe their drugs. There were half a dozen pieces at weekly intervals in the same Sunday newspaper and Jacqueline had read them all with great interest, but there was no real sign that Shilvers was a campaigning journalist of any kind. He had written one or two small articles about nuclear power in the distant past, but nothing recently, and nothing which indicated any strong opinion. That at least would be welcome news.

The bad news was that, having turned up at the funeral the day before, Anthony Shilvers had now visited Alfred Penshall's widow. Even with the sophisticated equipment available to her, Jacqueline could get no clue about their conversation, or even whether or not they had met before. She retained a faint hope that the pictures might reveal something which she had not seen herself.

As the enormously powerful telephoto lens had settled, Jacqueline had seen enough of Mrs Penshall's face to remind her of the shock she had experienced at first sight of her yesterday. The complete despair in her expression was difficult to put out of mind. She had not known Alf Penshall even remotely, but had passed on the information about his movements as she was obliged to do, and had been shattered by the news of his death. It made her question once again the worth of the many things she stood for. Another death. How many more would there be?

A few moments ago Jacqueline had paused before passing on the news of Shilvers' visit to Mrs Penshall. What would it lead to? Could she keep on telling herself that she was not responsible for the actions of others? In her head she knew that the situation in which she had put herself meant she had no choice but to pass on news of the visit. Others would know, and would know that she knew. If she failed to do her job she would come under suspicion herself. It was a risk she could not afford to take. In her heart she had felt reluctant and doubtful, but she had done it anyway. The news had been greeted with some alarm. Her opinion had not been sought or given. As she moved the light-sensitive paper around, waiting for the image to form, Jacqueline's mind wandered over the many dilemmas and contradictions of her life.

Half an hour later Jacqueline had a series of pictures of a man, shoulders hunched, in a heavy blue jacket walking towards the Penshall house. She could see him once again, knocking and going in, and there was another series of him coming away again. In some she could see his face quite clearly. Though not what she would have regarded as a handsome man, there was something about Anthony Shilvers that she liked. If pressed for an explanation of what she saw in his expression she might have resorted to desperately vague words like humanity or straightforwardness. Such characteristics were hardly in the vocabulary of her present occupation, and it was refreshing but disquieting to encounter someone from quite outside the world she was now part of, even at the long end of a zoom.

Jacqueline hung up the pictures and glanced over her other recent work, black and white shots of a woman whose vivid auburn hair and startling green eyes had made an impression on Jacqueline even through the camera lens. It had not taken long to find out who she was. Julia Somers was well-known to readers of certain up-market magazines, and now that it had been pointed out, Jacqueline realized that she herself had heard of her. She had seen photo-collections of a number of Julia Somers' designs, and despite her deeply-ingrained prejudice against spending large sums on fashionable clothes, she had on occasion been tempted. They were exactly the sort of clothes that Jacqueline would have liked to buy but would never be able to persuade herself to wear. In recent years she had cultivated an image which was designed to be taken seriously in a world where men find it difficult to take women seriously. She had adopted smart, no-nonsense clothes, and now the image was so much a part of her that she did not know for certain whether there was anything beneath the superficial skin in which she clad herself. Now thoughts about Julia Somers and the kind of life she must lead made her question once again the one she had chosen for herself.

Jacqueline looked more closely at several photographs she had taken of Shilvers and Julia together. The couple were walking down the cliffside path towards the village, and the woman was pointing at something far out to sea. But Anthony Shilvers' eyes were not following her hand, they were turned towards her. The image was sharp and clear, and Jacqueline looked hard at his expression. Julia had her back turned to Shilvers, and obviously thought he was looking where she pointed. Instead his face said that he was immersed in her. It was an unmistakable look of love, and it touched an emotion somewhere in her which Jacqueline usually kept very deeply buried. There was no man in her life. She had no time for one and she told herself that she had no need of one. Her work was everything to her, her commitment total. What she had to do was far too important to be complicated by romantic entanglements, or the games couples always and inevitably played with each other. Nonetheless, and now despite herself, Jacqueline found it impossible to take her eyes away from the face of Anthony Shilvers. No man had ever looked at her in that way. Her head said she did not want it, and her heart said something else.

She tried hard to concentrate on writing her report, but found her mind going over and over the same ground. In her turmoil she forced her thoughts back to the place they always settled when her doubts and fears crept up on her, her father. She was proud of him, she had looked after him, she had loved him after her mother had died, and she had nursed him after his accident. The many traumas had forged an extraordinary link between them. Her feelings on other things were often mixed up, but her feelings for Dr Graham Smedley were unambiguous. She loved him and was in awe of what he did, and his recent revelation to her had thrown all her thoughts into further turmoil. He was effectively in sole charge of a project which could potentially have incalculable beneficial results but which, even he admitted, could also bring about appalling disaster. Though she had tried hard not to show it, for Jacqueline to see him so uncertain and concerned when he was usually so confident and competent had a profound effect. She had turned the matter over in her mind endlessly since the conversation. When she had separated her feelings for her father from the rest of her emotions, she was once again left committed. She knew what she must do and now felt reinforced in her task. She put all doubt out of her mind and concentrated on her report. Nothing mattered more than what lay ahead of her. In a tiny recess, however, she hoped that nothing unpleasant would happen to Anthony Shilvers and Julia Somers.

CHAPTER SIXTEEN

Shilvers made some coffee and sat down with Julia to talk over the case so far. Her enquiries in the Register at Westermouth had yielded nothing. None of the six names was registered as a death. They agreed that it was now beyond dispute that I.N.I. had known about Penshall's concern and had decided to leave nothing to chance. There was nothing beyond suspicion linking them with it, but the coincidence of a mysterious death on the day after his visit to Shilvers was too great. Now the evidence of the note put the matter beyond doubt in both their minds.

The question Shilvers kept returning to was why I.N.I. had not just disposed of Penshall in the same way that they had disposed of the other workers from Dounscraig who were missing. If the company was capable of removing entire families from this close-knit community, then it was certainly capable of getting rid of Penshall without anybody making an enormous fuss. And now an even stranger inconsistency occurred to him. Having disposed of Penshall, why had they left Mrs Penshall in the village, able if she wanted to echo his doubts, and perhaps in her bereavement to do something which would jeopardize their entire operation? It did not make sense.

'Penshall went out of his way to convince me that his wife knew nothing of what was going on in the plant,' Shilvers recalled, 'so maybe he did the same with everybody else. Perhaps the word in the village is that she doesn't know about his worries, and that has been conveyed back to I.N.I.'

'So they feel confident enough to let her stay.'

'Maybe. But you can bet your life that they would need to be sure.' Shilvers was thinking out loud. 'And maybe that's why they turned up at the funeral, to try to guess from her behaviour whether she did or did not suspect that they were implicated.'

'And if that's what they had in mind, then the fact that she slapped Thornton will have told them everything they wanted to know.'

Shilvers and Julia sat a few seconds longer just looking at each other.

'Come on.' They grabbed their coats and a moment later were out of the door.

As they scuttled down the cliffside, Shilvers cursed his own stupidity. If Penshall had been killed for speaking to him, then they would now be watching to try to find out what he knew. If they were watching, they would know that he went to the funeral and that he had visited Mrs Penshall. Put all that together with her reaction to Thornton at the funeral and Mrs Penshall was in a very dangerous position.

By the time they reached the spot where the hire car had been, Shilvers and Julia were running. They slowed down to a brisk walk through the village, and Shilvers began to feel slightly less agitated. It was after all only four hours since he had called on her. If they had left her this long, they were unlikely to move in straight away. As they reached the bottom of the hill which led up towards the Penshall house, Shilvers began to wonder out loud what they would say to her.

'We'll need to be careful not to alarm her,' Julia agreed, 'maybe we might just say we were concerned about her being on her own, and enquire whether she has any family or someone she can go and stay with for a few days.'

Shilvers thought that was a good idea and was still considering the thought as the short row of cottages came into view.

'Is that it?' asked Julia. Shilvers was depressed but not surprised to see that she was far less out of breath than he was. He nodded.

A few minutes later they were at the gate and walking down the path to the side door of the house. As before, Shilvers hammered on the solid wood and waited. After a few moments he hammered again, this time harder and more urgently. His fears started to flood back. He watched for some movement of the curtains at the side window but there was none. There was no sight or sound of life. Shilvers went to the window and pressed his face against it, shielding out the reflection with his hand. He could see little through the nets but could make out no movement. Julia continued to hammer on the door.

'I'm going to break in,' Shilvers said.

'Don't be silly, you can't do that. She's probably gone to the shops, or even next door for a cup of tea. At least ask the neighbours.'

Shilvers did not answer. His concern was made worse by the feeling of guilt that he should never have allowed this situation to occur. He pulled Julia to one side, stepped back a few paces, and barged into the door with his shoulder. The door immediately burst open, tumbling him ungraciously into the hall.

'Mrs Penshall,' he called as he righted himself. 'Mrs Penshall, are you here?' Julia followed him into the house and started up the stairs, repeating his call but more softly in case she was asleep.

Shilvers continued down the hall and into the living-room. What he saw there made him step back in surprise. There was no carpet on the floor, there were no pictures on the walls, no settee or chairs. There was nothing whatever in the room. Julia had just reached the bottom of the stairs when Shilvers rushed past on his way into the kitchen where he had earlier made a cup of tea for himself and Mrs Penshall. There was no cooker, no refrigerator, no kettle. Shilvers opened the cupboard where Mrs Penshall had kept the teabags. It was empty. He went to other cupboards and opened them. They were empty.

In a frenzy Shilvers dashed from room to room all around the house. There was not a piece of furniture, not a carpet, not an ornament. There was no sign whatever that the house had been occupied for many months. Only the curtains at the windows gave the impression to the outside world that everything was normal.

'I can't believe it.' Shilvers seemed lost for sensible words.

'I just can't believe it.' He stared around the living-room in helpless amazement. 'I was in this room just four hours ago, sitting in an armchair and drinking a cup of tea. And now . . .'

Julia could only stare back at him, searching for some plausible explanation. In desperation she made the only suggestion she could think of.

'There can be no doubt that this is the right house?'

'Of course it's the right bloody house,' Shilvers exploded. 'Its the same wallpaper, the same curtains, the same bloody garden I walked through and the same front door that I knocked on. I may be mad but I'm not stupid for Christ's sake.' Shilvers' anger expressed his bewilderment at the absence of a logical explanation. 'A professional removal firm couldn't have completely emptied the house so quickly.'

Julia knew Shilvers well enough to know that a tactical withdrawal was advisable. She waited for several minutes before speaking again.

'Did she give any indication that she might be going away?'

'Not a word. Not a sign of it.'

As they contemplated the bare rooms, searching in vain for some clue, Julia thought she heard the faint sound of a car engine starting up.

'Tony, listen.' Both stood still for a second, and Shilvers was the first to bolt for the door. As he reached the corner of the house he caught a glimpse of a large car disappearing into the distance. It was accelerating hard, but he could just make out the registration number. He reached into his coat pocket for his notebook and began to scribble, repeating the letters under his breath as he wrote. 'ARH 998X. ARH 998X.' A moment later Julia was beside him. 'Did you see who it was?'

'No,' said Shilvers, 'but I've got a bloody good idea, and what is more I've got a bloody good way of finding out.' They set off down the hill.

Shilvers did not stop until he reached the village and Julia frequently broke into a run to keep up with him. They passed several people in the village, each of them grunting a greeting and being ignored by Shilvers. Still trying to catch her breath Julia smiled a half-hearted smile to make amends.

Shilvers' expression reflected the dark anger which had welled up inside him. Anger first of all at himself for his own lack of foresight in failing to perceive the danger to Mrs Penshall, and then at the mighty industrial machine which apparently had within its power the ability to move in and liquidate a household in a matter of hours, while nobody in the vicinity raised a finger to protest. The possibilities multiplied in his mind. What would become of her now? Would there be another mysterious hit and run accident? Or would Mrs Penshall go the same way as Alf's brother George and his family, and the rest of the families Alf had talked about? And if she did, would anyone in this godforsaken village give a damn?

Shilvers strode on towards the telephone-box. Once inside, Julia had to press herself against him to allow the door to close. Shilvers acted as though she was not there. He dialled the operator and asked for a transfer charge call to a London number he knew as well as he knew his own. A female voice answered and accepted the charge, as she did automatically no matter who or where the call came from. Shilvers identified himself and asked for the newsdesk. To his relief the call was answered by Frank Chaplin.

'Frank, do me an enormous favour will you? I want a registration number check.'

'Sure thing,' was the unhesitating reply. 'It might take a few minutes. Do you want to hold?'

'It's your phone bill so I will. The number is,' he referred to his notebook, 'ARH 998X. Got that?'

Chaplin repeated the number and asked Shilvers to hold. Chaplin would now call another number that Shilvers would have called direct if he had been using his own telephone. It was the number of a private enquiry agent who happened to be a retired policeman with friends still on the force. It would cost £50 to get a name and address. The *Sentinel* probably made two or three such enquiries a month, so the bill for this one might get laundered through the accounts. At this moment Shilvers did not care one way or the other.

Shilvers had to wait for Chaplin to get on to the agent and then the agent to get on to his friend at the computer terminal. From that moment it took only thirty seconds to find just about any registration number in Britain. Only the cars used by the official security services were not listed. The readout would give a name and address of the owner of the vehicle. There would also be a note of anything that was known about the owner, including information on previous convictions and whether there were any charges outstanding. That was rare, and in such a case the fee went up to £100.

Within five minutes Chaplin was back on the line.

'Are you ready for this?' Shilvers said that he was. 'Mr R. B. Thornton. Address, The Coach House, Downs Farm, Westermouth. Want me to repeat that?'

There was no need. Shilvers' shorthand was not that rusty. He read the details over.

'I'll remember you next time we're short of a court reporter,' said Chaplin.

'I'm likely to be around begging for more information before that happens.'

'That's O.K.,' said Chaplin, 'but remember when this story is ready we get first crack at it. That *is* the deal isn't it Tony? And don't try to give me any more crap about the Tourist Board.'

Shilvers thanked him and hung up. 'Thornton. The man at the funeral. I'm going to see him straight away.'

'I'm coming with you!' said Julia without hesitation.

'Not this time.' He was adamant. 'I'm going alone and I'm going to tell him everything we know and everything we suspect. I'll tell him that we'll reveal the lot unless he tells us where Mrs Penshall is.'

Julia put her hand on Shilvers' arm. Not for the first time recently she was thinking more logically than he was.

'Just think about that for a minute will you?' Her voice was urgent. 'You're planning to go storming in on a man who may be responsible for the disappearance of dozens of people, including an old lady this very day, and tell him you know all about it. Maybe you're going to tell him that you've written it all down in a sealed envelope and your solicitor will open it in ten days unless you turn up safe and sound? Use your head for Christ's sake.'

Her abruptness took Shilvers by surprise and he saw immediately that she was right.

'It may sound stupid to us, but how will they be sure that I haven't done exactly as you say? They can't take that risk can they?'

'Maybe.' Julia was still trying to think of arguments to prevent him from going.

'Anyway, I'm still going, and I'm going on my own. You are my insurance policy. If they're watching us, they have to assume that you know what I know, so they can't touch us separately. If they aren't, we've nothing to worry about. Take yourself home straight away, lock the door and don't open it in any circumstances until I get there.'

Julia had no choice but to agree.

'The bus to Westermouth leaves in a few minutes. I'll get that and then get a taxi back. I won't be late but don't start worrying before midnight.'

He gave her a long hug, and the last words of Mrs Penshall came back into his head. 'Look after your loved ones.' Julia tucked her head into his shoulder so he was unable to see the anxiety on her face. He held her under the chin and tried to raise her face towards him, but she only pressed herself harder against him. Then she quickly broke away.

'Be careful and get back as fast as you can,' she said and hurried away into the gathering gloom.

The ancient local bus clanked and shook and belched dark smoke into the cool air as it pulled out of Winderwath. It was an hourly service between Winderwath and Westermouth which stopped at very few formal bus-stops, but would halt to pick up anyone who hailed it in the narrow country lanes.

Shilvers looked out over the hedgerows and across the moor. The lights in the bus and the deepening darkness outside made it increasingly difficult to see anything beyond his own reflection in the dirty glass. He was not impressed by the tired face which glared back at him. Deep shadows filled and overflowed the craggy valleys which had replaced what had once been dimples. Thick cobwebs spread out from the corners of his eyes. It seemed that they had not cracked into a smile for years. He practised a smile and it felt as though his face was stiff. Across the bus a young woman with a pretty face and fashionable clothes tried to suppress a grin and went on reading her newspaper. Saturday night, Shilvers remembered. All around the world young girls were meeting young men for an evening out. None of them had the smallest reason to care about all this, the subject which was obsessing him. He looked again in the glass and saw that she was engrossed in her reading. He looked again at his reflection. He needed a shave and a haircut.

The sight of the girl made Shilvers think about Julia. Only thirty-two. Ten years between their ages, and while he was wearing very badly, she was wearing very well. His only consolation was that he had never allowed himself to get overweight. There had always been too much rushing around and too few regular meals. He weighed the same as he had when he worked with George Ffitch all those years ago. George had aged terribly. Maybe it was the business, Shilvers thought. Here he was, on a country bus, heading into he did not know what, without even a decent plan of what he intended to say. No wonder he looked old.

Minutes later Shilvers became aware that the bus was slowing down. The driver turned round towards him and called. 'This is Downs Farm Mister.' By now the bus had shuddered to a halt. 'The farmhouse is about half a mile down that lane.' The driver gestured towards a gap in the heavy dry-stone wall.

'Would that be the Coach House?'

'No. The Coach House is a bit further on still. It's nothing to do with the farm I believe. It's a converted place, belongs to a towny I think.' The driver realized his indiscretion. 'Meaning no offence like.'

'None taken.' Shilvers smiled another stiff smile. 'I daresay you're right.'

The bus spluttered and coughed its way down the road and Shilvers was left standing in almost complete darkness by the side of the lane. As the two red lights disappeared over the next hill, Shilvers was reminded that it is always much darker in the country than in the town. No street-lights, no buildings or headlights. Only the moon guided him towards the narrow track which seemed wide enough for only one vehicle to pass.

Shilvers looked up at the millions of stars. He turned in a circle to try to recognize the patterns his mother had so often pointed out to him. He could never see them then, nor could he see them now. When he looked ahead and started to walk he felt dizzy for a few seconds and had to put a hand on the stone wall to regain his balance. There were cows in the field next to him, standing quite still. Do cows stand up when they sleep, Shilvers wondered? He was not sure that he had ever known.

The bus sounded as though it was clanking its last as it pulled up at the stop outside the terminus in Westermouth. Two old women struggling up from their seats grumbled aloud as the young girl pressed past them to alight.

'Youngsters haven't got time to breathe these days,' said one.

The young woman with blonde hair cut short and piercing blue eyes did not rush into the arms of a waiting lover, but ran towards a telephone-box at the corner of the bus garage. She dialled and waited, then inserted her money.

'Gold? He's gone to see Thornton.' There was a pause. 'No, at his house. He's on foot. Better warn our man.' Without waiting for a reply she hung up. Before leaving the call box Jacqueline Smart checked her bag. There were no cosmetics or anything to indicate an evening out with a young man.

Only a camera, and beside it a small hand gun. She closed her bag and set off the way she had come.

Before long Shilvers saw lights which he assumed belonged to the farmhouse. There was a dim glow behind plain curtains in the downstairs windows. As he got nearer a farmyard dog began to yelp frantically. Shilvers heard what sounded to him like the thunder of a huge animal bounding towards him. The increasingly urgent and alarming barking ended in a sudden yelp as the chain reached its full extent with a metallic clunk. Shilvers could hear his own heart beating. After a short pause the barking continued, now with heightened pitch and volume. A light appeared in the doorway and a silhouette cast a long shadow across the farmyard.

'Shut up dog will you? Is there someone there?'

For some reason Shilvers considered saying nothing, but quickly realized the foolishness and possible consequences of remaining silent.

'Am I going the right way for the Coach House?' The light in the doorway was now totally eclipsed by an enormous shadow as the farmer stepped towards him, squinting in to the darkness.

'Straight on up the hill. Sorry about the dog. We don't get many visitors up here after dark, 'specially not on foot.' The remark invited an explanation but Shilvers did not feel like giving one.

'That's O.K. You don't happen to know whether Mr Thornton is in do you? You could save me a wasted journey.'

'Oh I think he's in all right. His car passed by about half an hour since. But isn't he expecting you? Mr Thornton don't like unexpected visitors.'

'It's O.K. Roger will be pleased to see me. I'm an old friend and it's a surprise.'

'Suit yourself.' Shilvers could see the shrug of the shoulders echoed in the vast shadow in front of the silhouette. 'Good-night.' The light from the doorway faded quickly away and once again there was darkness and silence. Back indoors the shape picked up the telephone and dialled. 'Gold? You're right.

He's on his way to see Thornton. He's not expected.'

Ten minutes later the farmhouse was out of sight and Shilvers began to make out the shape of what he supposed must be the Coach House. As he approached it became clear that this was the right place. A big car which looked black but could have been red was parked at the side of the house. ARH 998X. Shilvers put his hand on the bonnet. It was still warm.

The house had obviously been carefully and expensively modernized. There was a short gravel path from the heavy iron gates to the front door. The whole structure had been painted white, and window boxes overflowed from every ledge. The window-frames were of natural wood, and each downstairs window was shielded by oatmeal-coloured blinds, with strong lights behind them.

Shilvers looked up to see the macabre shape of a rook perched above him on a telephone wire. His eyes followed the wire to a box on the corner of the house, and now he could make out the shape of a person in an upstairs window, silhouetted against the blind. Shilvers stood quite still and watched as the person half-turned, the shadow revealing that he was speaking on the telephone. Shilvers could hear the faint sound of music.

He trod carefully as he approached the house, but still every footfall on the gravel sounded like a thunderclap in the quiet night. Shilvers wondered whether that was its purpose. As he drew level with one of the downstairs windows, Shilvers could now clearly distinguish the sound of opera. Perhaps it was Mozart. A passing shadow behind the blind of a downstairs window told him that there were at least two people in the house.

Only as he reached the big oak door did Shilvers realize that he had not given much thought to a cover story. What was he going to say? Julia would have planned better, he thought. It was too late to turn back. He must have been heard. He pulled back the heavy iron knocker and the crash reverberated across the hills behind him.

Immediately, as if he was expected, a shaft of light appeared in a single pane in the door and a robotic voice demanded, 'Who is it?' The sound of an aria distorted by the metallic filter wafted out into the darkness and into the surrounding fields. Shilvers could make out the concave shape of a face through the thick glass.

'My name is Anthony Shilvers,' he heard himself saying. 'I was a friend of Alfred Penshall.'

There was a long silence. Shilvers felt an irresistible urge to fill it. He was committed and had no choice but to go on.

'I wanted to speak to Mrs Penshall at the funeral yesterday but I didn't get the chance. Now I don't know where she is and I wondered if you could help?'

As his voice floated away in the darkness the silence once again closed around him. The face turned to one side, the distortion extending the nose to form a ridiculous caricature. The person seemed to be consulting. Then the panel went dark and the huge oak door swung open. Shilvers found himself squinting into the face of the man he had seen at the funeral the day before.

'And what makes you think I can help you?' The voice was educated but accentless. In for a penny, thought Shilvers.

'Well I went up to the Penshall house this evening, just to make sure that Mrs Penshall was all right. We had a short chat and she seemed to be fine. Later on I went to call on her again, and I found that she wasn't there, but I saw your car driving away. I recognized it from yesterday. I asked the ladies at the village post office if they knew your name and luckily for me they did. They seem to know everyone for miles around. Anyway, I couldn't see your number in the book, so I thought I'd pop out on the off-chance.'

The other man's expression gave no clue to his thoughts.

'You'd better come in.'

The man led Shilvers towards the living area. The furniture was high-tech, there were spotlights everywhere and tiled floors covered with multi-coloured rugs. The man went to a large modern cocktail cabinet packed with what seemed a hundred bottles, reflected and multiplied by more lights and mirrors.

'Will you have a drink, Mr Shilvers?'

'Brandy please,' said Shilvers. 'It's a bit nippy outside and it's a fair walk from the main road.'

The man half turned his head, and Shilvers saw his eyebrow arch as he poured. Shilvers examined his surroundings. There were no pictures of any kind. No photographs to give a fragment of information about the man in front of him.

'May I ask what is your business with Mrs Penshall?' said Thornton, heading towards him with a heavy crystal brandy goblet half filled with rich brown liquor. Thornton was in his mid-fifties, with greying hair, which was white at the temples, and cut short and smart. He had what Shilvers' mother would have called a distinguished look about him, with smooth skin and a firm jaw. Shilvers fancied that he could still make out the faint red traces of Mrs Penshall's furious slap the day before.

'Oh I'm just a friend of the family. Well to be precise I knew Alf reasonably well, but I hardly know Mrs Penshall. I thought I would just pop in and see if there was anything I could do. Then I remembered that I hadn't told her where she could find me if she needed anything so I went back. She doesn't have much in the way of family does she?'

'Only a sister in Manchester.' The reply was immediate.

'Anyway,' Shilvers continued, 'do you have any idea where she's gone? I'd just like to make sure that she knows where I am if she needs anything.'

'You must have been a good friend of Penshall's,' Thornton evaded the question, 'to be so concerned I mean. You must have known him well?' The man had been speaking loudly to dominate the opera coming from the hi-fi in one corner. Now the music stopped suddenly, and his last few words seemed unnaturally loud against the new silence. In that moment Shilvers thought he heard a noise upstairs and turned his head to listen. Thornton did not react.

'Yes, I've known him for years. Ever since I was a little lad actually. My folks used to bring me to this part of the country on holiday, year in year out. Alf was a farmer in those days and he used to let me ride the horses.' Shilvers was feeling pleased with himself. 'I knew his brother George too, but not so well. Haven't seen him for years actually. Odd that he wasn't at the funeral.'

Thornton sat in silence, cupping his brandy goblet in the palms of his hands. Shilvers could hardly conceal a smile as he realized that his story had taken Thornton completely by surprise. Eventually the older man spoke.

'When did you last see him?'

'Oh just before he died as a matter of fact.' Shilvers was now completely in charge of the situation and did not hesitate. 'I dropped him a letter a few weeks ago to say that I was coming up to do some work and asking him to call on me when he had a moment. He came up to the cottage where I'm staying on the night before he died.'

'Did he say anything?' For a moment Thornton had let his guard slip. His voice betrayed an unusual sense of urgency.

'Say anything?' Shilvers relished the moment. 'How do you mean, say anything?'

'I meant did he seem his old self. Was he worried about anything?'

'Worried?' Shilvers was determined not to let the man off the hook. 'Why should he be worried about anything?' He paused. 'You don't think that his death was anything other than an accident do you?'

Thornton put down his glass and got up. He walked swiftly to the far end of the room and turned around.

'Lots of hooligans flying around the countryside these days.' Thornton had recovered himself. 'They should tighten up on the drunken driving laws. But since you aren't driving . . .' He picked up a heavy decanter.

'Cheers,' said Shilvers, raising his glass.

Thornton sat back in his chair, but leaned forward as if to whisper. His voice indicated that he was imparting a secret.

'Look, it's all supposed to be very hush hush, but as you probably know Penshall worked for Imperial Nuclear Industries. I was his boss, and we're a company that prides itself on looking after the welfare of our employees. That's why I turned up at the funeral, and that is why I called on Mrs Penshall today. She was overwrought yesterday and I came to see if we could help in any way. Much like you. And like you I found her away. Presumably she's gone to stay with her sister, to get away from it all.'

And taken her furniture with her, thought Shilvers, but resisted the temptation to say it. They sipped their drinks for several minutes, assessing the situation, and examining each other. Shilvers wondered whether he should renew his attack, or retreat to consolidate. He decided to retreat. Julia, he reflected, would have been proud of him.

'Oh well, best be on my way.' He leapt to his feet, to the evident surprise of Thornton who jumped up after him. 'Do you mind if I call a taxi from here? I think the last bus from Westermouth has gone.'

Shilvers used the telephone, and the two men exchanged casual chat for fifteen minutes about the weather, the countryside and the local people. Thornton was still uneasy, Shilvers totally relaxed. When he heard a car outside, Shilvers reached for his coat and Thornton helped him on with it.

'By the way, Mr Shilvers,' said Thornton, 'what business are you in?'

Shilvers reached into his pocket and handed over a small white card. 'I'm a freelance journalist, working for the Tourist Board just now. If ever you have a story you think I might be able to use, please give me a call.' Shilvers headed out into the night. As he turned to wave good-night to Thornton, he was aware of a sudden movement at an upstairs window. Moments later, the car was sweeping down the lane cutting through the darkness with the confidence which only comes from having a local driver at the wheel.

Back in the Coach House, in an upstairs room, lay an open file with five ten inch by twelve inch black and white photographs spilling out across the table. Two men looked at the photographs, and then looked at each other, and they wondered.

CHAPTER SEVENTEEN

Julia kneeled on the chair beside the window at the front of the cottage and peered through the misted glass as the evening turned into night. She rubbed the window but only produced a damp blur, and wiped the cold moisture from her fingers on the backside of her jeans. Everything was dark grey. Grey sea, grey sky and grey clouds whispering across the horizon.

She looked at her watch. Nine o'clock. No need to start worrying before midnight, Shilvers had said. That was all right for him to say. She had been worried since the very first moment he had told her the story, and she was more worried now than ever. She was not worried for herself. It had not really dawned on her that she was in danger personally. Even the disappearance of Mrs Penshall, shocking to her though it surely was, had not properly persuaded Julia that she herself faced any threat. Now she wondered how she had reached that conclusion. It was illogical of her to have done so. If I.N.I. suspected that Penshall had told his worries to Shilvers, then they must assume that Shilvers had told her. If she knew, then she too was a threat.

Of course, I.N.I. could not be sure what Shilvers knew, but that had not worried them as far as Penshall was concerned. He was dead, and the reason was that they were not prepared to take the chance. Now they must be concerned about Shilvers. She was his insurance, he had said. That did not feel very reassuring just now. It would not be difficult for I.N.I. to move in on the two of them, separately or together, and they would meet the same fate which had befallen Mrs Penshall, whatever that was.

Did they dare do it? Julia wondered. Taking people out of a small, close community in which everyone knew each other and lived in fear was one thing. Shilvers, on the other hand, was a nationally known journalist. There were people, many of them, who knew he was here. The Tourist Board for a start, and the *Sentinel*. Frank Chaplin even knew that Shilvers was working on a story about Dounscraig. If something unexpected happened to Shilvers, Chaplin would begin making enquiries. Then would come another, and another, and for Dounscraig the whole thing would have gone too far. It would be out of control. There was also the matter of the sealed envelope. Absurd cliché that it sounded, I.N.I. could not be sure that Shilvers had not written down what he knew and left it somewhere for safe keeping. Surely they dare not take the risk?

Certainly that line of argument was reassuring, but then Julia wondered whether she was trying too hard to convince herself. This was an organization with enormous power and resources, which would clearly stop at nothing. Shilvers and she needed to take every possible precaution including, Julia thought, the hidden envelope with the whole story in it.

Julia wiped the window again and craned her neck to try to catch sight of Shilvers coming up the hill. There was no sound above the distant cacophony of sea and wind, and the monotonous tap tap tap of the branch of a shrub on the window-pane.

All this seemed far away from the short stay she had just had in Paris. There the work had been a success, and the life had been so fast and flashy that she had hardly had time to stop and wonder whether she was enjoying it or not. The friend from college with whom she had been staying had urged her to spread her wings and take what she could out of the glamorous life of the Paris fashion world. There were lots of fun people, and having fun with them could give a further boost to her already rocketing career. Why was she still hanging around with Tony? Sure he was a nice enough bloke, but what could he do for her? He wasn't even one of those gossip columnists who liked to be seen around with top models and fashion designers and who paid back the favours by writing titillating titbits about them in the popular press.

Julia had disliked such remarks but knew that she had done little to discourage them. She had just heard, shrugged her shoulders, and said that they did not understand. In the years they had been together, he had been a kind and considerate man, much more so than the skinny boys or the overweight men who waltzed around the fashion houses looking for their latest lay.

'Then why are you here?' her friend had asked. Again Julia had shrugged her shoulders.

There had been angry and frustrated words between her and Shilvers when they separated but there was still the care for each other and the wish not to hurt which was part of what remained precious in their relationship. Shilvers had not asked her to be faithful. She had given no undertaking, but would have been glad to have been asked. There were many parties in Paris, peopled with tidy men with style and plenty of charm. Julia knew that she was still attractive, but it was flattering to have it confirmed. She felt that she wanted to get away from everything English, and she did.

One morning she woke up, very early, in cold and unfamiliar sheets. Beside her in bed was what seemed in the dawn a mere boy, with curly black hair, and smooth deeply tanned skin. Julia looked out of the window into the blue foreign sky, and she thought about Tony, and she missed him. That same day, with no warning to her friends, she put her clothes and her passport and her drawings in a bag and took a taxi to the airport. Eighteen hours later she had traced Shilvers to this isolated retreat on a barren hilltop in the most remote part of England, and yet she felt at home. Only now, thinking about him and worrying about him, did she fully know the reason why.

Julia did not know much time had passed, but suddenly it was completely dark outside and she was aware of a figure passing across the window. Moments later there was a heavy knock on the door. She looked at her watch. Ten-thirty. Thank God, he was back. She hurried to the door and started to speak even as she opened the latch.

'Tony, how did you get – ?' Her words ended in a sharp intake of breath as she looked into the face of a large man in his sixties with bloated red features and dressed in a stained camel-hair coat. He was breathing hard from exertion, and when he spoke his accent was Scots.

'Sorry for startling you. You, I take it, are Julia?'

Julia just looked back at him, unable to react. She said nothing until the man spoke again.

'My name is Ffitch, George Ffitch. I'm an old friend of Anthony's. I met him the other night in the Huntsman.'

'Oh yes, of course. Come in.' Julia was still recovering from her surprise but she stood back and held the door open while the large figure came in from the cold. As he did so he removed his trilby hat. The thin hair had once been red and was now almost grey. The man carried a bundle of papers in his hand, which he put down on a chair and placed his hat on top of them.

'Sorry to burst in on you like this.' Julia was good at accents, and was narrowing this one down. Glaswegian – the working-class variety, completely and self-consciously ungentrified. 'Tony asked me to look out some information for him and I put these papers in the back of my car a week ago. I've been driving around with them ever since, and as I was passing the village . . .' Julia wondered where he could be going to be passing the village as it was on the way to nowhere. Ffitch was still talking. 'I didn't reckon on that bloody climb though.'

Uninvited, he practically fell into the only armchair in the room. Julia half-expected to see a cloud of dust blow up all around him and was relieved when it did not.

'Will he be back soon?'

'Any minute.' Julia did not know why she said it. She did so automatically, as if to ensure her own safety. She now remembered that Tony had told her about Ffitch. She did not know why, but for some reason she had decided that she did not much like him.

'What was he asking you about?'

Ffitch returned her gaze. There was no chance that she did not know the answer to her own question. If his old friend Shilvers knew something about I.N.I., he wanted to know it too. He saw this as a fortuitous opportunity to find out.

'Oh, just the business he's been working on.'

Julia was well up with him. 'Oh, you mean tourism? They don't look much like nature trails to me.' She nodded in the direction of the pile of papers Ffitch had put on the chair. Ffitch leaned across and shifted his hat to conceal them more thoroughly. 'Can I get you a drink?' Julia picked up the kettle and headed towards the sink.

'Don't tell me Tony hasn't got any Scotch in the house. You've certainly got him under control.'

Julia did not like the remark, and picked up a half-empty whisky bottle from next to the bucket of cold beer and handed it to Ffitch.

'Do you need a glass?' She did not expect an answer and did not get one. She wiped a thick tumbler with a tea-towel and handed it to him.

'Have you known Tony long?' asked the Scotsman, settling back with his legs outstretched. He poured himself a generous measure and put down the bottle.

'About seven years, have you?' Julia liked her visitor less and less. She did not like the fact that he visited at night without warning, she did not like his familiar manner, and she did not like him to make himself quite so much at home.

'Longer than I care to remember.' It was a cliché and Ffitch knew it. He looked at the ceiling as if trying to recall. 'Must be twenty-odd years. He was a slip of a bairn and I was . . . a lot younger than I am today.' He threw back his head and swallowed half of the contents of the tumbler. 'I'd like to say I taught him everything he knows, but I'm sorry to say it wouldn't be true. Between you and me, and I wouldn't tell him this, he is one of the best in the business. Came down the road of hard knocks – university of life and all that – like me.' He busied himself refilling his glass.

Julia knew she should have warmed to the compliment to Shilvers. Instead she saw behind it the implication that Ffitch too was one of the best in the business.

'He could have been editor of *The Times* by now. Could have been anything he wanted really. But he's got the bug, that's the trouble. He wants to be out and about, pressing his nose into other people's business. Not like those slugs back on the newsdesks. They don't know a good story from a forty-pound hammer. The problem is,' he emptied the glass again, 'good journalists don't get on in this business. It's just the arse-lickers that get promoted.'

'What were you on the *Sentinel*? Night Editor, wasn't it?'

Ffitch laughed out loud. This girl was sharp as well as lovely to look at. That bastard Shilvers, lucky as ever.

As Ffitch refilled his glass again Julia had a fleeting memory of her early days as a photographer at the *Sentinel*. She remembered delivering a batch of fashion pictures and noticing Shilvers, his feet on the desk, drinking coffee from a plastic cup and flicking through the day's papers. She saw that he was looking at her, and pretended not to notice. She had liked the look of him, and later he had cornered her in the lift and asked her to dinner. She had said yes, and that had been the beginning.

Julia was enjoying the memory when Ffitch's expression told her she was being asked a question.

'I'm sorry, I was miles away.'

'I was saying that Tony had that hungry for a story look when I met him in the pub a week or so back. He was asking about Dounscraig so I brought the cuttings over. What particular aspect is he interested in, do you know?' Ffitch now leaned over casually and picked up the pile of papers, pretending to be flicking through them. Julia was not going to take the bait.

'I think it's something about clean air, or pollution of the fishing rivers or something. He wants to make sure they aren't bilging smoke into the sky and pumping crap into the water supply.'

'Very conscientious,' said Ffitch sharply. He did not believe a word.

'It looks as though he's been held up,' said Julia. 'If you want to leave those I can tell him what they are. If you're in a hurry to get back?' Her voice indicated encouragement.

'No, I'll just wait a wee bit longer if that's all the same to you.

Mind if I help myself?' He did not expect an answer and did not get one. He reached for the bottle. Julia made herself some coffee.

The two sat in silence for a while, avoiding each other's eyes. Julia started to hum and then stopped. She picked up a magazine carelessly and flicked through the pages. She put it down again. Their eyes met and she looked quickly away, catching only a glimpse of the awkward smile which flashed across his face.

The silence was broken by the crunch of footsteps outside. Both moved to go to the door, but Julia gave Ffitch a look which froze him back into his seat. She had opened the door even before Shilvers could knock.

'That was well heard. I thought I'd . . . ' Shilvers' voice faded as he caught Julia's serious expression and followed her into the room.

'George. This is a surprise. What the hell are you doing up here at this time of night? Been making yourself at home I see.' Now he came right in and picked up the bottle. There was only an inch in the bottom. 'Nothing changes. Have you two got to know one another?'

'Well we haven't been sitting here in silence,' said Ffitch cheerfully. Only Shilvers was unconscious of the irony. His eyes wandered to a pile of papers on the arm of the chair.

'Oh you shouldn't have bothered to bring these up,' said Shilvers, nevertheless reaching for them with more enthusiasm than was consistent with his casual tone. 'Any time would have done.'

'It was nothing. Hardly out of my way,' said Ffitch. This time Julia was unable to hold back.

'Where in God's name is this place on the way to?' For some reason she would have been unable to account for, Julia's hostility was growing. This man was fishing for information. She wanted him to go.

'Have a beer,' said Shilvers, fishing in the bucket of water for a half-floating bottle.

'No thanks very much, I must be going. If you'll let me know which of those cuttings you're interested in I can photocopy them for you.'

Shilvers wasn't taking the bait either. 'Uncommonly generous,' he said, 'but not necessary.'

'Suit yourself,' said Ffitch, heading for the door. He turned. 'By the way, the boy who covers this area for the agency tells me there's a shindig down in the village hall tomorrow night. Annual event it is, dancing and whist drive, all that sort of rubbish. Apparently the whole village turns out, and sometimes one or two of the management from I.N.I. Something to do with good industrial relations with the serfs. *Noblesse oblige* and all that crap. I should think a smart up and coming journalist like you would get all his questions answered at a do like that.' Now Ffitch was striding away and was engulfed in the darkness.

'By the way, George,' Shilvers called after him into the night. 'Did you hear about that mysterious death a couple of weeks ago? The night we met in the Huntsman? The *Sentinel* asked me if there was anything to follow up.'

Ffitch was still just visible in the gloom. He stopped in his tracks and walked back a few paces. 'Alfred Penshall,' he said without hesitation. 'Hit and run wasn't it?'

Haven't a clue,' said Shilvers. 'It's only that I knew him slightly. As a kid I mean.' He felt Julia stiffen behind him and she put her hand on his shoulder to indicate her concern. Behind his back, Shilvers squeezed her other hand in reassurance. Ffitch walked back a few paces more and was now within the light thrown out from the cottage window.

'You knew him?'

'Yes. As a kid, when I used to come up this way on holiday with my folks. He was a farmer in those days.'

'So that's the reason for your interest in Dounscraig,' said Ffitch, standing quite still in the half shadows. His voice betrayed his curiosity. 'Penshall worked there. He must have given you a story.'

'If only it were true,' said Shilvers. He was pleased with how plausible he sounded. 'As a matter of fact he did come up the night before the accident, but all he talked about was old times. I was wondering, though, did you know about the accident when I saw you in the pub? There can't be too many mysteries around here, and I can't understand why you didn't mention it.'

'It doesn't do to give your best stories away to other journalists,' said Ffitch. He seemed satisfied and turned to go. 'You of all people should know that.' He waved his hand again and was gone.

'What the hell does that mean?' Shilvers called after him, but Ffitch was gone. Only a loud laugh echoed out of the night.

'What the hell did he mean by that?' repeated Shilvers, as he closed the door. 'Still, decent of him to bring these cuttings up.'

'Decent my arse,' was Julia's unhesitating reply. 'He was snooping.'

'Is that an expression you picked up at finishing school in Paris?' Shilvers immediately regretted the remark. 'He happens to be a very old friend and colleague, and is a damned good journalist, or at least he was in his day.'

'That's more or less what he says about you. Anyway,' she wanted to change the subject, 'how did you get on with the man who specializes in removals?'

They sat over coffee and beer and Shilvers told her the whole story. She was impressed. His account would add to I.N.I.'s confusion, and faced with a plausible and innocent explanation, they would now be less likely to act. It was a relief.

'But why did you tell the same story to Ffitch? You don't suspect . . . ?'

'Not in a million years,' said Shilvers. 'Ffitch may be an unscrupulous old bastard, but he is totally incorruptible. I'd stake my life on it.'

'Let's hope you aren't doing so,' said Julia.

That night, as Shilvers lay staring at the peeling whitewash of the bedroom ceiling, Julia's rhythmic breathing suggested that she was asleep. She was not. She was thinking about Penshall, and about Thornton. She was also thinking about

Ffitch, and wondering why she disliked him. Shilvers was surprised when she spoke.

'Are we going to this shindig tomorrow night? I haven't brought anything very glamorous.'

'You don't have to wear anything glamorous to stun this lot,' said Shilvers, and drew her into his arms for a long kiss. Clinging to each other, they made love in the cold wintry night on the edge of a cliff in the middle of the vast nothingness. Then they slept.

CHAPTER EIGHTEEN

The tiny green oblong flashed on and off the screen with hypnotic regularity and blurred into the surrounding numbers as Dr Graham Smedley's defective eyes wearied of their focus and his brain wearied of the concentration. With his protective specs pushed up on to the top of his head, and in near-darkness to ease the strain on his sensitive vision, Smedley was still obsessed with the elusive problem. For two days he had worked on nothing else, going over the suspect area time and time again, repeating calculations and running and rerunning programs. For the life of him he could find nothing wrong, nothing to justify the gnawing feeling of uncertainty which preoccupied his days and haunted his nights. Worst of all was the fact that he knew he would be unable to justify his dissatisfaction. What could he say? He thought he had felt a couple of near-earthquakes. But why had no one else apparently felt them? He was several floors above the experiment which he thought was their cause. Surely the people directly responsible for it would also have felt any disturbance? And certainly the extremely sensitive instruments which monitored so many aspects of the work twenty-four hours a day would have at least flickered some alarm. That was what they had been designed for. He himself, Dr Smedley, had designed them as he had designed the entire project. He must have been hallucinating, they would say. Perhaps he should take a few days off. Pay another visit to the company psychiatrist. After all, these accidents often left very deep wounds which could unsettle the best of us and make us act irrationally.

And yet, Project Nine Hundred was his child. He was its father. And he was sensitive to it as no one else was. Most of all it was he, not anyone else, who was responsible for it.

Smedley switched off the visual display unit. Now he knew what he had to do. The project had to be put on ice while everything was checked from top to bottom. It might be that the reason the alarm systems had failed to operate was that they themselves were incorrectly programmed. Perhaps something inside the project was dreadfully wrong and for some unpredictable reason the monitors were failing to pick it up. He knew there was no objective evidence, and his suggestion would be deeply unwelcome, but Smedley knew in his heart that it had to be done. In such matters there was no room for doubt. The consequences of failure, any failure, were too great. In this case they were far too great. A failure in Project Nine Hundred would have consequences which extended far beyond the perimeter fence. Smedley hardly dared to think of the outcome of a complete breakdown. Even the hint of such a possibility was enough to convince him that he must pull things up while the necessary checks were made. Smedley put his glasses on and turned on the light on his desk. He picked up the telephone.

'Please put me through to Mr Maddox.'

Ten minutes later Smedley was standing in front of the huge oak desk and listening to the raised voice of the Chief Executive of Imperial Nuclear Industries.

'You want to *what*? Is this a joke? Project Nine Hundred? It's our greatest success. Do you know how much is riding on Project Nine Hundred?'

'But that's exactly why I'm saying we have to shut it down temporarily, just because it does mean so much and we have to get it right. We have to be sure.'

'But how long for? How long would it take to check through the entire system?'

Smedley had already considered the answer and knew that it would not be well received.

'Maybe three months, possibly a few weeks more, depending on what we find.'

'Three months?' Daniel Maddox stood up abruptly and walked to the window, talking as he retreated. 'You can't be serious. Three months' delay on the strength of – what is the best you could call it, a hunch?' Maddox stood at the window for a few moments, punching his clenched fist into his open hand. Then he turned round. 'It's out of the question. We have budgets, work schedules, foreign orders, all sorts of work in the pipeline, all undertaken on the basis that Project Nine Hundred would be up and running by the summer. We just can't afford the delay.'

'You've done what?' Now Smedley was equally angry. 'You've taken orders from foreign countries on the assumption that we'll make a breakthrough which would be the single biggest achievement since splitting the atom? Just like that? You've assumed it? As though it could just be taken for granted that something which is beyond all our understanding, beyond nature itself, which could destroy the entire earth, would all fall into place in time for you to balance your books? That everything would work out like a simple addition?'

Now the two men were facing each other across the desk, one a smooth and well-groomed executive and salesman representing the industry in every country in the world, the other a hideously disfigured and shambling wreck who worked at the front line of the industry and remained aloof from the wheeling and dealing of finance and sales and public relations. The two men could not have had less in common, and yet neither could exist without the other. At that moment they both knew it, and both heartily wished it were otherwise. Their contrasting faces were the two faces of a very dangerous business, and what each was saying represented an unacceptable danger to the other.

'Now look.' Maddox had been taken aback by the unusual vehemence of Smedley's outburst and was trying to placate him. 'We have to do forecasts, budgets, plans, otherwise we couldn't function as an industry. You know the problems we've run into in many of the other areas, and you must know we've all been very much looking forward to the success of Project Nine Hundred.' He walked round the table and sat on the edge of it, close to Smedley. 'In a way you could look at it as a sign of the confidence the company has in you, Graham. The board knows your track record, knows your dedication, and knows that if anyone can deliver Project Nine Hundred to us, it is you. Now what is the board going to say when I tell them that Dr Smedley, in whom they have placed so much trust, is letting them down, and letting down a lot of our customers as well?' Smedley was about to answer, but it was not a question. 'I'll tell you what they'll say to me, Graham. They'll say, that's fine Mr Maddox. If Dr Smedley says the thing has to be shelved there must be a damned good reason for it. He's not an alarmist, he's not a hothead, he's our best scientist. May we know his reason? And what am I going to have to say to them? I'm going to have to say it's a hunch. That's all. There are no figures, there have been no mishaps, everything is going like clockwork. It's just a hunch, nothing more. Can you imagine how they're going to look at me, Graham? Can you imagine what they're going to say? We're expected to shelve a project which we're all counting on to get this industry and this company out of the biggest financial hole it has ever been in, on the basis of the hunch of a man who has been spooked by an accident?' Maddox went back and sat in his oversized armchair. 'They won't buy it, Graham. And you know what?' Now he sounded eminently reasonable. 'In their position, you wouldn't buy it either.'

Smedley sat down and for a long time remained still, looking ahead of him. Maddox was careful not to interrupt. Eventually he stood up again and walked silently and slowly towards the door.

'Graham,' said Maddox softly. Smedley stopped in his tracks but did not turn round. 'You wouldn't do anything silly now would you? I wouldn't want you to do anything that all of us might regret.'

Smedley remained motionless and spoke softly. 'Don't threaten me, Mr Maddox. You forget what I.N.I. has done to me already.' At that moment he turned and in a single movement removed his heavy-rimmed spectacles to reveal the ghastly disfigurement of his face. 'After this what can you do to me?'

Had Smedley been able to see, he would have noticed the colour drain from the face of Daniel Maddox. For a moment he was unable to speak, and seconds later the door closed quietly and he was alone. One minute later Maddox picked up the telephone.

'Bring me the file on Dr Graham Smedley will you.'

'Ah yes,' said Maddox as he studied the copious contents of a file which spanned a career as long as the history of the company. He was speaking under his breath to no one but himself. 'How convenient. Our Dr Smedley has a rather lovely daughter.'

CHAPTER NINETEEN

The alarming shrill of the seagulls seemed to scream a warning to Shilvers and Julia as they strode down the cliffside path on their way to the village. Once again the day was dull and misty and the gulls hovered level with them, appearing to fly out above the ocean, only to turn again and stream along on the wind until they appeared in imminent danger of crashing into the cliff-face just below the feet of the walking couple. Only at the last second would they pull out and up into safety, screeching as they wheeled away.

'Perhaps they have nests on the cliffside a little way down and think we're predators come to take away their eggs.' Shilvers preferred this explanation to the more superstitious one which had been bouncing around inside his head.

'Well, explain to them in a reasonable and civilized fashion that we're quite happy to do our shopping at the supermarket, and perhaps they would kindly stop scaring the shit out of me.'

They looked at each other and laughed, Julia pulling on Shilvers' arm and tucking her head against the shoulder of his donkey jacket. Minutes later, the rooftops of the tiny houses and shops which made up the village of Winderwath came into view.

'It's not easy, is it?' Suddenly Julia's tone had become intensely serious.

'What's not easy?'

'It's not easy to imagine that inside these tiny houses there are people who know about a company doing dangerous work which causes terrible accidents involving their neighbours, which gets rid of the victims and their entire families, and then breaks every bone in the body of anyone who dares to utter dissent. It's not easy to imagine that these people know all that, and yet they've been content to allow it to go on.'

Shilvers said nothing for several moments as they walked.

'Maybe they don't all know. Maybe some of them choose not to know, or at least not to think about it.'

Julia murmured agreement. They were nearly at the edge of the village when suddenly Shilvers stopped and stood quite still. Julia stopped too and looked at him.

'You're right of course, they must all know,' said Shilvers, 'which I agree seems strange. But then again, as Penshall himself described it to me, these people would regard something like this as *their* problem; not something that was anything to do with outsiders. It's probably something to do with never having had much help from the outside world in the past. They've had to face hardships, and poverty, and probably local disasters like flooding and droughts, without any help from the outside, and it just doesn't really occur to them that this problem is any different. It's their problem and they've just got to get on with it.'

The corners of Julia's mouth went down as she tried to absorb what Shilvers was saying. She felt as though she could understand it. The unrelenting battering which village and villagers suffered from the weather brought by the ocean, the poor soil, the absence of interest or assistance from outside, and the fact that all such hardships were held in common. All these things militated against looking to the outside for help.

'I suppose if you live in a city, there's always someone handy to turn to in times of crisis,' offered Julia.

'That's why it seems so strange to me that Ffitch knows nothing about all this,' said Shilvers. 'The newspaper or the local journalist is so often the place people turn to when things go wrong. Yet he knows not a thing about it, and it's right in his patch.'

Shilvers was genuinely bemused and Julia, unwilling to provoke him further with her opinion of his friend, said nothing. They began walking again and a few moments later they were standing outside the post office. Shilvers paused before opening the door.

'Seconds out, round one.' Julia looked at him in confusion

until he pushed the door and an enormous clang on the bell provided the punchline.

Molly and Doreen were both on their hands and knees stocking shelves behind the counter and stood up simultaneously, bumping into each other in their haste.

'So sorry about the bell . . . ' said Doreen.

'. . . but you often can't hear when you're in the back,' Shilvers finished the explanation. He was enjoying himself.

Doreen served Julia with some notepaper, envelopes and stamps, while Molly dealt with Shilvers' request for cigarettes and lighter fuel. There was consternation when the couple wanted to pay for all the items together. Shilvers was choosing the moment to put into action a scheme he had kept to himself.

'Damned shame about poor Alf Penshall.'

Once again the twins practically bumped into one another.

'Mr Penshall?' asked Doreen, as though she had never heard the name. Julia was also looking at Shilvers, unsure what he was up to.

'Yes. Alf Penshall. You know, the man who worked at Dounscraig. His funeral was the other day.'

By now Molly had begun to compose herself and was getting on with her business. 'I had no idea you knew Mr Penshall, Mr Shilvers. We thought you were a stranger to these parts.'

'Oh well, that proves that not everyone knows everything that goes on around here after all,' said Shilvers, relishing the moment. 'I used to come here as a lad for my holidays, and Alf Penshall used to let me ride horses on the farm he had in those days. But I assumed you knew that, which is why you held up the letter?'

'What letter?' the twins harmonized.

'Oh, I'm sorry,' said Shilvers, 'there must be some confusion here. I received a letter yesterday from Alf.' He studied their faces for some sign of understanding but identified none. A swift glance at Julia showed that she shared their confusion. He continued. 'The letter was written a fortnight ago, on the day before Alf was found dead. I assumed that you knew that I would be upset, and decided to hold it back until I got over the shock.'

Molly was first to speak. 'Mr Shilvers, my sister and I have been running this post office for twenty years, and we've never held up any letter for a single hour. Not a minute. It's against the law to hold up the Royal Mail. We wouldn't dream of it.'

Shilvers was well up with her. 'Well I thought it was a bit odd myself, but I couldn't come up with another explanation. I know the mail is sometimes a bit slow, but fourteen days to get from the village to me – and I've been in a few times since then to check.'

'Well we've seen no letter for you,' said Doreen without pause. 'I don't think you've had any mail through here for more than a fortnight. Registered letter was the last thing, if I remember right. Harry delivered it.'

'Well presumably Harry delivered this letter from Alf,' said Shilvers. 'Know where I can find him?'

'We've no idea,' said Molly, still indignant. 'We're not authorized to give out the private addresses of post office employees. We'll ask him when he comes in tomorrow.'

'Right you are then,' said Shilvers, refusing to respond to the abrupt tone. 'I'll pop in in a few days to find out what happened. Good day to you.' The bell tolled their departure.

'Well it was worth a try,' said Shilvers when they were outside.

'What did you expect to find out?' asked Julia.

'I don't know, but it's damned funny that this particular letter was held up. Perhaps our friend Harry the postman will be able to provide some explanation.' They went into the minimarket next door.

'Good-morning Mr Shilvers, er, good-morning Mrs Shilvers,' said the woman behind the counter.

'Good-morning,' said Shlivers. 'And by the way, this isn't Mrs Shilvers, my mother died some years ago. This is Julia, she's a friend of mine.' The two women nodded across the counter, both embarrassed in different ways by the weak joke.

'Well it's nice to see that you have a lady looking after you,

Mr Shilvers. Maybe now you'll eat a bit better. All that tinned stuff. I don't think you've had any fresh vegetables since you've been here.'

Shilvers resisted the temptation to say that he had not seen any. Instead he collected a basket and set off round the shop. Julia smiled at the woman and started loading potatoes and greens. Shilvers chose another bottle of Scotch from the meagre selection on offer. Minutes later they were back at the counter, the woman punching the till with her fingers.

'I don't know where it goes to these days,' she said with unconscious irony. 'Things always seem to be going up don't they, never coming down. That'll be fifteen pounds, nineteen pence.'

Shilvers counted out the money. Once again he was choosing his moment. 'It was a bit of a shock about poor old Alf Penshall wasn't it?'

The woman was looking at the till and did not look up. Instead she stood quite still, staring ahead of her.

'Are you all right?' Julia was genuinely concerned. The woman stayed unmoving for several seconds, apparently unable to react. When she spoke it was in a nervous stutter.

'I don't know anything about Alf Penshall. He didn't even come in here. I hardly even know his wife. And you don't want to be taking any notice of gossip, that's my advice. No good'll come of it.'

'Well what are people saying about Alf Penshall? We haven't heard,' said Shilvers. Julia looked at him. The subject had obviously upset the woman badly, but her reaction had been enough to further excite Shilvers' curiosity. 'This is a small village and you already told me that not much goes on around here without everyone knowing. What are people saying about Alf Penshall? What does the local rumour machine make of it?'

At this the woman dropped the money she was holding on to the counter, part of it spilling over on to the floor, and walked out from behind the checkout towards the store-room. As she went she brushed past several shelves, knocking stacks of tins all over the floor. The store-room door slammed shut behind her.

'Well I'm damned,' said Shilvers, the anger still growing inside him. 'She knows it, the twins next door know it, every person in this hole of a village knows it, and not one of them has the guts to get up and do something about it.'

Julia had been picking up the change from the counter and packing the purchases. Leaving the rest of the cash on the floor she took Shilvers by the arm and steered him towards the door.

'They deserve everything they get,' Shilvers was still shouting as they stepped outside. 'Maybe we should just stand aside and let these bastards up the road pick them off one by one.'

Julia said nothing but walked steadily back across the village green, with Shilvers a few paces behind her. She was angry too. Partly she sympathized with Shilvers' feelings of frustration, but she was also angry at the way he had behaved. Perhaps she understood better the reluctance of people to get involved in something which did not concern them directly. It was an understandable human instinct to draw the covers over your head and avoid trouble. It was up to the local police or the local politicians to do something about what was going on at I.N.I., but not necessarily up to the woman in the corner shop. It was hard to take it out on her, and she was angry that Shilvers had done so. Seeing the mood he was in, however, she decided that to raise the matter would only cause a destructive argument. She would be silent.

Both Shilvers and Julia remained immersed in their own thoughts as they began the steep climb up the hillside path. Julia felt precarious walking here, quite literally on the edge of the country, a very long way away from the things with which she felt comfortable and secure. Between her and them was a seemingly all-powerful organization which had almost certainly been watching, waiting for some move which indicated that Penshall had betrayed their secret. That, she now realized, was part of the reason she felt angry about Shilvers' pointless indiscretion. In spite of herself she clung on tight to his arm as they walked up the hill.

Shilvers turned over a different problem in his head. How was he to proceed now? He had lost his original witness, and now the man's wife as well. Neither had told him the names of anyone else in the village who might be sympathetic to the idea of exposing what was going on. All he had was a piece of paper with some names scrawled on, and a mass of circumstantial evidence. It was not anywhere near enough to persuade anyone to publish the story, even supposing he had enough to write it. Maybe I.N.I. realized that, which was why they were waiting. Somehow or other he would have to make them show their hand, without endangering himself or Julia. It was a difficult problem and he could see no obvious answers.

Neither had spoken and now they were within a yard or two of the cottage. Shilvers was a few paces in front, and turned to hand the shopping bag to Julia as he felt in his pocket for the keys. As he was half-turned to face her, the front door of the cottage swung suddenly open and two powerful hands reached out and grabbed him by the coat, jerking him inside. As he was propelled through the air towards the armchair, the same hands grabbed for Julia before she was able to scream. She too was dragged inside. The door slammed shut behind them.

Shilvers could make out the silhouettes of two men in the gloom of the sitting-room, and immediately pulled himself up from the chair. As he did so a large and powerful figure stepped towards him again and grabbed him by the lapels of his coat, hurling him headlong into a corner of the room. He fell with a crash. His hand went to the part of his head which had hit the wall, and it came away wet and bloody. Shilvers went to get to his feet again.

'No Tony, don't.'

Julia's shout contained enough urgency to stop Shilvers and the enormous man who was closing on him again. Both looked round to see that she was being held by another man who had both of her arms held tightly behind her back, and was pushing her upwards so that she was forced to stand on the tips of her toes.

'All right all right, let her go,' said Shilvers, getting up slowly and reaching for a handkerchief to mop the blood from his head.

'That's a more sensible fella.' It was the bigger of the two men. 'Now get back into the chair and behave yourself.'

Shilvers looked more carefully at the man and realized that he knew him. It was Roache. The man he had talked to in the Huntsman on the night he had overheard the argument. The other man had eased his grip on Julia's arms and sat her heavily down in another chair by the window. He was dressed in an unfamiliar manner, but Shilvers thought he knew him too. Yes. Shilvers could scarcely recognize him now, but it was Harry, the postman.

'Well well,' said Shilvers, 'is this your day-job? I hope you aren't expecting another fiver for this.'

'Let's get down to business,' barked Roache, 'and none of your lip or make no mistake Mr Shilvers, I'll break your back.'

'I don't doubt you would. So take whatever you want and get out of here. There's nothing much of value, but have whatever you can find.'

Roache crouched down in front of Shilvers' chair and spoke more calmly. 'I'm afraid you haven't got the picture at all, Mr Shilvers. I'm surprised, intelligent fella like you. We haven't come to take anything from you, we've come to give you something. A piece of very good advice as it 'appens.'

'And what might that be?' asked Shilvers. He was beginning to think he could guess.

'Simple really,' said Roache. 'Keep your nose out of other people's business, and bugger off to whichever big city you crawled out of. Then forget anything you ever heard about Winderwath.' Everything about Bernard Roache was oversized, and Shilvers recalled his earlier impression that he might be a bit crazy. He wanted to evade the point, but was anxious not to antagonize him.

'I don't know what you're talking about, and I don't like threats,' said Shilvers. 'I came here to do some work for the

Tourist Board. Now if you don't like tourists that's fine by me but – '

His words were cut off as Roache swept his enormous arm out in front of him and crashed his fist across the side of Shilvers' face. Julia screamed 'Don't!' but the word caught in her throat as Harry tightened his grip on her shoulders.

'Don't play silly games with me, Mr Shilvers. I'm talking about what that bloody fool Alf Penshall told you on the night he came up here. We all warned him not to cause any trouble. But he wouldn't be told, and he was made to pay for it, wasn't he?'

'I still don't know what you're talking about. Sure, Alf Penshall did come up here, but he was an old friend of mine. He didn't tell me anything except that the weather round here doesn't improve.'

'Dear Mr Shilvers.' It was Harry reading aloud from a piece of paper he had drawn from his pocket, 'Just a note to say that something funny is going on since we met. I think I may be being watched, and it could be I.N.I.'

Everything now came together and Shilvers breathed deeply and looked at the floor. 'So that's why the letter was late,' he said. 'Opening other people's mail is a very bad habit, Harry. You should try to get out of it. Anyway,' he looked at Roache, 'what does that prove?'

'I told you we didn't come up here to play games with you, Mr Shilvers. But we've got plenty of time, and since you obviously like games, my friend Harry here is rather fond of them too. Aren't you Harry?' Roache turned to face his friend, who smiled at both of them and immediately plunged his hand down inside Julia's woollen pullover and on to her left breast. Shilvers saw Julia stiffen in pain as the hand squeezed. He leapt forward only to be shoved immediately back into the chair by Roache's powerful arms.

'For God's sake Tony,' pleaded Julia.

'O.K., O.K., leave her alone,' said Shilvers. 'Let's talk.'

Roache turned to Harry and the jerk of his head indicated

to him he should stop. Harry looked disappointed as he withdrew his hand from Julia's breast.

'O.K.,' said Roache, 'but this time talk sense.'

'Penshall did tell me what's going on at Dounscraig. He told me about the accidents and the disappearances. I've made a few discreet enquiries, but so far I haven't turned up anything to suggest what he told me was true. That's all of it.'

'Well no doubt Penshall also told you that some of us don't care for meddling by outsiders. Certainly we have a bit of a problem with I.N.I., but it's our problem, and we aren't going to solve it by having the plant closed down and putting everyone around here out of work. So what you've got to do is stop your snooping, get out of this village, and forget you ever heard of the place. Otherwise I'm going to come looking for you. And Harry is going to come looking for your attractive friend here, aren't you Harry?' Harry laughed.

'But these people are your neighbours,' Julia said. 'Alf Penshall was your friend. You can't want to just let them disappear without trace and do nothing about it? None of you knows who will be next. It could be you, or your families. Don't you want it stopped?'

Roache turned to her. 'We don't need the likes of you to come up here telling us how to look after each other. We've been getting by long enough without outsiders coming in and giving us advice. We'll keep an eye on our neighbours in our own way. And we don't see how it'll solve the problem putting everyone around here out of a job like they was before Dounscraig came here. All the trouble ever caused round here came from outsiders. Even I.N.I. fall into that category if truth be told, but at least they brought something with them we want. That's jobs. We don't like relying on handouts from city folk like you. We want to pay our way, and that's what we're doing. And we want you to keep out of it.' Roache turned back to Shilvers. 'Understand?'

'Oh I understand all right. What you say is crystal clear.' Shilvers thought for a moment before continuing. 'And what's more it makes perfect sense. I'll forget what Alf Penshall told me, and forget all about I.N.I. and I'll even forget about your little visit.'

'Don't take us for idiots, Mr Shilvers,' said Harry. 'We may not be sophisticated city folk like you are, but we aren't stupid. Why should we believe that you'll forget all about all this?'

'Because I haven't any choice. What could I do with it anyway? I don't know enough to write anything that anyone would print. If I tipped off another journalist or newspaper they would come up here, and both you in the village and I.N.I. would deny it. Who could prove anything? Even if someone could get to them no doubt all the records have been falsified. No,' said Shilvers, 'without your co-operation, I could do nothing anyway. And I'm not stupid enough to risk another visit from you and your friend here.'

The two local men looked at each other for a moment and seemed to agree.

'All right Mr Shilvers,' said Roache. 'We're going to trust you. But if I even suspect that you've been poking your nose around things that don't concern you, I'm going to come up here and break your back.'

'That's as clear as day,' said Shilvers.

Roache jerked his head and Harry let Julia go. Without speaking again the two men headed for the door.

'By the way,' Shilvers called after them. 'What was the point of the slashed tyres?'

They turned back to face him. 'What the hell are you talking about now?' said Roache.

'The tyres on my car. Someone slashed them the other night. Are you trying to tell me it wasn't you?'

They laughed. 'We wouldn't waste our time slashing your tyres, Mr Shilvers,' said Harry. He reached down into his boot and produced a long-bladed knife which he held loosely in his hand. 'We're simple people, and if we have a point to make, we believe in making it a bit more directly. Got the idea?'

Now they were closing the door behind them. 'It looks like you got enemies, Mr Shilvers.' The roaring laughter of the two men was swallowed by the wind as they disappeared into the distance.

Three large glasses of whisky later, Shilvers was just beginning to absorb the implications of what had happened. Julia had been silent, but had eventually said she needed a shower to wash away the smell and the feel of Harry the postman. Now Shilvers heard the water stop and Julia emerged wearing the white towelling dressing-gown, her hair tied up above her head.

She poured herself a glass of whisky. 'How are you thinking of handling it?'

Shilvers held his glass in front of him and looked over the rim into the liquid, revolving his hand so that it washed over the whole inside surface.

'We have no choice. I don't think they were sent by I.N.I. but it must be a possibility. And I don't know which of them there's more reason to be afraid of.' Shilvers looked down into the brown liquor in his glass. 'We'll have to forget it. We can't risk having those monsters turn up here again, and even if we go back to London they could find us within hours.'

'Tony? You are joking aren't you?'

'We haven't got a thing to go on anyway. We'll just have to forget it. I'll finish my stuff for the Tourist Board and we'll head on out by the end of the week – ' Shilvers' words were interrupted by a crash as Julia brought down her glass hard on the table in front of him. She stood and looked down at him.

'Tony? I've seen you do work on the criminal gangs of South London, on the black drug pushers of Tottenham, and even the goddamn Mafia. I don't believe you're going to let a couple of these country bumpkins put you off the best story you've ever had in your life.'

'I know that Julia but – '

'But bloody nothing,' she shouted. 'And don't give me any of that rubbish about having nothing to go on. I know what it is about this that's different, and don't think I damned well don't. It's me, isn't it?'

'Well Julia you haven't been involved before and it's one thing me taking risks with my own safety . . . '

'Just forget it Tony.' Julia was heading for the door. 'Put all ideas of leaving this alone out of your mind. We're going on, and we're going on together. Now get ready because we're going to meet all these assholes at the shindig at the Winderwath Waldorf. But just do me one favour will you? If Roache or the friendly postman are there, don't mention Dounscraig.'

She was about to close the door behind her when Shilvers called her back.

'Julia.' She halted and her head came back through the gap in the door. 'I love you.'

'And do you think I don't know that?' she smiled and was gone.

CHAPTER TWENTY

'Well, will it interfere with our operation or won't it?' Once again, for what seemed the twentieth time that day, James Gold was shouting. 'It's a simple enough question, and God knows there are enough of you out there telling me you're dedicated to the cause. Why the hell can't I get a straight answer?'

Jacqueline Smart sat still. She resented being spoken to in this manner and felt that she should not have to tolerate it. Around her the bare walls of the military-style prefabricated hut did nothing to alleviate the bitter cold, and beyond the thin walls the wind whistled through the rusting barbed-wire perimeter fence. She waited for the long silence to emphasize the difference in volume between their voices before speaking.

'The reason you cannot have a straight answer – ' despite her indignation she still had to be careful not to be insolent, ' – is that there isn't one. All we know is what we can see, and what he is saying.' She got up and walked towards Gold. He thought she was approaching him but instead she passed him by to refer to the scores of blown-up black and white photographs pinned to the cream and green gloss painted wall.

'He's been to the police station to look at the electoral register, and she has been to Westermouth to look at the register of births, marriages and deaths. Both acts are entirely consistent with the project we know he is working on for the Tourist Board.' Jacqueline picked up a short wooden pointer from the otherwise bare desk and jabbed it at another picture on the wall. 'We know that he was visited by Penshall and that he seemed surprised to see him. Everyone assumed that this was their first meeting and that Penshall was blowing the whistle. Now,' she was looking directly at Gold and altered her tone just barely enough for him to recognize the criticism, but not enough for it to be too obvious, 'we don't know whether there was any reason for Penshall to die or not.'

Gold watched her walk back to her place at the other side of the room, dressed all in black, her outfit a mass of zips and pockets in which she carried the various tools of her trade. He had to try not to think of her as the attractive woman she unquestionably was. She was a colleague, and one who was excellent at her work. He knew it was unfair and perhaps even unwise to criticize, but the organization had to know the answers to his questions.

'Well, what do you suggest? Do we call the whole thing off? Do we cancel the operation and waste months of hard work? The consequences could be disastrous. The press haven't been entirely sympathetic to our political people recently as it is. If all this gets out, and it becomes known that we're involved, we'll lose our financial backing and the whole bloody thing will collapse.'

Gold turned away to examine the photographs again. Jacqueline felt she had nothing further to add. Eventually he spoke again. 'Should we bring him in?'

Jacqueline walked over to the wall so that she was inches away from Gold.

'If we do we'll have to bring her in too. There will be a lot more questions. And we don't know how they'll react to us. Maddox has asked to see me tomorrow. Maybe I'll get a better idea then.' She paused. 'I think we should wait a bit longer.'

'Very well,' said Gold. 'We'll back your judgement.' He paused. 'But God help us all if you're not right.'

CHAPTER TWENTY-ONE

In spite of the ordeal of a few hours earlier, Julia assured Shilvers at least a dozen times that she wanted to go to the Winderwath annual village social.

'We'll chat to locals and ask questions to make them think we're still interested in information about local landmarks and the countryside. That'll help to convince them that you're still working on the project for the Tourist Board. Then at the same time we'll carefully look out for anybody who looks like an outsider. If we think they come from I.N.I. we'll see how they get on with the locals; in particular with our two visitors. Maybe we'll be able to reassure ourselves that I.N.I. doesn't know as much as those two know.'

'But for Christ's sake Julia. If we look as though we're remotely interested in anything to do with Dounscraig, or if we even find ourselves involved in a casual conversation about it, we run the risk of those goons coming up here and massacring me and doing heaven knows what to you. It's a crazy risk.'

Julia was undeterred. 'We're not going to let those bastards think we're scared. They believed the undertaking you gave them, and if we don't give them any reason to think otherwise tonight, it will just look as though you're trying to get the information you want for your Tourist Board articles. We can even tell a few people that you're nearly finished, and anything we say is bound to get back.' She smiled and slipped into a poor imitation of the local accent. 'Not much 'appens around 'ere you know . . . '

Shilvers gave her a lukewarm smile. He felt confused, but also impressed by Julia's ability to cope. Instead of terrifying her as he might have expected, the incident with the two men seemed to have made her more determined. At the same time he had an uneasy feeling deep inside. Clearly they were making very little progress which would help him to tell the story. This latest episode was an enormous setback. He wondered what he would be feeling by now had she not been here. Certainly part of his fear was for her safety, but now he would readily admit that he was also afraid for himself. Were it not for her support he might very well be wondering whether he had any real chance of getting the full story and living long enough to tell it. His emotions were a mix of pride in Julia and apprehension.

Julia put on what she always referred to as her 'little black dress'. She spoke of it as if it was the only one of its kind that she owned. In fact every time she said she was going to put the dress on it was a different one. Shilvers always noticed and it was part of a game they played that he pretended not to.

'Not that drab old thing again,' he would joke. They would laugh and know they were going to have a good night out together. Tonight, though, Shilvers felt far from sure.

Julia had washed her hair in the cold shower and tied it in a mass above her head, so that when she appeared from the bedroom Shilvers was astonished by how beautiful she seemed. Her face looked radiant and her eyes bright. Shilvers thought, as he had so often before, that a large part of her beauty came from within her in a way which would not be diminished by time and wrinkles. It was a generosity of spirit which seemed to flow out of her and to warm up everything around her. Shilvers put on the smartest jacket and trousers he had with him, and knew that even in a relatively poor community like this one he would be the scruffiest person present. That part bothered him not a bit.

The night was still and calm as the couple walked arm in arm down the hill towards the village. From the vantage point of the cliff road they could see the village hall from several hundred yards away. It was next to the church, set in a street immediately behind the row of shops which fronted on to the green. Through the gloom they could hear the muffled sound of music playing and several times a shaft of light beamed from the opening door into the street as couples arrived from every direction for the event, and a burst of music belched out to be swallowed up in the vast darkness.

There was no hint of anything other than welcome as Shilvers and Julia entered and paid their fifty pence each admission at a table set up in the lobby.

'Proceeds go to the church flowers fund,' said the comfortable old woman in floral dress reassuringly. Julia's face lit up in her friendliest smile. 'Have a lovely time you two,' said the woman.

'Oh we will for sure,' said Julia and sounded for all the world as though she meant it.

The doors into the main hall opened to expose them to a wall of uncomfortable heat and amplified music. Much of the heat was provided by the twenty or so couples dancing with a determination to enjoy themselves which Shilvers had seldom seen. All of the noise came from a five piece country-style band with banjo, bass, fiddle, drums and singer. They were in the middle of a deafening and badly distorted version of 'Tie a yellow ribbon round the old oak tree' when Shilvers and Julia entered. Both had to force themselves not to retreat.

They weaved across the floor between bobbing dancers towards the bar, Julia squeezing Shilvers' arm as she spotted Bernard Roache slumped against it with a pint glass in his hand. He was deep in conversation with several men whom Shilvers did not recognize, and there was no sign of Harry. Roache looked up as the couple came near and Shilvers noticed the look of disarmed surprise flicker quickly back to the more familiar threat. Shilvers did not now feel physically afraid and he hoped he did not look it.

With drinks in their hands Julia and Shilvers wandered away to find a table as far from the speakers as they could get. Julia nodded a greeting to the twin sisters from the post office who, despite their hostility to one another, seemed inseparable. In return their faces smiled but their eyes remained cold.

As they sat down at a table in the further corner from the stage, Shilvers looked around more carefully. He tried to sort out the locals from any visitors there might be, and found that it was not difficult. While most of the men wore cheap and well-worn suits with shiny but heavy black shoes a few, dotted around the hall, were plainly city types. Shilvers saw a face he recognized and quickly identified it as Roland Dixon, the local M.P. who was now retired on the back benches having been an Energy Minister in the distant past. Shilvers pointed him out to Julia.

'He was a lush then and he's a lush now. He was well known for having his own corner in the Strangers' Bar. He could always be relied on to be propping it up, night after night, glad-handing everyone whoever they may be. The only time he ever left it was when the whips forced him into the Chamber to vote. Then he never knew what the hell he was voting for.'

There were several other conspicuous groups of smart-looking middle-aged men, looking uncomfortable with pint glasses in their hands, engaged in earnest conversation with local people.

'That, no doubt, is the condescending industrial relations policy of I.N.I. that Ffitch was talking about. Management pretending to be democratic once a year by talking to their workers,' said Shilvers.

'My my, we are sharp and bitter tonight,' said Julia, then she said something almost to herself. 'I wonder why Ffitch mentioned this do to us?' She had to repeat the question directly into Shilvers' ear for him to be able to hear her.

'Just his bloody mischief I guess. Why else? If there was anything really interesting he'd be here himself.'

'No doubt it's being covered by one of his "boys",' shouted Julia.

Shilvers gave her a reproachful smile. It was clear that they were not going to agree about Ffitch.

Then something jogged in Shilvers' memory and told him that a face in the crowd that he had noticed earlier was familiar to him. He glanced across the hall towards a large and prosperous-looking man in his fifties talking loudly in a distinctly upper-class southern accent. Beside him stood the slim and petite figure of a young woman. She was smartly dressed and had eye-catching blonde hair cut short and in a fringe across her forehead. Shilvers struggled to remember where he had seen her before. He felt that it was recently, but he could not recall when and it irritated him.

'Good evening, Tony Shilvers isn't it?' Shilvers looked round in surprise to see the bloated figure of Roland Dixon leaning precariously over Julia towards him. 'I haven't seen you for years. When will it have been?'

Shilvers reminded him that they had last met at a Department of Energy reception for the press seven or eight years earlier. Shilvers decided not to remind Dixon that he was as drunk then as he was now. Instead he introduced the man to Julia, deliberately omitting her surname. There was no sensible reason to do so, but it felt like a precaution.

'Who is that chap over there,' Shilvers asked the M.P., 'talking to the little blonde girl.'

'Daniel Maddox, Chief Executive of I.N.I. Why, want an introduction?'

'No thanks. What about the girl?'

'Haven't a clue,' said Dixon. 'Some sort of Personal Assistant I'm told. Rising star. Wouldn't mind an introduction there myself.' Dixon was slurring his words and leering repulsively.

While Shilvers wrestled with his memory Dixon engaged Julia with an anecdote about his relationship with the press which Shilvers had heard several times years before. He gave up the effort to listen in favour of the deafening music. Moments later he was wondering how they could extricate themselves from the reminiscences when Shilvers caught sight of another familiar face which he was even less keen to see. He turned round slowly and tried to hide his dismay. It was the man he had met at the Coach House, Roger Thornton.

'Ah, Mr Shilvers.' Thornton had crossed the dancehall and was stretching out a hand and smiling broadly. 'How nice to see you. You're even more well-connected locally than you let on.'

Shilvers shook hands and introduced Julia, once again deliberately omitting her surname. Now feeling edged out, Roland Dixon said he would 'catch up with you later', and headed towards the bar.

'As a matter of fact George Ffitch told me you might be coming,' said Thornton, 'so I brought along someone else who I think you know. Just hang on a moment.'

Thornton disappeared into the hallway, leaving Shilvers and Julia wondering who it could possibly be. A few moments later he returned, followed by an older woman dressed in a smart tweed suit and expensive-looking shoes. At one moment Shilvers thought there was something familiar about her, and at the next his jaw fell open.

'Mrs Penshall?'

'Hello Mr Shilvers. How nice to see you again.'

Shilvers was unable to disguise his astonishment as the woman approached him, her right hand outstretched. For several moments he was still not completely sure that it was her. She looked identical to the woman he had seen at the funeral and on the following day at her house, but at the same time somehow completely different. Her hair had been styled in smart curls and she was wearing a make-up which took away the deathly pallor. She looked ten years younger. Shilvers became aware that her gaze was fixed on him, her expression unchanging. He tried to collect himself.

'Mrs Penshall, let me introduce my friend Julia. Julia, this is . . .' he hesitated, 'this is Mrs Penshall, Alf's wife, er, I beg your pardon, his widow.'

'After your visit I felt a bit concerned and so I made some enquiries.' It was Thornton speaking above the deafening noise from the band. Shilvers kept his eyes on the woman. 'I found that Mrs Penshall had wisely gone to stay with her sister for a few days. I telephoned and told her about your concern and as she was coming back to pick up a few things she kindly agreed to come along here to reassure you that she's all right. Didn't you, Mrs Penshall?'

The woman had not moved her eyes from Shilvers' face. Several seconds passed before she spoke.

'Yes. That's right.' Something about her voice made Shilvers concerned.

'Are you all right, Mrs Penshall? You don't seem quite yourself. Are you sure everything's O.K?'

Once again there was a lapse of several seconds before the woman replied. When she did her voice was calm, but seemed monotonous, without normal inflexion.

'Oh yes, quite well thank you. Mr Thornton has been very kind.'

Shilvers glanced at Thornton and saw that he was looking intently at the woman. This was the man he had seen Mrs Penshall slap a few days ago, but who was now being described as very kind. Was it his imagination? For a moment it seemed to Shilvers that he was like a parent watching a child giving a stage performance. There was pride in the event but it was coupled with fear that the performer might stumble or forget the lines.

'Are you quite sure you're all right Mrs Penshall?' repeated Shilvers.

The woman was motionless. Then her mouth opened, but no sound came out. The band seemed even louder and Shilvers strained hard to try to catch anything she said. For the first time her eyes seemed to flicker into life, and they flashed towards Julia and back to Shilvers. For a second Shilvers thought she would speak, then there was an interruption.

'She's still suffering from shock, naturally.' It was Thornton. Shilvers saw that he was holding her by the arm and beginning to draw her back away from them. 'But time is the great healer. We'll look after Mrs Penshall until she's quite recovered, you can rely on that, Mr Shilvers.'

'Where will you be going now Mrs Penshall?' Julia called out above the music.

'She's going back to stay with her sister for a few weeks. We'll see she gets transport.'

'Where's that, Mrs Penshall? Where does your sister live?' said Shilvers still more urgently.

But Thornton was now ushering her away from them, towards the door.

'I think Mrs Penshall has had enough for her first outing. She's still not quite herself. I'll take her back now. Nice to see you again, Mr Shilvers.'

Shilvers was on the brink of following, but realized that he could only pursue the matter by making a scene. He glanced across the hall to see that Harry the postman had now joined Bernard Roache and both were staring at them intently. He cursed aloud and the sound was swallowed under the jangle of discordant music.

Three hours later Roger Thornton and Daniel Maddox from Imperial Nuclear Industries were sitting in the back seat of a large chauffeur-driven car. Between them sat Mrs Penshall, quite motionless, her eyes still staring directly in front of her. In the front seat, next to the driver, Jacqueline Smart sat quietly, listening to the conversation.

'It was a bit of a risk. Do you think it came off?'

'I don't know,' said Thornton. 'Shilvers was suspicious.'

'The top and bottom of the problem is,' said Maddox, 'that we just don't have a clue how much or how little the bastard knows. Whether Penshall told him anything or not.' There was a brief silence. 'Is there really no chance of getting anything out of her?' The question referred to the woman sitting between them, but she did not acknowledge it, or show any awareness of it.

'Not a chance I'm afraid. Far too far gone.'

'Those bloody idiots,' said Maddox.

In the front seat, Jacqueline Smart shared their anxiety. Her sudden and unexpected promotion to Personal Assistant to the Chief Executive, Mr Maddox, had put her in an excellent position to find out much more about what was going on in I.N.I. and she had her own reasons for wanting to find out as much as she could. At this moment she wanted to know as badly as they did how much Shilvers and Julia had been told. She smiled to herself as the car whisked them away into the night.

CHAPTER TWENTY-TWO

'What in God's name did you make of that?'

Shilvers spoke for the first time as they closed the cottage door behind them, and with one movement he took off his coat and threw it angrily across the room into a chair. In the walk from the village he had searched every corner of his mind and imagination for an explanation which made sense. Julia had not wanted to speak first. Her thoughts wandered over a dozen possibilities, even entertaining the idea that Shilvers had entirely misunderstood his conversation with Mrs Penshall. Maybe she had intended all along to move away immediately. Maybe they had after all returned to the wrong house by mistake. She hardly dared think the thoughts, and did not dare give them voice.

'There's something badly wrong with her, didn't you think so? She didn't seem herself. She didn't, did she?' Julia thought he sounded as though he was trying to reassure himself.

'Remember I haven't seen her before. And she's bound to be a bit subdued. Perhaps she's in a sort of delayed shock.' Julia was treading as carefully as she knew how.

'Yes, that's it. Maybe she's in shock. Did you think so?'

The tone of Shilvers' voice indicated that his search for an explanation was a desperate one. It was born of a mixture of genuine confusion and guilt over whatever might have happened to Mrs Penshall.

'Or,' now Shilvers was pacing the floor, one hand on his brow, the other beating the air, 'maybe she's been hypnotized.'

Julia looked at him, confused and concerned.

'Sure, that could be it,' he continued. 'That would be a terrific idea from their point of view. She goes around telling everyone that it's all O.K., she feels all right. I.N.I. are being very kind to her, but all the time she's under hypnosis.'

Julia continued to study him. She thought his idea implausible but was sufficiently perturbed by his mental state to feel inclined to go along with anything which would satisfy him.

'Maybe. Maybe,' she said slowly. 'I'll make some coffee.' Shilvers finished pacing up and down the room and slumped down in the armchair.

'They're cool though,' he said eventually. In the reflection of the window he could see Julia busying herself. 'You've got to hand it to them. Cool as a bloody cucumber bringing her there like that.' Julia came towards him and put down a steaming hot cup of coffee in front of him. 'It's a bloody masterstroke, bringing her there like that.'

Julia sat in the chair opposite him. There was a long silence, then she said, 'I don't know what the hell is going on, but I'd bet my life that your friend Mr George Ffitch is involved in it right up to his slimy neck.'

'Oh no,' Shilvers' hand came down flat on the table with unexpected force. 'That can't be right. You don't know him. Ffitch wouldn't ever, not with those bastards. He's a journalist for Christ's sake.' Shilvers spoke as though it was the equivalent of taking holy orders. Julia decided not to pursue the point but Shilvers continued to chase the thought around his own head. 'Sure he was having some fun with us there. But that's only because he's got no idea what's involved here. Do you think if he did he'd be pissing around like a clown up there? He'd be on to the story. Every journalist in Britain would give his right arm to get a story like this one. If Ffitch even had a smell of it, he'd be all over it like a swarm of bees. No one can resist the prospect of their byline over the story of the decade, least of all someone like Ffitch.' Shilvers looked at Julia, as if appealing to her to agree with him. She could accept his logic, but in her heart she did not believe it.

'Maybe.' Her eyes went down to her coffee cup. 'Then again . . .'

'You don't know him like I do. I've known him for years. He could never resist a scoop, not in a million years.'

Shilvers was convinced. Julia was not. She turned and looked out into the darkness. Even in the reflection she could see the lines of anxiety on Shilvers' face. He held his head in both hands, and gently, almost imperceptibly, moved it from side to side, pondering the extraordinary events of the day.

When Julia awoke the next morning the bed beside her was empty. She looked at the cheap alarm clock on the cheap bedside table. It was seven-thirty. She realized that she had been woken by the wind whistling through the holes between the tiles. Above the billow she could hear the intermittent tap tap tap of Shilvers' typewriter in the next room. They had both slept badly, keeping their thoughts and their doubts to themselves. Julia felt unable to share her concern with Shilvers. He was the largest part of it.

Eventually she slipped out of bed and covered her nakedness with his dressing-gown. She liked the feel of it against her skin, and it reminded her of home. As she brushed her long auburn hair, she knew that when she thought of home, she thought of Shilvers' flat, not her own. And when she thought of home, she thought of him.

He looked up when she entered the room but did not pause in his typing. 'Morning,' he said out of the corner of his mouth, now stopping to take a sip of coffee. 'Coffee's hot on the stove.' He was immersed in his writing in a way which Julia had not witnessed for a very long time. This was how he used to work when the minutes before a deadline were ticking away. It always excited her to watch him in top gear, unable to make his fingers work quickly enough to get his thoughts down on the page. This was usually the moment when he had done all his research, on the telephone or on his travels, sorted out his notes, and was getting on with his favourite bit – sitting down and just telling the story. Julia had poured coffee and once again sat opposite him.

'Your memoirs?' she teased.

'Not exactly.' Shilvers stopped work and held up the page which was still in the typewriter and started reading. 'Rural

Cumbria, the county of the poets.' He looked up. 'Has a nice ring to it, don't you think?' He looked down again and Julia watched his eyes following the lines in front of him. A slight frown creased her brow. 'The unique and unspoiled beauty of rural Cumbria is much the same today in many parts as it was one hundred and fifty years ago when some of the greatest men of letters of their age wandered across its moorlands seeking inspiration for verse which would excite many generations.' He looked up again. 'Not over the top is it?'

'Tony?'

'Through many decades and many changes in the outside world, Cumbria has resisted the ravages of the urban developers and the motorway builders to retain the panoramic land and seascapes which have always been a favourite of the discerning traveller.'

'Tony?'

'Even today a well-planned route can take the visitor over many miles of breathtaking countryside without the fear of ever meeting another vehicle – '

'Tony. What is this garbage?' She was shouting to be heard above him. Her abruptness stopped him in mid-flow. He sat silent, looking at the paper in front of him, as though puzzled.

'Garbage? It may be garbage to you but it pays the bills you know. How do you think I can manage to keep you in all this luxury?' His arms described an extravagant gesture at the cold room.

'Tony for God's sake.' But Shilvers had not finished.

'Garbage it may be, but at least someone will be prepared to pay good money for it, unlike any crap I might eventually write about disappearing families and furniture. Whoever in their right mind would pay for that shit?'

Julia was looking at him intently. 'A few days ago it wouldn't have occurred to you to wonder who would pay for it. The important thing then was not who would pay for it, but getting the story. And that,' now she reached over and pressed her open hand over his forearm, 'and that is what is important now.

So put this rubbish away. And I mean it. Now.' Her last word left no room for misunderstanding.

Shilvers looked at her, and she saw his eyes mist over. He turned suddenly to look outside, and shielded himself from her. The brightness of the sky made him screw up his face until a small tear trickled out of the corner of his eye and penetrated through the folds of his face as he pressed his hands against it. He forced himself to look at the great grey clouds drifting across the sky. Nearer and perilously nearer to the cliff edge and the roof of the cottage itself, the gulls veered and screeched on the wind. After a minute Shilvers took away his hands and turned again to Julia. Without speaking his hand went slowly forward and took the paper from the typewriter and methodically he tore it into a dozen pieces.

'You know what,' said Julia brightly, 'I haven't even seen the damned place yet. Let's go for a walk.' Without hesitating she got up and went to the bedroom door, undoing the cord of the white dressing-gown as she walked. As she reached the door, she slipped the robe from her shoulder and drew it down her back so that it revealed the full beauty of her nakedness.

'Julia.' She stopped and turned her head, half of her body now obscured behind the bedroom door. 'Come here will you?'

Julia stood still for a second, then, dropping the robe to the floor, turned and walked back towards him. She reached the table and gently took his head and held it close against her. He put his arms around her waist and pressed his head against her firm and naked body, still warm from their shared bed. They stood still and silent for many moments, until Shilvers looked up at her and lightly brushed his face against her breasts, which he took in his hands and gently kissed.

'I'll have to write this garbage for the Tourist Board some time you know,' he said.

'Yes. But not right now.' He stood up and she gently led him towards the bedroom.

* * *

An hour later Shilvers and Julia were striding out across the openness of the moorland landscape, with a good following wind pressing them onwards to their destination. For once the wind seemed warm and not damp, but it gusted strongly, blowing the hair into their eyes. Over each small hill groups of sheep bleated their protests and retreated from the intruders. Shilvers reckoned that a course directly north-east from his cottage would be the shortest route to Dounscraig. Previously he had walked up the coast and then directly inland. Julia now strode on ahead of him.

'Come on old fella,' she shouted over her shoulder, not slowing down.

'O.K., that does it.' Shilvers set off at a run and overtook her straight away, ploughing on over a hill and down the other side on a steep bank into a valley. Julia set off after him and soon found the momentum of the run taking her feet from her as she scrambled down through the rough grass. By now Shilvers was at the bottom of the slope and starting on the equally steep run up the other side. His chest was hurting as he pounded on, determined if it killed him not to allow Julia to catch up.

'You cheat,' shouted Julia. 'But cheating won't help you old timer.' She was now beginning to narrow the gap between them as she benefited from the momentum of the run downhill. Shilvers was not about to waste precious breath replying to the taunt. Instead he put his head down in a powerful last effort to make the summit of the hill before his wind gave out. His chest felt as though it would burst and his legs rebelled against him. Even so he could feel Julia only a few paces behind him as the summit appeared ahead.

There were two small hills in front of them as they ran, and a further larger mound beyond, reaching up into the small clouds scuttling across the brilliant blue sky. Shilvers could hear his heart and his breath as he reached the top of the first hill, and glanced over his shoulder to catch sight of Julia only a few paces behind him.

'Do your worst,' he called out at the top of a breath, and renewed his effort as he began to gain momentum on the steep slope leading towards a gulley and then on to the next ridge. Julia said nothing, but tucked her head down, her arms flailing wildly as she struggled to catch up. She was still gaining ground. Shilvers' feet were falling heavily on the soft grass. He could feel the muscles in his legs jerking in protest at the unaccustomed stress.

'First one to the top of the next hill,' he shouted, aware that only momentum and determination stood between this moment and humiliating defeat which she would not let him forget for weeks.

'Unfair,' yelled Julia, but her gasped shout was lost in the gusting wind, and she struggled again to close the few paces' gap.

As the gradient got steeper, they had to slow down and heave themselves up the hill. By now Shilvers could hear nothing except the wind, and his own body screaming at him in alarm at what it was being told to do. With only a few steps to go Julia sensed that Shilvers had done his best, and she lengthened her stride, throwing herself towards the top of the hill. As they gained the summit, a strong gusting wind struck them full in the face together and a huge shape loomed large up towards them and seemed to overshadow them. Shilvers had a momentary impression of a deafening screech and bright lights flashing into his eyes. Beside him Julia fell to her knees and raised her arm over her head in a futile gesture of self-protection. Shilvers stopped dead in his tracks, and as his mind wrestled with the image in front of him he felt his legs give way. The shape stopped immediately ahead of them. The blitz of the senses and confusion were total, yet over in a second. Shilvers opened his eyes to take in what seemed an enormous military vehicle with caterpillar tracks and camouflage paint, silhouetted against the sky.

'What the f—?' Shilvers had not time to finish the expletive before he heard the heavy metallic sound of the door and running feet coming round the truck towards them. Julia was now on her hands and knees. Shilvers glanced at her and saw that she was more in control of herself than he was. She stared with a mixture of anger and indignation at the two men standing immediately in front of them.

'Who the bloody hell are you?' she demanded.

'We might well ask the same question.' The voice of the older of the two men was calm and controlled. Both wore what Shilvers had learned in recent years to call paramilitary uniform, complete with berets and some insignia on their epaulettes. The jackets and trousers were of a pale-blue reminiscent of the R.A.F. but of a material which better suited the army. 'This is private property and you two have no right to be here. Do you have any identification with you?'

Only his temper enabled Shilvers to ignore the pain and protest from his limbs as he struggled to his feet. 'Now just a minute . . .' But Julia wasn't going to abdicate command.

'Now look,' said Julia, 'I don't know which country or which century you guys come from, but this is Britain and though you may have cause to regret it, it's still a relatively free country. So either explain yourselves or get the hell out of our way so that we can take a number from that piece of metal and get on our way to report you to the local police.'

The two men were looking directly at Julia with open mouths. Shilvers was too, in mixed admiration and amazement. He could hardly breathe, let alone deliver a speech. He looked back at the two men, and the younger of them slowly turned to look at his senior, his eyebrows practically forming the shape of question marks.

'We are the site patrol police for Imperial Nuclear Industries. Behind us is the Dounscraig nuclear installation which is a restricted area under the terms of the Restricted Sites Act of April this year. You are within the boundary of that restricted area and we are empowered under the Act to detain you if necessary to discover the purpose of your trespass.' The senior of the two glanced at the younger man who, his confidence restored, resumed his hostile gaze at Shilvers and Julia.

'That's fine Mister,' said Julia, unbowed. 'Then take us directly to your superior whoever he is, so that he can offer us some explanation of this infringement of our rights that doesn't come directly from the pages of the Mr Plod manual.' Shilvers could hardly believe he was hearing this from Julia, and he was nonplussed that she was so much more in command of the situation than he was.

The younger man's regained confidence appeared to evaporate as quickly as it had returned. But Julia had not finished.

'Before we go I require you to mark the spot at which we are now standing as independent evidence of the fact that we are outside the site boundary or any notices indicating any restriction. Perhaps a nuclear shell from your vehicle would be appropriate?'

CHAPTER TWENTY-THREE

Julia refused to ride in the military vehicle, and she and Shilvers marched down the hill with the officer and his younger colleague behind them. With the large camouflaged machine on caterpillar tracks trundling behind them they made a bizarre procession across the English countryside. The junior of the two men spoke in a muffled voice into a two-way radio.

Inside the site, the vehicle peeled away to leave the group of four marching down an inner road, alongside a series of enormous concrete structures which could have been mass air-raid shelters. Shilvers guessed that they were storage tanks. He looked up to see grass growing from guttering forty feet in the air, and stains from dripping liquid down the outside of the walls. He recalled what Penshall had said about the wear and tear which inevitably occurred in any industrial premises over several decades. Dounscraig showed all the signs of fairing no better than any other such installation. They walked for perhaps a quarter of a mile, looking all around. No one spoke.

The couple were taken into a Sixties-style system-built office-block, and then to a large room with completely blank walls, a large wooden table and half a dozen chairs.

'Someone will see you in a moment,' said the officer. 'Please wait.'

'Whoever it is make sure it's someone important enough to put your arse in a sling,' Julia called after him. Shilvers raised his eyebrows. In spite of his discomfort, he was entertained by her indignation.

There were blinds at the windcw, and as soon as the door had closed behind them Julia was pulling at the strings to look outside. She wasted her time. The only view was of a sheer brick wall ten feet away from the glass. It stretched out of sight in all directions. Julia let the blind fall noisily.

'What do you make of this then?' she asked Shilvers. For practical purposes she had forgotten all about the story they were concerned with, and just regarded the incident as an infringement of her civil liberties. She was seething with anger. Shilvers was calculating.

'A ruse to get us in here without a struggle?'

Julia paused. 'Oh shit. You don't think . . .?'

There was a noise in the corridor of approaching footsteps. Shilvers stood up and walked over to the window where Julia was. The door opened.

'Ah Mr Shilvers, Miss Somers. This is a surprise.' Something about the man was familiar. 'Maddox. Daniel Maddox. I believe I saw you both at the Winderwath village social. We have a mutual friend in Mr Dixon. A very pleasant evening I thought.'

'Ah yes,' said Shilvers. 'Happier circumstances.'

'Never mind the small talk Mr Maddox,' Julia interrupted. 'We'd like to know just what the bloody hell is going on here. We were taking a casual walk on the moor, and have been arrested by two goons in military uniform and frogmarched in here like we were foreign spies. Is this Britain or East Germany? Who the –?'

'Please calm down Miss Somers,' said Maddox politely. He was pulling up a chair and opening a file in front of him on the desk. 'I'm sure we can get this sorted out in no time.'

Maddox indicated two chairs on the other side of the desk. Julia paused but Shilvers took a seat and gestured for her to do likewise. Maddox studied his file without speaking. Then he looked up.

'Now.' Suddenly he seemed much more like a policeman. 'You say you were out for a casual walk on the moor . . .'

'You bet your life we were,' said Julia, 'if it's any business of yours, which it isn't. Where the hell do you guys get off asking these questions anyway? I came here to complain, not to be put through the third degree.'

Maddox didn't flinch. He looked up and clasped his hands in front of him. He directed his speech mostly towards Shilvers in a manner which irritated Julia still further because it was intended to make her feel like an errant schoolgirl who had allowed her mouth to run away with her.

'Now I know that this must all be a dreadful bore for you, but I do hope you will understand. We are required under the terms of the Restricted Sites Act simply to ensure that the Dounscraig plant is secure from prowlers, or, not wishing to sound too melodramatic, industrial espionage. You'll appreciate that there are lots of foreign powers who would be very glad to get their hands on the technology involved in this plant.' His patient look pleaded for understanding. 'Now obviously neither of you would be involved in anything of that sort, but we are required to satisfy ourselves.' He paused again. 'It's a statutory obligation. Mr Shilvers?'

Shilvers looked at Maddox and at Julia. All this was a disaster. He had badly wanted to get into Dounscraig for a look around, but not like this. This man was as smooth and slick as they come, and so far everything he had said was reasonable.

'Sure. I can see there's a problem. But you already know who we are and what we're up to. I'm working for the Tourist Board for Christ's sake. What could be more harmless than that?'

'We already know that you're working for the Tourist Board. They have been most helpful in confirming your credentials. But what they weren't fully able to explain, and what I am still, I must confess, a little confused about, is why you found it necessary to photograph the site? They told us that your work was merely in providing the literature, not the scenic views for their brochures.'

'Photographs? I don't understand.'

Maddox reached in the file and brought out a blown-up black and white photograph of a man in a battered coat with a camera to his eye, pointing it directly into the lens. Even upside-down, Shilvers could recognize it as himself.

'November 14th last, I think. We sent an officer to enquire about your business at the time, but when he got to where you had been, you had long gone. We didn't worry about it at the time, but then you came back a few days later, and now you have come back again. Why the extraordinary interest in Dounscraig Mr Shilvers?' The placatory tone in Maddox's voice had all but vanished and he sat silent, with eyebrows raised, waiting for an answer.

Shilvers noted that Julia was now leaving things to him. He kept his composure. 'There's no mystery, Mr Maddox. I'm here for the Tourist Board. Dounscraig isn't exactly a tourist draw, but it is a curiosity sticking up in the middle of nowhere like it is, and I wanted to write something about it. I photograph lots of things that I want to write about, to keep their image in front of me as I write. I find it helps. Anyway,' Shilvers was beginning to regain his confidence, 'as far as I know it's still a free country. We were well away from the site, and there was no indication of a restricted area or any problem taking photographs.' Maddox was listening intently as Shilvers continued. 'Presumably the industrial secrets of which you speak are not available to be discovered by a cheap telephoto lens from half a mile away – otherwise no doubt they are being photographed as we speak from a satellite. Anyway, we came here for an apology from you people and we expect to get one, otherwise I'll be making it my business to write a quite different style of article about the place, for a quite different publication.'

'And what sort of article might that be?' asked Maddox.

'An article in a Sunday newspaper which asks how it is that two ordinary people minding their own business, and taking a walk on the moors, can find themselves arrested by men in paramilitary uniform, driving an offensive-looking military vehicle, in peacetime, from an organization which has no police powers outside its own premises. I think our friendly M.P. Mr Dixon might want to get on the bandwagon with a few indignant quotes, don't you?'

Now it was Julia's turn to be impressed, but Maddox was still smiling.

'I'd be surprised if Mr Dixon wanted to join an anti-Dounscraig bandwagon. All the same, we have nothing to hide from politicians and the public, except our technology. Everyone knows everything that goes on here. We have a productivity and safety record to be proud of, and we would be surprised if a responsible journalist such as yourself would wish to create sensation and alarm about an industry which is such an important employer in these otherwise difficult times.'

'I'm ready to be convinced, Mr Maddox. I've never been here or anywhere like this before. I'd be delighted to get the guided tour.'

Julia looked at Shilvers. She was astonished by his nerve.

'I'll have to check on that,' said Maddox, 'but in principle I don't see why not. As I said, we have nothing to hide and much to be proud of. Please wait a few moments.'

Fifteen minutes later Shilvers and Julia were dressed in neat white overalls and construction site helmets with I.N.I. painted on the front, following a yellow line down what seemed like miles of corridor. In front of them a smart-looking woman dressed in a navy-blue two-piece suit delivered the potted tourist guide, scarcely looking round at the couple.

'Nuclear reactor . . . major achievement for British technology . . . envy of the world . . . dedicated to the peaceful production of energy . . . safety record second to none . . . major foreign currency earner . . . two thousand three hundred employees . . .' The propaganda washed over Julia but Shilvers was listening intently for any clue about what was being done apart from the reprocessing which he already knew about. 'Spent fuel rods are taken to the decanning plant . . . immersed in coolant liquid in conditions of absolute safety . . . restricted areas are constantly monitored . . . all employees are subject to regular safety screening.'

At last Shilvers and Julia were taken into an enormous locker-room where their guide showed a pass and was given three further sets of overalls and overshoes. She turned to her charges for the first time in ten minutes.

'Please put these on. They are to be discarded once you leave the restricted area. Please also wear these personal radioactivity monitors. They must also be left at this desk when you leave the area. Please be assured that there is no danger. This is merely a routine precaution for your own comfort and safety.'

The spiel was directly from the airlines, thought Shilvers, as he squeezed his fell-walking boots into the plastic overshoes. Beside him, Julia was stepping into another layer of overalls. In large red letters on the floor were written the words RESTRICTED AREA, and beyond them a six-inch-high barrier, with yellow and black diagonal stripes. 'It's only for the tourists.' Once again Penshall's words rang round Shilvers' head as his cushioned feet padded softly along the metal walkways. Shilvers and Julia continued following their guide, who had stopped talking, and now merely glanced over her shoulder periodically to ensure that they were following.

Shilvers looked about him. The hall they had entered appeared to be made entirely of metal and was shaped like an enormous cylinder. The walkway was half-way up the side of the cylinder, which was perhaps two hundred feet high. In the centre of the circle was a massive complex of pipes, wires and tubes, leading into what seemed like a glass container with some kind of boiler inside it. Shilvers had not the slightest understanding of how technology of this kind worked, and could only ever see a spaghetti of stainless steel with dials and controls. Men in silver suits and what looked like space-helmets patrolled the walkways which intersected the metal complex. Some carried clipboards and consulted dials, others pushed small trolleys of instruments around the installation. It could have been the inside of a nuclear power station, or the working bits of the space command station at NASA for all Shilvers knew. He did not understand it, and even as he realized his inadequacy, he reflected that this was why so many people were simply relieved to be told that the scientists had it all under control and that there was no need to worry.

At last the guide reached the doorway of a glass-fronted control room overlooking the installation, and turned round to beckon Shilvers and Julia inside. She went ahead to speak privately with one of a dozen or so men in the module, who half-turned from his work to glance at Shilvers and Julia. Without changing his expression, the scientist looked at the couple from across the huge room and nodded a greeting, and turned back to exchange quiet words with the guide. While Julia was obviously more interested than he in the elaborate technology all around them, Shilvers kept his eyes fixed on the scientist. He wore heavily shaded glasses and his white coat was shabby and dishevelled. Shilvers could only see the man's profile, but there was something about him that especially interested him. Now the conversation had finished and the scientist and guide approached. Shilvers saw that the guide deliberately broke away to speak to Julia, while the other man came towards him.

'Mr Shilvers? May I introduce myself? I'm Dr Graham Smedley.'

The name struck a chord somewhere in Shilvers' memory, which was trying to trace it even as his head turned for the introduction. The memory and eyesight reached the same conclusion at the same moment. An enormous scar on the side of Smedley's face was impossible to avoid. It looked as though his skin had melted, and Shilvers remembered Alf Penshall's story of the evacuation. Smedley. 'One of the top boffins', Penshall had called him. 'Seen around in a wheelchair and badly scarred', he had said. Alf's brother George had been involved in that accident. The only difference was that George had not been seen again, neither were his wife and two children.

'Car crash. Two years ago. If you think this is bad you should see what it was like before the plastic surgeons did their stuff.' Only now did Shilvers realize that he had been appallingly rude. All other thoughts were submerged beneath embarrassment.

'I'm dreadfully sorry. I didn't mean to stare. It was only . . .'

'Oh please don't apologize. I quite understand. Everybody stares, but some manage to disguise their curiosity better than others.' The voice of the scientist was calm and controlled.

Shilvers struggled to sort out his thoughts and find the right words not to express them. 'It was only that I've seen quite a few crash scars and burns in my time, but yours seem unfamiliar. I'm terribly sorry. I hope I haven't offended you.'

'Not at all,' said Smedley. 'People always want to, but they seldom talk about it. There was indeed a very hot fire. The accident involved an articulated lorry on the motorway. The petrol tank exploded. I was lucky to get away with my eyesight.'

Shilvers looked at the dark glasses. Smedley's story was no doubt well rehearsed. It would be the one he had given to friends and relatives, or even curious members of the local press should they be lucky enough to meet him. Shilvers thought about Ffitch. Would he buy a story like that? Five years ago he wouldn't have, but now perhaps he was too comfortable. Running a local news agency meant being friendly with the local industrialists and swallowing too many press releases and publicity handouts.

'Would you like an explanation of what goes on here or would I be wasting my time?' asked Smedley. 'I don't mind giving you the rundown but, as we're being refreshingly frank, if you've seen as many people feigning interest while mentally glazing over as I have, you learn to recognize it. You look to me as though you're about saturated with it.'

Smedley's casual approach had broken the atmosphere, and Shilvers was relieved.

'To tell you the truth, it doesn't mean that much to me. If you had any enormous problems I don't suppose you'd be telling me anyway. And I hate to confirm prejudices about the press, but in my business, if everything is going wonderfully well it's not of much interest. So perhaps we'd better not hold you up.'

'I'd appreciate that Mr Shilvers. Hard though it may be to believe, we do a pretty difficult job here, and this is a particularly difficult time.' Shilvers was about to turn away towards the door when Smedley's next remark stopped him in his tracks. The scientist leaned over towards Shilvers and spoke softly. 'Maybe I could tell you about the reasons why it's a difficult time over a drink. But not in the Huntsman.'

Shilvers turned back, trying to confirm that he properly

understood what was being said. The expression on the scarred face told him that he did. The two men shook hands.

'Be very glad to accept,' he said quietly. 'Any time.'

'Perhaps the Travellers in Westermouth. Ten o'clock?' Shilvers could hardly believe what he was hearing, and his journalistic instincts went on to autopilot.

'I'll be there.'

Maddox was back to his bland and charming self when Shilvers and Julia returned to the office. 'I'll get a car to run you back to Winderwath if you like. It's raining now and getting dark.' Julia was about to accept.

'No thanks, we'd prefer to walk. We'll just get back before nightfall if we set off now.' Shilvers took Julia, still half-protesting, by the arm and headed towards the door.

'I'm sure you won't mind if we escort you to the gate. More regulations I'm afraid.' Maddox shook hands. 'And if there's anything else you want to know about us here, Mr Shilvers, you have only to ask. It's as well not to stalk us from our blind side. It makes people jumpy, you understand.'

Shilvers did not comment, and the couple walked in silence behind a commissionaire in a blue uniform and peaked cap. When they got outside and away from earshot Julia was the first to speak.

'What a snow-job! I've never met such a slimy bunch. You'd think that butter wouldn't melt in their mouths. I'm really going to enjoy bringing those bastards down a peg or two – or at least I'm going to enjoy watching you do it.' Shilvers hadn't spoken. 'Well, what did you think?' Shilvers still did not speak, but walked on briskly, deep in thought.

'Tony, I was talking to you. What did you think?' Her sharper tone brought Shilvers back from his racing thoughts.

'What do I think? I think we've struck gold, that's what I think. Race you back to the cottage.' Shilvers darted off over the hills as the sun began to set over the horizon.

'What the . . . ?' but a gust of wind blew her words away.

CHAPTER TWENTY-FOUR

There were only a half-dozen people in the lounge bar of the Travellers public house when Shilvers and Julia came in at 9.45 that evening. On their journey Shilvers had been anxious to ensure that they were not followed. They had caught the last bus from Winderwath together, but Shilvers had alighted first so that Julia could watch who got off with him. An old lady and a younger woman, apparently her daughter, had moved from their seats shortly after Shilvers had headed towards the door of the bus. Had they been getting up anyway? Julia thought so.

Shilvers crossed the road from the bus-stop. The two women headed off slowly down another side-road. Shilvers waited in a doorway on the other pavement for Julia to walk back from the next stop. As arranged she went beyond his stop for two hundred yards before circling back towards the spot where Shilvers was waiting. There was no sign of anyone following.

The couple bought drinks and went to a table in the furthest and darkest corner of the lounge. It was ten o'clock. There was no sign of Smedley.

'Do you think he'll come?' Julia had asked for the third time when they had reached the shepherd's cottage earlier that evening.

'How the hell do I know? But if he wasn't going to come, why would he suggest it?'

Julia thought for a moment and his earlier remark echoed in her memory. 'Maybe it's a trap?'

Shilvers had considered the possibility, but if it was what would it prove? A journalist accepts a whispered invitation from a scientist in a secret nuclear installation to meet him for a drink. There wasn't a self-respecting journalist in the country who would decline such an offer. There was no law against meeting for a drink.

'We'll keep the thought in mind when we see what he's got to say. It's even illegal to sit and listen to information you know is covered by the Official Secrets Act. You're supposed to cover your ears and sing "Land of Hope and Glory" if anyone tries to tell you an official secret. Maybe it is a trap. Maybe.' But Shilvers did not think it was.

'I don't know why. I've got a bad feeling about this.'

'It may be of some comfort to you to know that I've brought my friend from Cyprus with me,' said Shilvers, and with two hands he clasped the pocket of his jacket to reveal the outline of a small pistol. Julia had seen the gun before, when he had brought it back with him after doing a story about the British military bases in Cyprus. It had been given to him by a friendly officer because of the tense situation on the island, and the same officer had deliberately overlooked it when Shilvers had taken the R.A.F. flight back to Britain.

'Tony, for heaven's sake! I didn't even know you had that up here with you.'

'Just extra insurance,' said Shilvers, taking another drink.

Ten-past ten. No sign. Perhaps in the other bar? Shilvers did a tour of the pub. Maybe Smedley is under suspicion and is being followed. Maybe he decided it was too dangerous. Several more locals had joined the half-dozen at the bar and the volume of chatter was higher. A good venue, thought Shilvers. An unlikely haunt for a nuclear scientist, but plausible. If the worst came to the worst it could seem like a coincidence. Shilvers wondered whether he was trying to convince himself or testing the explanation to see if it was plausible to anyone else. Their glasses were empty. The couple caused a stir of interest when Julia went to get them refilled. Townies for sure.

As Julia returned from the bar and put down the two glasses, her attention was drawn to another table in the next alcove. A man was sitting alone in the shadows, his peaked cap still on despite the warmth of the lounge. She saw the flash of his tinted spectacles as she sat down.

'I think we've hit the jackpot,' she told Shilvers. Even as he went to turn round the man had left his seat and was carrying his drink towards them, his other hand outstretched.

'Glad you could make it, Mr Shilvers. This must be Miss Somers.' Smedley, wearing a shabby grey raincoat and cap, took the spare stool at their table. 'Did you enjoy your sightseeing tour this afternoon?'

'Very interesting, though I'm not sure that we saw much of what really goes on,' said Shilvers, 'did we?'

Smedley took a long drink from his pint glass. Despite himself Shilvers watched as the scarred tissue on Smedley's face remained still while the other side moved as he swallowed the beer. The empty glass came down on the table.

'Let's not waste time Mr Shilvers, Miss Somers. I.N.I. suspect, but they can't be sure, that Alf Penshall told you everything he knows about Dounscraig. They thought they were certain, but then when you came up with that story about knowing him when you were a small boy, they weren't so positive. Getting rid of workers who get into accidents or cause trouble is one thing, but disposing of a journalist of some national reputation takes a bit more thought. They can't afford to take any chances, so they're watching you like a hawk.'

Though he had half expected it, the information was still alarming. Shilvers once again looked around the bar for anyone taking an interest in them. He saw nothing to cause concern.

'No need to fear this evening, I think. I watched you come in here and then watched for another fifteen minutes before coming in myself. Either they've slipped up or given themselves a night off. It's the sort of carelessness that has got them into the trouble they're in right now.'

'And what trouble is that, Dr Smedley?' Julia spoke for the first time.

'I think you have a pretty good idea. Penshall is dead, so we just have to hope that he didn't die for absolutely nothing.' Smedley looked directly at the two of them.

'There's just one thing that troubles me,' said Shilvers, looking up from his drink and returning Smedley's gaze. 'What are we all doing here? You are a very highly paid nuclear scientist who has presumably spent his life dedicated to what is going on at I.N.I. Yet if what you seem to be suggesting is true, you're about to spill the beans on something which will put them out of business, and set back the industry twenty-five years. I don't get it.'

Smedley had been watching Shilvers carefully, but now he looked into the distance, focusing on nothing as he spoke.

'If Penshall told you what I think he told you, then you know the real reason for this.' His fingers went to the disfigured side of his face, the tips touching it ever so gently as though there was still pain. 'But it isn't only this. It's what happened to the others who were less lucky. Sure, you're right, I am dedicated to the nuclear industry. I still believe it is our only hope to avoid a freezing planet when all the fossil fuels run out, as they eventually will. It's the only conceivable long-term and renewable source of energy for a world which has based future survival on the need for energy. So yes, I am dedicated to it. But,' now he looked directly at Shilvers and Julia, his eyes darting from one to the other, 'but not at any price, and the price we have been paying at I.N.I. is too high. Much higher than even you two suspect. Excuse me.'

Smedley picked up his glass and went to the bar. Shilvers watched him and tried to lip-read his words to the barman. A pint of best bitter. Nothing more. Smedley turned his head so that he faced away from the couple. Was he indicating something to someone in the other bar?

'What do you think?' asked Julia.

'Shh. I'm watching.' Shilvers was watching Smedley, and trying to detect any hint of a signal or alert to anyone around him. He could see nothing. Smedley paid for his drink and came back to the table. Maybe even the act of buying the drink was some kind of signal. How could he possibly be sure?

'Dr Smedley, I hope you'll forgive me. You know everything that I.N.I. knows about us, which presumably includes the interest payments on my mortgage, and we know nothing about you. Now suppose Penshall did tell us some secret information about I.N.I., and suppose we were trying to find out more. Wouldn't I.N.I. send in someone just like you, who would approach us in exactly the way you have approached us, to find out what we know?' Shilvers swallowed his beer. 'I'm not saying we know anything at all, you understand, I'm just saying supposing.'

Dr Smedley smiled. Half of his face remained still. He stared into his drink. 'I appreciate the point. In fact I had already thought of it. And I realize that the only way you will be able to trust me, is if I tell you something I feel pretty sure you don't already know. Would you agree?'

Shilvers and Julia looked at each other. 'I guess so. And the sum total of what we don't know about what is going on around here could fill several encyclopaedias,' said Shilvers.

Smedley moved his chair a little closer to the table, and spoke at still more muted volume. 'I'm assuming that Penshall told you all about the series of bad accidents we've had at Dounscraig which haven't been made public. I assume he's told you about the many evacuations which haven't been talked about, and, most important of all, I can guess that he's told you about the many disappearances there have been of the personnel involved in those accidents. Would I be right?'

Shilvers didn't alter his expression. 'Please go on.'

The unscarred part of Smedley's face moved into another half-smile. 'What I know he didn't tell you is something the poor bastard never had a chance to know, and that is how he died. The coroner was right in speculating that he was hit by a vehicle. What he didn't speculate on was what kind of vehicle.' Smedley looked intently at the pair of them, waiting for a reaction. There was none. 'Alf Penshall was run down on the site of Imperial Nuclear Industries, by a twenty-ton earth-moving vehicle with caterpillar tracks, and taken at dead of night in a large brown car to the spot where he was later found dumped. The car, you may be surprised to discover, was driven by someone who I gather you already know.'

Julia was ready for what was to come. It hit Shilvers like a pole-axe.

'Mr George Ffitch, manager and proprietor of the West of Britain News Service with offices only about two miles from where we are sitting.'

'That's bollocks and you know it is.' In his surprise Shilvers had raised his voice and attracted the attention of several drinkers at the bar. Julia put her hand on his arm. He lowered his voice. 'Dr Smedley, I can believe every syllable you've told me about Imperial Nuclear Industries. I have no problem believing anything about the nuclear industry, but I've known George Ffitch for nearly fifteen years, and in the last few days I have to admit that it has crossed my mind that his old instincts have been blinded or compromised a bit by the exigencies of operating in a small backwater like this piss-hole.' Shilvers was now under control, but his voice still betrayed anger. 'But never, never in my wildest imagination, would I be prepared to accept that he would be involved in the death of anyone, let alone an old man like Alf Penshall, just for doing what journalists encourage everyone to do at all times, and that is to tell us the truth.' Shilvers caught the look of concern on Julia's face. 'I'm sorry Julia, I just don't believe it, and what scares the shit out of me is that for you, Dr Smedley, to tell me that must cast doubt on everything else you say to me this evening, and even your motives for meeting me. I'm sorry, but that's the way it is.'

When Shilvers had finished the three sat in silence for several seconds. Smedley appeared unmoved by Shilvers' outburst, and took several sips of his drink before speaking again.

'I appreciate your views about your old friend. I wouldn't have raised it at this point because it is not central to what we have to discuss. I merely wished to give you information which, if you choose to, you could use your journalistic talents to check on, and if I am proved to be right, you might feel you can trust me. As I said, I fully believe that Mr Penshall, whether he be a childhood friend of yours or not, told you all the other things I have mentioned tonight. I know he was unable to tell you the manner of his own death – an incident which should remind us all of the dangers in what we are doing, and even in meeting here like this tonight. For myself I feel that perhaps I have pressed my luck too far for one evening already.' Smedley drained his glass and got up to go. 'I will say no more for now. My information about Mr Ffitch has obviously undermined whatever little faith you had in me, and I understand your caution over other matters. If you are half the journalist you are by reputation, you will be able to confirm what I have told you about your friend. If you are unable to do so, and still don't accept my word, we will not meet again. If it is otherwise, call this number at any time, ask for Mr Dawson and give the number from which you are speaking. I will return your call on a secure line within ten minutes. Nothing is totally secure, but this system should be safe.' Smedley handed over a small piece of card, blank except for a six figure telephone number written in pencil. 'I hope we meet again.' He turned and was gone.

Shilvers and Julia were battling through the blustering wind and raising their voices over the roar of the breakers below before they began to make any headway in a conversation which had gone round and round for the last hour of their journey home.

'You admit you haven't seen or heard anything from Ffitch in several years. A lot can happen to a person in that time. Don't forget, everyone has their price. Everyone can be bought. And the bottom line is,' shouted Julia into the wind, 'how do you actually know he *isn't* involved?'

Shilvers stopped in mid-stride and turned, his back to the ocean, and looked at Julia. He took a deep breath. 'Because, my dear Julia, on the night that Penshall died, George Ffitch was with me in the Huntsman, five hundred yards from where we are standing right now.'

A huge breaker smashed with full force into the cliff several hundreds of feet below. The rock held firm, and used the force of the wave itself to push the water back with equal ferocity, into the path of another oncoming wave.

CHAPTER TWENTY-FIVE

'He would have to have been at I.N.I., watched Penshall being literally shattered by a twenty-ton truck, taken the body and put it into his car, dumped it at the side of the road outside the village, gone for a wash and brush up and a cup of tea, and then come to meet me in the pub. I start asking him about I.N.I. and he answers me, as cool as a cucumber, having just been involved in the death of a man because I.N.I. suspected him of having talked to me. Now,' Shilvers was sipping coffee and addressing Julia from across the room, 'does that seem plausible to you?'

'But you admitted yourself that the police had found the body by the time you met, and that Ffitch must have known about it. Why didn't he mention it to you in the pub that night?'

'Because there was no reason to connect it to Dounscraig. At the time it was just another traffic accident.'

'Come off it Tony. When Ffitch was sitting where you are now the other night you wanted to know the answer to that question yourself. There can't be so many mystery deaths around this small country area that it wasn't worth mentioning. It must be big news for an agency like Ffitch's. The man worked at I.N.I. He would surely have mentioned it, unless he had some reason not to.'

Shilvers recalled how Ffitch had fingered the side of his nose in that irritating manner. He remembered how he had wanted to know then why Ffitch had failed to tell him about Penshall's death. Now his omission seemed perfectly ordinary. Was he losing his perspective on this story? He had to be aware of the possibility.

How to proceed? Homework. However unlikely he thought Smedley's account, he must do his homework. That's what Ffitch would have told him in the old days. If he was half the journalist his reputation made him out to be, Smedley had said, he could find out the truth. It was right, and he knew he should not need someone like Smedley to remind him of it. He would find out the answer to the allegation, then he would know how to handle Smedley. If Smedley was a plant, part of a trap, he would have to take Julia and get out fast, dealing with the story as best he could from a distance. If Smedley was on the level, he would have an invaluable ally. But he could not be. What he had said about Ffitch could not be right. It could not.

By morning Shilvers had devised a plan. At nine o'clock he called Ffitch from the telephone box in the village to arrange a meeting. Then made a second call, this one long-distance, to another old friend. The friend had been intrigued by Shilvers' mysterious tone of voice, and had agreed to drop everything and meet him at Westermouth station this afternoon. Yes, he had rashly agreed, Shilvers could have preliminary results within twenty-four hours.

'I'm sorry about this old man,' said Shilvers over sausage and mash in a pub near Ffitch's office, 'but after an unfortunate incident with the tyres of the last car I hired, the local firm has me on its blacklist. I've been promising Julia I'd drive her up the coast for a week now, and she's run out of patience. I'll have it back to you by the time you leave the office.'

'That's O.K. Tony. Be careful though,' Ffitch knocked back his third large whisky, 'it's a bit posher than you're used to. Automatic. And it's got one of those new-fangled mobile phones, so no calling your friends in Australia.'

'I'll bring it back in one piece, even if I have to push it.' Shilvers smiled with his eyes and picked up the keys from the table in front of him. He suddenly felt uncomfortable about trading on the goodwill of an old friend in order to check him out. He felt momentarily guilty for even entertaining the idea that what Smedley had said might be true. Too late now, he thought, in for a penny . . .

'Hope the trouble and strife likes our local coastline. It strikes me she doesn't like much around here.'

'Now don't be like that,' said Shilvers, 'it's just that she's a towny like me. It takes us a while to appreciate the charm of sheep-shit, but I'm sure we'll see its beauty in due course.'

As Shilvers waved goodbye to Ffitch on the pavement outside the pub, Julia drew herself back into a doorway to avoid being seen. She watched Ffitch head off towards his office, not looking back as Shilvers got into the driver's seat of the large brown car. Fifty yards on, Ffitch still had not looked around as he walked into the shop-doorway which was the office entrance of the West of Britain News Service. Shilvers didn't even glance across at her. He signalled and pulled out into the traffic.

Julia still watched while a white Ford Escort car with two men inside pulled out from the row of cars on the other side of the road, and fell in three cars behind Shilvers. She hurried towards a nearby telephone-box and waited. Two miles down the road Shilvers parked the brown saloon at the side of the road and went into a telephone-box. He took a piece of paper from his pocket and dialled the number. In the box outside the pub where Shilvers and Ffitch had been drinking, the telephone bell rang. Julia picked up the receiver and waited for the caller to put in his money at the other end.

'A white Ford Escort,' she said calmly. 'Two men inside. Nothing else that I can see.' There was no reply. Julia left the telephone box, walked back to the doorway opposite the pub and waited.

Back in Ffitch's car, Shilvers joined the light afternoon traffic and headed out of town, glancing carefully in the mirror as he drove. He headed for the open country road which would lead eventually to Winderwath. He did not hurry and neither, apparently, did anyone else in the line of half a dozen cars behind him. Shilvers looked at his watch. 1.45. A little early. He slowed down still more and several cars behind overtook. Shilvers glanced in the mirror. A white car was still there, three behind him.

Into the hilly countryside, Shilvers began the long climb to the top of a ridge which overlooked a wide valley below. As he reached the brow of the hill, he could see the road snaking through the countryside in front of him. At the bottom of the valley was a winding river, and beside it, a railway line with occasional small viaducts smoothing out its path. River and railway were visible far into the horizon to the left. Shilvers slowed his car almost to a standstill. The car behind tooted in irritation and Shilvers waved it past.

The white blur in the mirror hung back in the distance behind him.

Shilvers looked again towards the horizon. Then he saw what he was waiting for. Emerging from behind a distant hillside, the intercity train. Wait for it. Wait. Wait. Don't go in too soon, the advice echoed around his head. Gently. Wait for it. Now.

Without warning Shilvers pressed the accelerator hard down to the floor. The automatic gearbox screamed in protest as the car leapt forward, leaving the nearest car behind him disappearing in the mirror. Down into the valley he raced as if for collision with the oncoming train. Shilvers looked again into his mirror. In the distance the white car tried to pull out to overtake but was forced back by a lorry travelling fast in the other direction. Down the hill he sped, the hedges flashing past on each side. Maybe he had left it too late. The train had disappeared behind the hillside, and would emerge into sight in a few seconds. Once again a distant blur in the mirror indicated the white car, this time successfully overtaking the three cars ahead of it. It spurted down the valley behind him.

In the distance over to his right, Shilvers saw the train emerge from the tunnel. He must be nearly there. Where was it?

A small bend in the road revealed in front of him what he had been looking for. Five hundred yards away he saw the blur of flashing lights, and glanced in the mirror to see the white Ford screeching up behind him, narrowing the distance between them at every second. Shilvers pressed the floor still harder. Eighty-five. Ninety miles an hour. Now the hedgerows blotted out his view of the train, and in the distance beyond the screaming roar of his own engine, he could hear the clanging bell as the level-crossing gate began to descend. Shilvers' right foot felt as though it would go through the floor. One hundred miles an hour. There was no stopping now anyway. The white car was perhaps fifty yards behind when Shilvers felt a bump under the suspension, and the crossing gate missed the roof of the car by inches. Nearly took Ffitch back a convertible, thought Shilvers. Behind him he heard the squeal of brakes and in his mirror he saw grey smoke rising as the tyres of the car behind him skidded on the tarmac. Shilvers smiled and slowed down.

Twenty minutes later he was back in Westermouth. It had been a simple matter to conceal his car in a farmyard as the white Ford flashed by on its way to Winderwath, and then double back towards the town. As he slowed down by the telephone box Julia was in the car so quickly that it was scarcely necessary for him to stop.

'Lose them?'

'Lost them.'

'Bloody well done,' she thrilled. 'Next stop, the station.'

Five minutes later the brown car was pulling into the crowded car-park next to Westermouth railway station. Even as they slowed, Shilvers recognized the familiar shape of his friend Paul Reade approaching them, his equally familiar Gladstone bag bouncing off the side of his knee as he walked.

'Hullo Tony. This had better be good. I've left a dismembered body on ice to come down here this afternoon.' He put out his hand. Shilvers shook it warmly.

'I hope you've washed thoroughly since you've been playing with dead bodies, you nasty necromaniac.' By now Julia had come around from the passenger side of the car.

'You haven't met my friend Julia Somers. This is my old friend Paul Reade, known to his colleagues as the Professor. Professor of Forensic Medicine, to be precise.' The two exchanged greetings.

'Let's get to work. Is this the car?' Reade opened his bag and placed it on the passenger seat of the brown saloon. His eyes were scanning the back seat even as he reached into the bag for several small bottles containing liquid, and swabs. Inside the lid of the bag were fixed a variety of steel instruments. Reade selected tweezers and went to work.

'We've kept samples of hair and clothing from Penshall, but even if he was a passenger in the car, I doubt if I'll be able to tell you if he was dead or alive at the time.'

'Don't worry about that,' said Shilvers. 'If you tell me that Penshall was in the back of this car recently, I'll know the rest.'

Shilvers and Julia watched, fascinated, as the scientist thoroughly examined every square inch of the back seat of the car, picking up the most minute traces of what seemed to Julia like dust and fluff.

'Of course, if this was official, I'd be doing this in the laboratory, not in a bloody station car-park,' said Reade.

'Yes, but look at it another way. If it was official, you'd be getting paid and not doing it for old times' sake.'

'Don't remind me. I must be potty. Think about my pension.'

'If this turns up what some people around here expect it to,' Shilvers glanced at Julia, 'they'll be giving you a medal for exemplary detective work.'

'I doubt that. As far as the Penshall file is concerned, only a hit and run has been committed. The local police have their work cut out to reduce the figures of existing serious crime without adding to their problems by looking for a murderer they don't think exists. I'm finished here. What about the boot?'

Reade put half a dozen samples and swabs into separate test-tubes and carefully labelled them. Meanwhile Shilvers opened the boot and was surprised to find it completely empty and apparently recently swept.

'Either your friend is obsessively tidy, or he has something to hide,' said Reade. 'Still, he obviously doesn't know much about my business, because a quick clean with the vacuum cleaner won't get rid of what I'm after.' Reade set about his exhaustive examination with tweezers and sample jar.

Twenty minutes later the forensic scientist had finished and Shilvers and Julia were walking with him back into the station.

'Telephone me at the lab tomorrow afternoon. Since you only want a simple match, it shouldn't take five minutes once I get the opportunity to do it. I might even get one of my post-graduates to do it as an exercise.'

'Don't do that if you wouldn't mind,' said Shilvers, not altering his pace. 'No disrespect to the students, but this is very important to me, otherwise I wouldn't have asked for the favour. If the tests come up with a positive match, I have to be one hundred per cent certain of it. I will be if you tell me. I hope you understand.'

Paul Reade stopped on the platform and turned to Shilvers. 'I do and I will. Even if I have to give up my lunch of recently dried corpse to do it. You have my word.' He shook hands with both of them. 'Now, get off and enjoy some of the countryside for a couple of hours, and leave the gruesome stuff to the experts.'

As the couple drove in silence along the coast road north of Winderwath, Julia looked out over the ocean. She thought about what would happen when all this was over, and they returned to London, and their more familiar lifestyles. Already she had been out of touch for longer than was sensible in a business where being new and being around were everything. Nothing was of less interest than yesterday's styles, and if you were the one who had designed them, you were yesterday's designer. She thought that maybe she would take some time out to do some drawings while Shilvers pursued the story.

As the sea and clouds flashed past to her left, Julia glanced towards him and watched that slight twitch below his left eye which indicated he was thinking hard as he drove. He had become obsessed with the story in a way that she had not seen for several years and yet his mood was unstable and unpredictable. It was a dangerous situation, but she was glad to see him so absorbed in something which was clearly important to him. Too often in recent months he had done work which was only for the money. Maybe she would not do any drawing after all. Maybe she would just stick around and help him.

'Do you feel any better about it?' she asked.

'About what?'

'Borrowing Ffitch's car and then using it to check him out.'

There was a silence.

'It's just professionalism. In the old days Ffitch would have been the first to accept that.' Shilvers slipped into his poor impression of a Mafia boss. 'It's nothing personal, just business.' He paused. 'It's a lead and I have to check it. If, as I expect, it turns up negative, it will tell me something important about Smedley. That I.N.I. are trying to lead us into a trap.'

'If I.N.I. are clever enough to do that, they're also clever enough to plant incriminating evidence on Ffitch's property.'

'I've thought of that, but I don't think they would have been smart enough to deposit Penshall's body in his car before it was found. They had no reason to do so at the time.' Shilvers drove in silence for several miles. As the road began to turn away from the coast he looked at his watch. Four o'clock.

'Maybe we had better be getting Ffitch's car back.' He looked at Julia and they smiled warmly at each other. She put her hand over his and held it tight.

'You know that I'm back to stay, don't you?'

Shilvers kept looking at the road ahead.

'Yes,' he said at last, 'I think I do.'

CHAPTER TWENTY-SIX

'I don't know whether this is good news or bad, but at least it's unambiguous.' Reade was speaking in a muted voice and Shilvers had to press the receiver hard against his ear. He pushed a finger into the other ear and shouted.

'You'll have to speak up Paul. I can hardly hear you.'

'There's a definite match,' was the scarcely more audible reply. 'Hairs from Penshall's head match hairs from the back seat, and traces from the coat Penshall was wearing when he was found were also in the car boot, despite some pretty thorough vacuum cleaning. Penshall was definitely in that car some time not long before he died, if he wasn't dead already.'

Standing next to Shilvers in the telephone-box, Julia was burning with curiosity, but his voice betrayed nothing.

'And there can be no doubt? No possibility of a mistake?'

'None whatever. I have two perfect matches. It's been enough in the past to send men to the gallows. Shall I send this to the local police?'

'No, don't do that,' said Shilvers abruptly. 'I'd like you to wait a bit, but keep the file safe, and in no circumstances tell anyone about it. This couldn't be more important, for everyone's safety, including yours.'

'This puts me in a difficult position, Tony. I'm an employee of the Home Office . . .'

'I know that Paul,' shouted Shilvers, 'but you said yourself, the file on this is closed. Just give me a few days. It can't make any difference after this amount of time. Just trust me.'

'O.K. Tony. I'll give you until the end of the week. Then the file goes to West Cumbria police.'

'Thanks Paul. I'll be in touch.'

Shilvers put the receiver down but continued to stare at it. Julia was able to guess the outcome, and this did not seem like a good time to gloat. A few seconds passed. Shilvers' hand was still on the receiver when he heard the single faint ring of the bell. He waited and heard another single ring. He picked up the receiver and carefully and deliberately pushed down the cradle twice. He put the handset to his ear and listened.

'O.K. Tony. I'll give you until the end of the week. Then the file goes to West Cumbria police.' It was Reade's voice.

'Thanks Paul, I'll be in touch.' His own. Shilvers put down the receiver again.

'Holy shit.' He looked through the glass all around, his heart beating rapidly. Parked a hundred yards away was a white transit van without markings, but with elaborate aerials and with tinted rear windows. 'Holy shit,' he repeated, 'now we're for it.'

'What the hell's wrong?' asked Julia. But already Shilvers was dialling the Manchester number on which he had just spoken to Paul Reade. The seconds ticked past agonizingly slowly as he waited for the connection. Shilvers imagined the cogs turning and interweaving at exchanges between himself and Manchester, and believed that each cog was conspiring to hold him up for as long as possible. He crashed his fist against the glass in frustration. The unobtainable tone. He dialled again. Again a single continuous tone. Now almost frantic, he called the operator and asked for a test on the line. The seconds ticked away. Neither of them spoke.

'I'm sorry, that line is out of order right now. I'll inform the engineer.'

'I have a feeling he already knows,' said Shilvers, and slammed down the phone. 'We've got to get to Manchester to see Reade. The poor bastard is deeply in the shit and he doesn't even know it.'

Shilvers called the nearest taxi firm in Westermouth. He knew it was dangerous to wait where they were, but also that any other venue he gave to the taxi would be overheard. He thought the post office was public enough to be as safe a place as any. It would take twenty minutes to get there, said the taxi-operator. 'Where will you be going to?'

'I'll tell you when you get here,' said Shilvers, and replaced the receiver.

On the walk to the post office Shilvers told Julia what had happened. It could only be I.N.I. listening to the conversation, and now that they knew what had passed between him and Reade, they must assume that he had the whole story. They would have to close in soon. Julia walked along in silence for several minutes then took Shilvers by the arm.

'Have you got your friend with you, you know, the one from Cyprus?' Shilvers tapped his right hand pocket. 'Next stop Manchester,' said Julia.

Five miles away Mr Roger Thornton, General Manager of Imperial Nuclear Industries Ltd, was sitting in his office staring out of the window towards the mass of concrete and steel which was the heart of the Dounscraig nuclear reprocessing plant. All around him, far in the background, he could hear and feel the deep hum of immense power under harness. It was always there, in the air, in the walls, in the furniture, even outside. Always there. Sometimes he could go for days and weeks on end and never notice it. Today Roger Thornton looked out of the window of his office, and listened to that sound. It seemed deafening.

On the desk beside him lay a plum-coloured file, the colour of secret files in I.N.I. Most of the files were plum-coloured. This one was secret for good reason. Glancing down at it, Thornton could see the edges of several black and white photographs. With one finger he slid them out on to the table. He did not pick them up, but just looked.

The first picture, taken from great distance and at dusk, showed the grainy shape of an old man, back to camera, standing outside an old wooden door. Behind it, just peeping round the edge, a younger man. Remarkable really, thought Thornton, even at that distance and in that light, the expression on the face of the younger man was discernible. Surprise. Even slight apprehension. No sign of recognition there, that was for sure. Yet Shilvers had told him that Penshall was a friend from childhood. Thornton stared again through the glass. Could Shilvers have been telling the truth? If he had not seen Penshall for twenty years or more, he would be bound not to recognize him. That would explain the expression. On the other hand . . .

Then there was a second picture, this one in daylight, but still from great distance. The younger man walked up the hill towards Mr Penshall's house. The date on the back reminded Thornton that it was taken on the day following Penshall's funeral. His hand went automatically to the side of his face when he remembered that slap from Mrs Penshall. Still, he thought, all those wounds were now healed. Even hers. He allowed himself a smile at the thought. It did not make him look happy.

If this had involved one of the workers, or even a local journalist, he would not have worried. He would have taken action, taken no chances. He had found it necessary to do so several times before. But Shilvers was something else. He had a reputation, and friends with resources and influence. In the worst possible scenario Shilvers might already know nearly everything and have told others. If Shilvers vanished, they would come looking. Time, it seemed, was running out. And yet, it might still all be all right. Shilvers might really have known Penshall from childhood holidays. The call might have been purely social. Thornton had not known Penshall personally, but from all accounts, he would scarcely have had the courage to bring in outsiders. Maybe it was all right after all.

Thornton placed his hand flat on the top of his solid mahogany desk. It was almost as though the deep hum was coming from within it. It felt like putting your hand on the bonnet of a Rolls-Royce with the engine running, except that the engine was a million times more powerful, yet even more quiet. He leaned forward, and put his head sideways on the desk-top, pressing his ear to the cold wood. The sound did seem louder. It was as if the contact made his head a part of the massive machine. The sound was inside his head and all around him. Thornton felt very tired.

A sharp knock on his office door made Thornton sit bolt

upright, and nervously shuffle through the papers on his desk. As he shouted 'Come in', he slipped the photographs back into the folder and turned it upside-down so that the title was hidden. An I.N.I. security guard in uniform entered the office with a sealed blue envelope. He placed it on Thornton's desk, and stood to attention behind it. It was a standard company envelope, with the message 'TELEX – URGENT' on the outside. Thornton reached for a brass letter-knife on his desk and slit it open.

'Just came in sir,' said the guard. 'Security said you'd want to see it straight away.'

Thornton was expressionless as his eyes scanned the ten-line message. It was from the security department's mobile unit in Winderwath. A verbatim report of a telephone conversation. He finished reading, and without speaking, raised his eyes to look outside again at the tangled mass of pipes, wires and cables which connected every building in the complex. Suddenly they all seemed to merge into a single grey blur.

'Will there be a reply sir?'

The guard's question jolted Thornton back to reality. 'No. That will be all.' The guard did a military about-turn and left.

Thornton leaned over to an intercom and pressed a button. 'Joan. Get me our security people in Manchester, will you? Then get me Mr Ffitch.'

Two hours later, with a confused and harassed taxi-driver waiting outside, Shilvers and Julia walked into the offices of the North-Western Forensic Science Laboratory on Oxford Road in Manchester. From the outside it was indistinguishable from any other building in the university. Shilvers rang a bell at reception and a commissionaire in grey uniform pushed back a glass partition.

'Is Professor Reade here?'

'Is he expecting you?'

'No, but he knows who I am. Could you say that Anthony Shilvers is downstairs?'

The commissionaire shuffled over to a desk and began to look in an enormous directory. Shilvers watched in growing frustration as his finger followed a long column of names, and heard the man muttering 'Reade, Reade' under his breath. 'Ah yes.' He picked up the handset from a small switchboard and poked out a four figure number with exaggerated care as though he had never used the telephone before. His eyes darted around as he waited another lifetime for an answer.

'I have a man in reception for Professor Reade. Name of . . .' He put his hand over the mouthpiece. 'What did you say your name was?'

'Shilvers. Anthony Shilvers.'

'Mr Chivers. In reception.' There was a long pause. The man started taking notes. 'Righto, I'll tell him. Right. Got that. Thank you.' He shuffled back to the counter. 'Professor Reade went out about an hour and a half ago with some visitors. They don't know whether he'll be back this afternoon.'

'Who were they? Did they have an appointment? Did they leave names?' Shilvers' voice was rising as his concern for Reade's safety mounted.

'I don't know as they did. Anyway . . .' the man was reacting to Shilvers' tone, 'I don't know that it would be appropriate to tell you. What's done here is confidential.' The commissionaire seemed to have second thoughts. 'Most of it is anyway.'

Julia stepped forward. 'Mr Shilvers is Professor Reade's brother-in-law. The Professor's sister, Mr Shilvers' wife, has been taken ill and is asking for him. We want to know where he is so that we can try to contact him.'

'Well why didn't you say so?' said the commissionaire. 'Let me look.'

Shilvers looked at Julia in amazement. Once again he was very impressed. The corners of his mouth turned down forming a compliment.

'Yes. Here we are. I remember now. Two men arrived for him at three o'clock. Didn't have an appointment. He came down and they went straight out.'

'What did they look like?'

The man looked confused again, and Julia added some further explanation. 'They could be other relatives. We're trying to work out whether someone else has taken him to the hospital.'

'Oh, I see. No, no, they didn't look to me like they knew him at all. Had to introduce themselves. Smartly dressed they were. But there was one thing . . .'

'What's that?' Shilvers' impatience was verging on rudeness.

'Something I especially noted. They were in a very smart car. Dark red it was. And something you don't see very often these days. They had a chauffeur.'

Shilvers reacted instantly. 'Wearing a brown uniform?'

'Yes, that's right. Is it family then?' Now the man was trying to be helpful, but Shilvers had turned away, his face very pale.

'Sounds like a messenger from Uncle Roger and Dan,' said Julia. 'Thanks very much indeed. Come on Tony.' She took Shilvers by the arm.

'Mr Dawson please.' With the taxi-driver from Westermouth still waiting, Shilvers and Julia had walked to a telephone box outside the laboratory, and dialled the number written in pencil on a crumpled piece of paper. There was a pause at the other end.

'This is Mr Dawson speaking. What's your number?'

'061 499 9834. That's 061 499 9834. It's a call box.'

'Please wait,' said the voice on the other end, and the line went dead.

Shilvers looked at his watch. Five minutes, Smedley had said. Shilvers wondered if it was Smedley answering the telephone himself, and calling back later from a more secure line. If it was not Smedley, but a colleague, he would also have to be in on the betrayal. It added to the risk. Still, Smedley had been right about Ffitch. Even now he could scarcely believe it was true. How the hell had Ffitch allowed himself to get mixed up in a thing like this? And with an organization like I.N.I.?

'Maybe it was the money,' he said aloud.

'What?' said Julia, who had been standing silently next to him.

'Sorry,' said Shilvers, 'I was miles away. I was wondering what made Ffitch throw in his lot with I.N.I. It must have been money, I suppose. It's a long way from the rest of the world up here. Maybe he just lost sight of reality.'

Julia remained silent. She had not liked Ffitch from the beginning, but she reflected that she had not known him in the days when he first met Shilvers. She had seen what he had turned into, and none of the revelations really surprised her.

'What happened to his wife and children?' asked Julia. 'Didn't you say he had two daughters?'

'Gone to live in Scotland, he told me. Which is odd, since it was he who came from Scotland, not her. She originally came from around here I think. Maybe that was part of it,' said Shilvers, 'maybe when the family split up it sent him a bit off his rocker.'

'Maybe,' said Julia. She did not think so.

Both jumped when the telephone bell rang. Shilvers picked it up instantly.

'Mr Shilvers?' said a more familiar voice.

'It is.'

'Dr Smedley. You called.'

'We have to meet,' said Shilvers. 'I've confirmed the information, and now it is very urgent that I receive more. I think the time in which I will be able to operate may be running out. I can be in your area in two hours.'

There was a silence. 'This line is secure, but the situation is now very dangerous. I will meet you at your cottage in two hours from now. I will approach by the cross-country route. Are you being followed?'

Christ, thought Shilvers, in the hurry and excitement he had not even checked.

'I don't know.'

'Then you probably are. Set off in another direction and try to lose them. Then come back here. If you're late, don't worry. I'll wait.'

The phone clicked and the line went dead. Shilvers waited for any further indication that the phone had been listened to.

There was no sound. He picked up the receiver and tapped the cradle twice. Nothing untoward. Outside the telephone box Shilvers looked around him. There was heavy traffic and many parked cars. It could be any of them. The couple got into the back seat of the taxi.

'This has cost you thirty-seven quid so far. Do you want to go back and double it?'

'No. We're heading towards North Wales.'

The taxi-driver turned to look at Shilvers as if to check that he was not actually raving mad. Saying nothing, he turned back and switched on the engine. As the car crawled through the south-western suburbs of Manchester, Shilvers shuffled down in his seat and kept a constant watch through the rear window. Julia said nothing. She understood.

Instinctively Shilvers was looking for a white Ford Escort, but he knew it was naïve to think they would use the same car twice. He wished that he was driving himself. How would this taxi-driver from a quiet and sleepy seaside town take to being told that they were being followed, and by people who would gladly kill them all if they thought it necessary? Shilvers was in no doubt that he would have to handle this carefully.

Eventually Shilvers decided that the beige-coloured Saab with three men inside had sat three vehicles behind them for too long to be coincidence and decided to test his suspicion. Waiting until they were nearly level with a narrow sidestreet, Shilvers leant forward and spoke quickly. 'Turn right here. Yes here, here.'

The taxi-driver reacted instinctively and wheeled the car round without warning. There was a blast on the horn from the car immediately behind. A second later and they were in the sidestreet.

'Christ almighty, are you daft or what?' said the driver. 'Shouting things at me like that you'll get us all killed.' Shilvers was too interested in what was going on behind to take much notice. He watched the Saab cruise by, and saw that both passengers had turned their heads to look down the sidestreet as they passed. Just before the car went out of sight, he saw the brake-lights go on, and the indicator flashing that it was pulling in.

'Sorry, friend,' said Shilvers. 'I suddenly remembered a friend of mine lives in this area, but this isn't the road after all. I think it's the one before. Can you do a right here?'

The taxi-driver had sunk into an indignant silence and was beginning to resign himself to do just as he was told, and collect a fat fare at the end of it all. He turned sharp right.

'Now left. First left.'

The car swung immediately left. Shilvers saw a tiny alleyway on the right of the road, leading probably to garages behind a row of suburban houses.

'Just pull in here a minute will you?' The taxi pulled in. 'Now bear with me a second. Could you just turn off your engine and lights?'

'Now what the bloody hell is going on?' The driver turned off the engine and turned round. 'What sort of a game are you playing, mate? This could be a mugging for all I know.'

Shilvers reached into his pocket and produced his wallet. He took out five ten-pound notes and gave them to the driver.

'Have this to be going on with. I'm sorry about all this. We can be off in a minute.' Shilvers turned round again to watch from the back window as the driver tucked the notes into a pouch underneath his seat. 'Lights are off are they?'

'They're off,' said the driver, resigned once more.

Five minutes passed before Shilvers saw the beige Saab, still with three men inside, cruise slowly past the narrow entrance at the end of the alleyway.

'There it is,' he said to Julia. 'We'll give it a few minutes longer.'

Three more minutes passed. Shilvers asked the driver to go ahead and turn around while he walked back to the corner. The driver shrugged and did as he was told. Shilvers looked carefully in every direction before waving the taxi forward to pick him up.

'Now we can be on our way,' he told the driver.

'Towards North Wales?'

'Hell no,' said Shilvers with a smile. 'Winderwath.'

CHAPTER TWENTY-SEVEN

Five minutes away from Winderwath, the sky was pitch dark and Julia was sound asleep, her head slumped on Shilvers' shoulder. For most of the journey he had gazed out of the window and watched day turn to dusk and into night, so that all he could see was the blur of trees and bushes as they dashed along the motorway, on to busy side roads, and eventually down narrow country lanes.

The many events of recent days filled his thoughts as the car ploughed on through mud and puddles towards Winderwath. He remembered his own drive along these roads, returning from Alf Penshall's funeral. How much had happened since then. This story. At some times he had thought it was the most outrageous thing he had ever heard in his life, and had even rebuked himself for wasting time on it. At others it seemed perfectly plausible that an industry which regarded itself as so far above the rules of behaviour governing mere mortals might feel justified in taking any actions it thought necessary. Now, with luck, he was within hours of finding out the truth, and being able to prove it.

He thought about Smedley. It had been an enormous piece of luck meeting him. Had Smedley already made up his mind to blow what was happening before Shilvers came along? Was he just waiting for the right moment? Even now there was something about him which seemed as though it might not be entirely on the level. On a sudden instinct he told the driver to pull over at a telephone box at the side of the road. Julia woke up as he started to get out of the car.

'Are we here? What's happening Tony?'

'No, not yet. I'm just making a phone call.'

'Who to?'

'To my life insurance agent.'

In the call box Shilvers dialled his London flat and listened to his own voice on the answering machine. He waited for the tone and then spoke clearly.

'This is Anthony Shilvers on Monday 15th December. Should I meet what looks like an accidental death within the next few days, please be assured that it is not accidental, and begin enquiries with one Dr Smedley, who works for Imperial Nuclear Industries at Dounscraig. After that try Roger Thornton, and Dan Maddox. They will claim to know nothing, but one of them will be guilty.'

As he returned to the car Shilvers realized he had been melodramatic. Who would even listen to his message if he was the victim of a car accident? No one. Then again, maybe Frank at the *Sentinel* might. Anyway, Shilvers felt better having done it.

'On to Winderwath,' he told the driver.

Two minutes later the taxi was fast approaching the village green. It was a narrow country road with no space for two cars to pass each other. The only other way out of the village was along the two footpaths running up the hills on either side. A real cul-de-sac, thought Shilvers.

Shilvers was reaching for his wallet to pay the driver when suddenly the car braked hard and the tyres squealed.

'What the . . .?' Shilvers and the taxi-driver shouted at the same time.

'Oh shit,' said Julia as she recognized more quickly what was happening. Twenty yards in front of them perhaps forty men were standing across the road. At their head, right in the centre, Julia could just make out the enormous silhouette of Bernard Roache. The group was advancing on the car.

'What the hell is going on?' said the driver.

'Don't talk. Just reverse. Hard, hard. As fast as you can.'

The taxi-driver slammed his car into reverse. The wheels spun and there was smoke and burning rubber as the car leapt backwards. As it did so the crowd, led by Roache, broke into a run.

'Stop them. Stop them for Christ's sake.' It was Roache.

'Do a turn. Turn right around,' Shilvers was shouting.

The driver turned the steering-wheel hard and the car lurched on to the grass of the village green. He changed into first gear and pressed the accelerator hard. Again the wheels spun. This time the car did not move. The crowd of men was now only thirty yards from the car.

'Lock the door Julia,' shouted Shilvers, and his hand went to his pocket where he held the handle of the revolver, releasing the safety catch with his thumb. Still the wheels turned and Shilvers could see and smell smoke rising from the rear tyres. With the mob only feet away, suddenly they took hold and the car sprang forward, back on to the tarmac. Shilvers saw Roache's snarling face lunge for the side window as the car gathered speed back towards the only route out of the village square. The taxi was twenty yards from it, and beginning to open a gap between itself and the still running men, when a large brown car appeared at the junction ahead of them and stopped. Julia was looking through the windscreen.

'Ffitch, that bastard Ffitch.'

The taxi-driver rammed on his brakes and the car shuddered to a halt, stalling inches away from the side of Ffitch's car. Immediately Shilvers grabbed Julia by the hand and leapt out of his door. Now the revolver was out of his pocket.

He practically dragged Julia round to the front of Ffitch's car, just as the large figure in a camel-hair coat was emerging from the driver's door. Roache and the crowd of men were ten feet away when Shilvers raised the revolver and shouted.

'Stop! Stop you bastard or I'll blow your head off, so help me I will.' The men stopped in their tracks. Ffitch was walking slowly round to the front of his car. Shilvers waved the gun briefly in his direction.

'That goes for you too George. Don't think I wouldn't, because you know me better.'

'I don't doubt it for a minute,' said Ffitch calmly. He stopped in the brightness from his own car headlights. 'But equally you should recognize that some of us have little to lose. If you leave this village, I'm going to spend the few years I have left in jail, and that, believe it or don't, is the least of my worries. You have to believe me when I tell you that dying here and now is preferable.'

Now Shilvers pointed the gun direct at Ffitch's forehead. In the corner of his eye he could see looks of apprehension on the faces of several of the villagers. He recognized the postman, Harry, who had visited his cottage with Roache that night. None of them would move for the moment.

'I told you what would happen if you kept on poking around didn't I?' It was the aggressive voice of Roache. 'You've come up here, and you've stirred up trouble. More trouble than you know how to handle, even with that little toy you're holding.' Roache slowly advanced towards Shilvers. 'We're country people. We've been around guns all our lives. I can tell a fake when I see one, even in this light.'

Without hesitating, Shilvers swung around and fired two bullets into the ground next to Roache's feet. Julia clutched her ears and screamed as the group of men retreated half a dozen steps. Roache yelled out, 'Hold it!'

They stopped. Behind his back, out of Shilvers' line of vision, Roache gestured to the men behind him. Waiting for Shilvers' attention to be concentrated on Ffitch, Harry the postman edged sideways away from the group into the darkness of the village green.

'Tony for Jesus' sake.' Once again it was the soft Glaswegian drawl of Ffitch. 'We must be able to work this out. None of these people wants any bloodshed. They just want their livelihoods. They're protecting their families. No one wants to hurt anybody here.'

'Oh sure,' said Shilvers. 'Like nobody wanted to hurt Alf Penshall. And nobody wanted to hurt his brother George. Or Thomkins. Or Parsons. Or Aldwich, Erly and Morrison. Or about thirty others and their families who have just been wiped off the map for the sake of these people's livelihoods and their families. What about *their* livelihoods? Eh? What did you care about Alf Penshall?'

'Look,' said Ffitch. Shilvers was glancing round all the time to make sure the men were all standing still. 'Tony. You don't understand. If you only knew.'

'O.K. Tell me about it, George. Tell me how much you got paid to dump Penshall's busted-apart body in a country lane, and God knows what else over the years. Tell me in round figures, then maybe I will understand. Maybe it was your livelihood too. Maybe it was your family you were concerned about?'

Ffitch was silent. No one moved. For a few seconds Shilvers could hear the sound of the ocean in the far distance, the strong wind still beating the waves against the headland.

'You're nearer the truth than you can guess,' said Ffitch softly. Shilvers craned his head to hear him better, and as he did so he felt a movement in the air behind his head and wheeled around. As he turned and Julia lurched after him he heard a thud, and saw Harry falling to his knees, blood already streaming from an open wound at the top of his head. Behind him Shilvers could make out the shape of another man, standing still, a thick stump of wood in his hand.

'Smedley.'

In the same second Roache let out an appalling yell and hurled himself towards Shilvers and Julia. Shilvers raised his hand and squeezed the trigger twice. Roache was so close that Julia saw the explosions as the bullets ripped into his chest. He sunk to his knees but his momentum carried him on so that he crashed into Julia and Shilvers, spattering great globules of his blood over them both. Julia recoiled in disgust and horror. Then all was quiet as the light fell on Roache's face, staring vacantly up into the moonless sky.

'Let's get out of here,' said a voice in the crowd of men, and together they edged backwards into the darkness and scattered. Shilvers heard an engine start up, and looked to see the wheels of the taxi spin, then grip. He made no move to stop the car from speeding away. Now Shilvers looked down and saw Harry lying face downwards in the mud, thick blood oozing from his head, and Smedley still standing next to him with the club in his hand.

Ffitch stood still, staring blankly at Shilvers. Shilvers lowered the gun. Taking Julia and Smedley by the arm he walked past Ffitch towards the brown car. He opened both passenger doors on that side and gestured for them to get in. Ffitch had not turned around, but just stood, looking across the green towards the sea. The wind was whipping up and the surf was louder. He was still standing there as Shilvers reversed the car and turned the wheel, so that the headlights silhouetted him against the blackness, and then left him standing alone in the night. Seconds later the brown car was heading out of the village.

'O.K., start talking Dr Smedley. And if you give me just one tiny piece of bullshit I'll splatter your brains across the countryside. What has happened to all those people in the accidents and their families? What have you bastards done with them all?'

In the back seat, Smedley coughed a deep chesty cough before answering.

'The real problems began about ten years ago.' He spoke in a calm and quiet voice so that Shilvers had to strain to hear him over the roaring engine. 'As the reprocessing work got under way and more experimentation to try to find ways of reducing the risks of spent nuclear fuel, all sorts of techniques were talked about, some were experimented with. But you have to understand. This was the frontier of technology, handling the most dangerous substances known to mankind. We didn't really know what the hell we were doing. You could say we don't know now in some ways.'

As Smedley talked, Shilvers drove as fast as he could away from Winderwath into the blackness. He did not know where, nor did the road or the direction register in his mind. All became a blur as he concentrated on Smedley's words.

'You've seen those pictures of servicemen in the Fifties standing looking at the mushroom clouds. It seems ridiculously irresponsible now, but you have to put yourself in the shoes of the scientists at the time. We had no way of knowing what the harmful effects would be. It was the same with neutralizing radioactive waste. How can we tell what we've achieved unless we go near the stuff?'

'So you use people as human guinea pigs, just like they did in the Fifties?'

'No. In no way.' Smedley was indignant and emphatic. 'But doing all these experiments, moving all this harmful stuff around, there were bound to be accidents. There weren't very many, but there were some. Some people got hurt, and it was difficult to know what to do with them.'

'What was wrong with sending them to hospital and informing the public?'

'Because if we had done that we would have been closed down in a week. Most politicians haven't got the bottle to accept the risks that their own policies make necessary. They are the ones that demand the cheap energy, that want to win votes by cutting fuel bills, that want to take away the power of the coal miners. But then when there's a problem because they're pushing too hard, they're the first to squeal "enquiry". The one thing everyone in I.N.I. agreed on at the time was that the politicians should be kept out of it. And they were.'

'None of them knew?'

'Very few. But that doesn't mean their civil servants didn't. We couldn't have done what we have had to do without Whitehall behind us. They could see the necessities just as easily as we could.'

'And just like you, they know better than elected representatives. Democracy can't always be relied on to do the best thing, therefore we, the ruling classes, feel entitled to go around governments when we feel we know better what is good for the country than they do. That's the rationale of military dictatorships all around the world.'

'Don't be naïve, Mr Shilvers,' said Smedley. 'You want to turn the switch and have the light come on just like everyone else. But you don't want the bad news that comes with it.'

Shilvers thought his temper would explode, but he restrained himself. He had not yet found out what he wanted to know.

'Well. Get to the point. What did you do to the casualties of all this fine work?'

There was a long silence. Shilvers looked at Julia. Her eyes were fixed in their gaze through the windscreen. She did not return his glance, but looked as though she might be in shock.

'To be honest, if I tell you, you won't believe me. So I suggest we find somewhere safe to spend the night, and tomorrow morning I'll take you to see everything you want to know.'

CHAPTER TWENTY-EIGHT

Shilvers woke up still at the wheel of the car. His seat was pushed back and Julia's head rested on his lap, her feet curled up on the front passenger seat. A heavy coat was pulled up around her ears, but her breath turned to mist in the cold. Over his shoulder Shilvers could see the rumpled shape of Smedley asleep on the back seat. He wiped away some condensation from the side-window to reveal, just inches away from the car, the wall of a barn.

Aware of the dangers of stopping overnight at any public place, they had pulled into a field and parked behind a farm-building. Shilvers wiped away the mist from the windscreen. They seemed to be miles from anywhere. He stretched, and Julia stirred.

His mind wandered over the trauma of the previous night, and for a moment he could hardly decide whether it had all been a bad dream or whether it had been real. He had shot someone, Bernard Roache. Probably he had killed him. It was self-defence; Roache was at the head of a large and angry gang, who looked bent on murder. It was clear cut. Then again, thought Shilvers, how would that sound in court, should all this ever end up there? The truth was that he had seen no weapon in Roache's hand. Although a big and threatening man, he was unarmed and Shilvers had shot him with a gun; a gun he did not even have a licence to keep.

Would the police even now be patrolling the countryside looking for Ffitch's car? Shilvers doubted it. The villagers were unlikely to have alerted anyone other than Charlton, and he was undoubtedly already a part of the conspiracy. There remained the taxi-driver, who would undoubtedly have gone directly to the police. But Shilvers was increasingly convinced that Penshall had been right. The local police must all be involved. There was no way, otherwise, that the disappearances could have been kept so secret for so long. It was much more likely that Ffitch or one of the villagers had tipped off I.N.I. and they were handling the situation. On their record to date they would have no trouble disposing of Roache's body, and having done so they must now be looking for Shilvers. If they found him, there was now no doubt about what they would do.

Shilvers realized that he did not care about the legal consequences of the killing. Neither, if he was honest, did he care much about having taken Roache's life. The discovery surprised him. The man was dead and he was probably a murderer, and all because Roache was standing between him and a good story. Yet Roache had indisputably been abetting a situation in which men and their families were vanishing, presumably being killed. Had he succeeded in getting rid of Shilvers, that situation would continue. At least now, when Shilvers was able to blow the story open, all that would have to end. And that time was near.

Smedley had said that he could not tell him the truth last night, because Shilvers would not believe it. After all that had happened, what could there be left that would surprise him? He smiled at the irony. In the last few weeks he had met a man who had told him the most fantastic tale he had ever heard and who had been murdered for doing so. He had talked to the man's wife, who was in one moment distraught, in the next calm, in the next had vanished, and had then returned behaving as though nothing had happened. He had found out that one of his best friends was an accomplice to murder, and he had killed a man himself. Now here was Smedley saying he could not tell him the real story because it was too incredible.

A shuffle and yawn in the back of the car indicated that Smedley was waking. Fifteen minutes later, with the heater on full blast, the big brown car edged out of the field and cautiously on to the country road. Now Smedley was giving directions. First they headed back towards Winderwath, then along what seemed a maze of side roads which took them back inland, and then north, parallel to the coast. After twenty miles of heading in one direction then another, Shilvers began to feel concerned.

'Where the hell are we going? Back to Dounscraig?'

'Not on your life. We're not far away now. Take this lane on the right.' Now the car was twisting and turning over small hills and through valleys. Five miles further on they reached a crossroads. The left-hand turn had a sign reading 'Unsuitable for motor vehicles'.

'It's left here.'

'If we get stuck we'll all be in trouble,' said Shilvers, nevertheless obeying the instruction.

Half a mile further on Smedley spoke again. 'Stop at this next gate.' Fifty yards ahead a clump of trees flanked the road, and in the deepest part, on the left side, was a wooden gate. Shilvers drew up beside it and Smedley got out and opened the gate, then got back into the car.

'Drive on down this path, through the trees. You'll come to another gate on your right.' Shilvers looked around him. As the car emerged from the trees he looked over miles of barren moorland in every direction.

'This must be the remotest part of England. Where the hell are we?'

'An Ordnance Survey map wouldn't help you,' said Smedley. 'Stop at this gate.' In a dry-stone wall a rickety wooden gate displayed a notice: 'PRIVATE PROPERTY. KEEP OUT.' Once again Smedley got out of the car. As he walked to the front, Shilvers stared at the ghastly disfigurement which made half of Smedley's face totally expressionless.

To Shilvers' astonishment Smedley removed a brick from the stone wall and took what looked like a credit card from his pocket. He inserted the card in a gap in the wall, and the gate swung open.

'Neat,' said Shilvers, as Smedley got back in the car. In the mirror behind him he watched the gate swing shut.

'It's about a mile down this track where we're headed. Prepare yourselves for a surprise,' said Smedley.

Now Shilvers and Julia were craning their necks to see over the brow of each of the many small hills on the road before them.

Shilvers noticed that the road surface had improved, and it now seemed as though they were back on a country highway, except that they were in the middle of nowhere.

Ahead there was a blind bend and Shilvers had to slow down to ten miles an hour to get around it. As they did so, the couple had to shield their eyes from the bright winter sun. On the horizon they could just make out the silhouette of a village. They looked at each other. Julia shrugged her shoulders. One hundred yards further on they could see the thatches of tiny cottages and the thin smoke curling up from red-brick chimneys in the rows of perfectly matched buildings. To Julia it looked like a model village from a picture postcard.

'Drive straight on into the main street,' said Smedley. Shilvers continued at ten miles an hour. There were small groups of people walking on the pavements, a mother with a pram talking to a shopkeeper, a telephone box and letter box outside the post office. Everything seemed perfectly normal, and yet something made Julia feel uncomfortable.

'It's the prettiest village I've ever seen,' said Julia, straining her eyes across the road at a group of four people who had stopped their conversation to stare at the car. She fell silent as one of the men left the group and began to walk towards the car. As he got closer Shilvers noticed that he walked with a slight limp. Shilvers looked again at the men he had been talking to. He saw that one of them had one leg of his trousers pinned up against his waist. He supported himself on crutches. Now the first man was coming nearer. Julia focused on his face, and put her hand to her mouth.

When he was only a few paces from the car, Shilvers could see that where the man's face should have been was a mass of discoloured and disfigured skin. One hole roughly in the middle was where his nose should have been, and a tight eyelid stood above a misshapen orb which was a single eye. Beneath the nose, where his mouth should have been, the face faded sharply away into a neck which was craggy and swollen. On top of his head, a few tufts of grey hair looked as though they had been planted at random. As the man came level with the passenger window, Julia buried her face in her hands. Despite himself Shilvers looked away in horror.

Behind them, Smedley wound down the window.

'It's all right Mr Morrison. These two are visitors. Everything is all right.'

Shilvers and Julia heard an unearthly croak, and from the corner of his eye Shilvers could see the man nodding his head. What little there was of the bottom of his face moved in something like a smile. Shilvers looked away again.

'Is that Mr Erly and Mr Crane with you?' said Smedley. The man nodded again. 'All right. See you later.' The man grunted again and limped back towards the group in the distance. Now Shilvers could see that they, like Morrison, had grotesquely scarred and discoloured heads, like hideous masks stretched over their skulls, squashing ordinary features beneath the tightness. Shilvers' eyes screwed up, emphasizing the deepening lines on his face, as he tried to understand.

'We can get out of the car and walk around if you like,' said Smedley, opening his door. Shilvers followed him and went round to Julia's door. At first she sat still, looking at him. He took her by the hand and helped her to her feet.

'It's perfectly all right,' said Smedley, 'everyone here is harmless, and they know me. After all, I lived here myself for four months.'

As they crossed the road to a row of half a dozen shops, Julia saw a mother and two small children on the other pavement. As they approached she was relieved to see that they were perfectly normal. Julia prepared to greet the woman, but she and both children walked past, eyes staring to the front and looking neither left nor right. It was as though they had not seen her.

On the left as they walked there was a small butcher's shop. A few paces on Shilvers and Julia turned to look in the window. Julia felt her knees about to give way and Shilvers supported her. It was the traditional butcher's shop, with a man in blue striped apron and straw hat chopping meat. But as he turned to look at them they saw that he too was revoltingly scarred. To Julia, looking through the shop window, his face looked like a molten mess of purple flesh, with holes crudely cut where eyes, nose and mouth should have been. Again the lower jaw seemed to be missing altogether, but Julia could see a row of top teeth below what should have been a top lip. She closed her eyes tight and shuddered.

'What have you bastards done?' said Shilvers. 'What on earth have you done?' As the repulsive images of horrifying faces crowded in on him, Shilvers thought he could feel and hear the deep growl of power vibrating through the ground beneath his feet. He looked down, and imagined for a moment that the sound was reverberating into his feet, up through his body, and into his head. Again he felt at one with the massive and overwhelming power, which seemed to draw energy from deep within the earth itself. His head seemed to spin, and he felt on the brink of swooning.

Then Shilvers noticed a woman emerge from one of the neat row of cottages which fronted on to the street in between the shops. She had her back to Shilvers, but there was something familiar about her. She had a long grey coat and carried a shopping basket. She closed her door behind her and turned to cross the road. Shilvers recognized her at the same time as Julia grabbed his arm and pointed her out.

'Yes,' said Shilvers, 'Mrs Penshall.' He stepped forward to greet her. 'Mrs Penshall. How are you?' From staring directly ahead, Mrs Penshall turned slowly to look at Shilvers. Her expression seemed totally blank and vacant.

'Mrs Penshall. Do you remember me? It's Anthony Shilvers. I came to see you at your house on the day after your husband's funeral. Do you remember?'

Mrs Penshall's expression did not alter. After a few seconds she spoke. Her voice was calm, and yet mechanical.

'Ah yes. Mr Shilvers. How very nice to see you. I must hurry now, I have my shopping to get. Good day to you.' She turned her head away and walked on. Shilvers called after her.

'Mrs Penshall. Just a moment. I'd like to ask you . . .'

She did not look back. She just walked steadily away from the small group, and entered the butcher's shop.

'Are you beginning to get the idea?' asked Smedley.

'I'm sure as hell not,' said Julia.

Shilvers looked at Smedley and his eyes narrowed. 'I think I am.'

Smedley looked around him. 'I can take you to see Alf's brother George if you like, and his wife and kids. George had his accident at the same time as me, except my injuries were not as serious. That's why he had to stay. I was lucky.'

'But he'll never get away?'

'No,' said Smedley, 'not ever.'

'And his wife and kids? Are they doped or brainwashed, or whatever it is you do to the normal ones so they won't try to get away?'

'Yes,' said Smedley without apparent emotion, 'I'm afraid they are.'

'And will be for ever?'

'That's right.'

Shilvers looked at Julia. She was staring into space, and then she looked back at him. Her mouth dropped open as at last she fully understood what was happening. 'Oh my God.'

'How many people live in the village?' asked Shilvers.

'About two hundred and fifty. There are forty-five former workers who had accidents of one sort or another, then there are their families, sometimes even aunts and uncles. There are a few others who seemed unstable and looked likely to spill the beans. They are of course under permanent sedation like the relatives. Those who've been in the accidents are only occasionally sedated.'

'And they just run their own little community here? The butcher, the baker, the bloody candlestick-maker. And nobody knows that they are here except I.N.I.?'

'That's right, and the relevant Whitehall departments. Home

Office, Department of Energy, Defence. We have a nuclear police force which collects anyone who is so close to the family that they won't believe a disappearance story, and we spread the word to more distant friends and relatives that a great opportunity suddenly came up with I.N.I. in Australia and the family has emigrated.'

'And presumably the families and friends then get occasional letters from Australia?'

Smedley nodded. 'You catch on very quickly, Mr Shilvers.'

'But surely some people must get suspicious. What happens when old friends plan to visit them in Australia or something like that?' asked Julia.

'I.N.I. intercepts letters from this country to Australia, and we have a sophisticated system of discouraging such propositions. We'll send a slightly unfriendly letter. It's amazing how few people will pursue even lifelong friendships if they think they are getting the cold shoulder. If the person here persists we might invent an illness in the family, or say that the family is about to move to another district. Or even that the family is thinking of coming back. There's no end of plausible excuses for a fertile mind. And if and when friends or relatives get too suspicious, as a last resort they might also end up here. Unfortunately they too have to be drugged, but that has happened surprisingly little.'

'And the telephone?'

'Well, there are amazingly clear lines to Australia now. You could almost believe you were speaking to someone as near as Cumbria.'

Shilvers paused to try to take in what he was hearing. Surely even I.N.I. could not believe they would get away with this indefinitely?

'The police, the authorities, what about the people from the nearby villages or even ramblers? What about them?'

'That was a problem at first because this area is one of particular geological interest. There's a fault in the rock which means the whole district is surrounded by a naturally occurring sheer wall, and beyond that is a fence and signs saying this is a restricted area. The way we came in is the only way by road, and that has the security measures you saw, and some that you did not. As for the rest, M.O.D. have told the R.A.F. and civil authorities that this is the site of a top secret underground nuclear research establishment with a model village on the surface for camouflage. All aircraft are instructed to keep clear.'

Shilvers' mind was still racing over the difficulties in trying to keep something like this a secret.

'But what happens when the ones with the scars try to get away? You crush them under earth movers I suppose?'

'No,' Smedley paused, 'and we don't shoot them either.' He waited for the significance of his remark to sink in. 'Hard though it may be for you to believe, no one who is scarred like this wants to go back into the real world. You've seen a couple of these people. If you looked like that, would you?' Shilvers could scarcely imagine. 'I've got an idea myself what it feels like to be stared at wherever I go. Think what it would be like for these people, hideously deformed as most of them are.'

'Which is why they are prepared to co-operate in making phone calls to their relatives pretending that everything is perfect far away down under in sunny Australia.'

'Precisely.'

'And that suits I.N.I. down to the bloody ground.'

'It does,' said Smedley.

'But what about the phone box and the letter box? What happens when one of the sedated community tries to call up friends or relatives?'

'Mere props, I'm afraid. It adds to the atmosphere of normality which I.N.I. tries very hard to create.'

'Normality?' Shilvers was incredulous. 'You people must be the sickest . . .' Shilvers stopped talking as he saw two women walking down the pavement towards them, one of them old, perhaps sixty, the other about thirty. The younger of the two was attractive and smartly dressed. Once again both seemed to be in a daze, but as Shilvers looked he thought there was something about the older woman that was familiar. It had been years, very many years. It was difficult because her blank expression altered her, and it was such a long time since he had seen her, but yes, it was.

'Mrs Ffitch.' The women were now level with him, and he repeated her name. The older woman did not turn or respond to his call. The younger merely looked at him with a blank stare. They walked on.

'Yes,' said Smedley. 'That's George Ffitch's wife and one of his daughters.'

'Well what the hell are they doing here? They're supposed to be in Scotland.'

'You see how ready people are to believe such stories about people they know?' said Smedley. 'Unfortunately for them, four years ago George Ffitch heard a rumour about some of the accidents at I.N.I. and began making enquiries. He did rather well as a matter of fact, and started to get a bit too near to the truth. But on this occasion I.N.I. decided that if they took him in, he would eventually be replaced by another inquisitive journalist. So they decided that Mr Ffitch would be more useful left outside, warning us if anyone else came snooping around, and putting them off the scent. It's a service I'm told he has performed a number of times. He's very plausible.'

Shilvers shook his head. At last all became clear and he understood why Ffitch had behaved the way he had. He was, as he had hinted in the village, afraid for the lives of his family. For Shilvers, it was almost a relief.

'So I.N.I. kidnapped Ffitch's wife and daughters, forcing him to keep quiet?'

'Yes. More unfortunately still the other daughter whom you haven't seen today managed to avoid her sedation on one occasion and tried to escape. She became I.N.I.'s only fatality here. It's all worked remarkably efficiently considering.'

'So if it's such a marvellous solution, why the hell have you brought us here to blow it all to the world,' asked Julia.

'Good God Miss Somers,' said Smedley calmly, 'don't you understand yet?' Shilvers and Julia turned to look at him. 'You probably won't believe me but I really am sorry.' Now he was gazing far into the distance, his voice fading. Had their vision been able to penetrate the shaded lenses of his spectacles, Shilvers and Julia would have seen Dr Smedley's disfigured eyes filling up with tears. 'You see, they own me, just in the same way that they own Ffitch.' Once again he turned to face the couple, and for a moment Shilvers noticed a distinctive nervous twitch irritating the scarred tissue on the corner of Smedley's left eye. 'He had a wife and daughters. I only have a daughter. She works for I.N.I.'

'And she has been threatened?' asked Julia.

'No,' said Smedley. 'Far from it, she has been recently promoted so that she is within easy reach should I fail to do as I have been told. It is I who have been threatened. You see I too recently made the same mistake Penshall made. Though I still believe in the nuclear industry, I felt they were going too far, too fast, and that the cost might be too high. Like him I made the mistake of talking about it.' Now Smedley's voice and mind once again seemed distant. 'I.N.I. has already taken away from me just about everything I have which could be of personal interest. My daughter is the only thing left, and now they are threatening that they will take her away too unless I carry out their instructions. Mr Shilvers, Miss Somers, please forgive me.'

Smedley said nothing more, but shrugged his shoulders and turned away, walking slowly down the pavement in the direction of the car. Shilvers put his hand in his coat pocket and gripped the handle of the pistol. Julia looked at him without speaking.

'Your guess is as good as mine, but it doesn't sound wonderful.'

Seconds later the question was answered by the deep growl of heavy vehicles in the distance. Shilvers and Julia looked upwards and strained their eyes to focus on the point where the moors met the grey sky. The air vibrated with the rumbling noise, and at last they saw them. First one, then another and another. A convoy of five of I.N.I.'s military vehicles was heading down the only road into the village, blocking any chance of escape.

CHAPTER TWENTY-NINE

'How the hell did we let things get this far? Why didn't we know they would end up in the village?' Gold's clenched fist came down hard on the table, blowing clouds of dust from the long-neglected desk up into the air.

Jacqueline Smart was sitting bolt upright in her chair, trying her best not to be intimidated by Gold's outburst.

'We knew that I.N.I. intended to set them up, but we assumed that it was to get them back into the plant. None of our operatives thought there was any possibility of them being taken to the village, least of all by my father.' Jacqueline was genuinely confused and concerned. 'I have no idea whatever how they can have persuaded him to go along with it. It's just not his style, not his department.' Still she was trying not to let her concern about her father cloud her judgement. 'There is no reason to take them to the village. By any rational analysis it's a very stupid thing to do.'

'Rational analysis?' Gold's voice was even louder than before. 'You've been on the inside there for five years. You're supposed to be a trusted intelligence officer, confided in by top management. You've even been promoted so you're right next to the bloody Chief Executive, and you're talking to me about rational analysis? I don't want to know about rational analysis. What I want is inside information and that is the entire purpose of your existence, and the years and years we have expended on getting this operation right. Now we have to be taken by surprise by something like this. By a second-rate investigative reporter.'

Jacqueline knew there was little to be gained by pointing out how unreasonable Gold was being. She had managed to keep up with every move inside I.N.I. Now they had acted totally unpredictably, and she was being blamed.

As James Gold studied the file and photographs of the Shilvers surveillance, Jacqueline Smart looked around her at the walls of the prefabricated hut which had been the local base of the Direct Action group since long before she had joined it five years before. The ghastly skulls on the posters which roared their anti-nuclear message and which she had found so persuasive when she had been recruited into the organization suddenly seemed hollow and empty. Now that it was nearly over, her time spent inside I.N.I., working her way up the ranks and into the trust of the management, seemed like someone else's past. It had been a challenging and schizophrenic existence. Even her own father, a colleague at Dounscraig had no idea what she did, either officially or unofficially. She had traded on the endemic secrecy of the nuclear establishment to keep her own cover.

I.N.I. had paid her to keep an eye on protest groups like this one, and nosey individuals like Shilvers, and had given her all the best surveillance facilities to do so. That included cars, helicopters, and all the most sophisticated telescopic and photographic equipment available anywhere in the world. She had given I.N.I. the occasional piece of inside information about the less serious protest groups like Greenpeace and Friends of the Earth, just to keep them happy. Meanwhile she had used the facilities they had given her to find out about I.N.I.'s operations for her group, which she believed was the only one with any chance of bringing about a radical reverse in the nuclear establishment. The reason was that unlike the others it was prepared to take direct and, if necessary, violent action. Though the covert nature of her own activity meant that she saw little of it, she knew that her group was the only one with the funds, the training and the will to intervene physically with force as and when the situation demanded it. That time seemed as though it might have arrived.

Now Jacqueline recalled the small publicity successes the organization had been able to win because of the tiny bits of information she had been able to provide. They had seemed like great successes then, vindicating the enormous effort she was going to on the organization's behalf.

In the long silence Jacqueline remembered her own disbelief when she first learned about the existence of the village. Ironically it had been her father, who was totally loyal to the nuclear industry, who had unwittingly given her the information. After the accident she had been told that he was to convalesce at a special installation in Kansas. When he had returned after four months he seemed reluctant to discuss what it had been like. Then one day she had overheard him speaking on the telephone at his home to the Dounscraig management. She had heard it all.

Now she remembered the astonishment and wonder in the organization when she had passed the information back. How fêted she had been then, and what a contrast it was to the way she was being treated now. She recalled the group's elaborate plans to locate the community, and then all the trouble they had gone to in order to choose precisely the right moment to reveal the news to the world. They had selected the date of an international convention designed to boost the reputation of the industry across the developed world, and to persuade the developing world to buy yet more of the hardware of nuclear energy. That conference was due to meet in London in two months' time, and the Direct Action group had planned to use its military capability to bring a selected group of the world's press and television to the village on the day of its opening. The plans had been careful and painstaking, but there was now a risk that they had been overtaken by events, overtaken in fact by the man Gold was now calling a second-rate investigative journalist.

It especially angered her that her competence appeared to be in question. In fact she had been tuned in to Shilvers' appearance on the scene from the very first moment. Penshall was one of the workers on whom I.N.I. kept an occasional watch because informers from the village had reported that he had voiced some disquiet. As luck would have it Penshall was being watched on the day of the first visit to Shilvers. She had delayed telling I.N.I. for several hours but had of course reported the incident to Gold straight away. He had ordered continued monitoring and she had been in charge of carrying it out. He had also ordered, without her knowledge, that Shilvers' car tyres be slashed as a warning to him to keep away. When she had heard about it she had been angry at the clumsiness, but had said nothing.

How had he managed to discover so quickly what it had taken her so long to discover? And what was her own father doing bringing the couple to the village? She found it frustrating that she did not know the answers. Jacqueline resisted the temptation to point out to Gold that the man he was deriding had managed to find out in a matter of weeks what the organization had taken several years to put together. This was not the right moment. There was a long silence before Jacqueline spoke.

'We ought to act now. Time is very short.'

Gold looked directly at her. His piercing eyes screamed his anger, anger made worse by the knowledge that she was not properly to blame, and yet he had blamed her. He was acting unreasonably and he blamed her for making him do so. So he was angry.

'Right,' he said at last. 'I will summon the others. We go.'

CHAPTER THIRTY

'There had better be a damned good explanation for this. I'm supposed to be briefing the Secretary of State for his annual speech to Chief Police Officers.' Sir Roger Greaves briskly unpacked the heavy files from his Home Office issue briefcase and placed it beside him on the floor. At his side were Sir Clive Banner from the Department of Energy and Sir James Connor, recently appointed Permanent Secretary at Defence. Across the wide mahogany conference table sat Dan Maddox and Roger Thornton.

There was only one other person in the room. Sitting alone at the end of the table, conspicuous by his dejected demeanour and shabby clothes, was the local Member of Parliament Roland Dixon.

The two men from I.N.I. glanced at one other, each apparently reluctant to be the first to speak.

'Well? What's it all about? What's so urgent that we all have to drop everything and coming hurtling up to this godforsaken . . .?'

'We have run into some problems with Project Nine Hundred,' Thornton interrupted.

'And with security at the village. We've got a problem there too.'

'Good God,' said Sir James Connor. 'What the hell has gone wrong?'

'There's a safety scare at Project Nine Hundred. There've been some problems. Dr Smedley, the Chief Scientist in charge, came to us a while ago and said he thought something was seriously wrong. He said he wanted to shut the thing down for tests.'

'You haven't let him?' asked Sir Clive. His question implied that no one could be so stupid as to have done so, with the possible exception of the two men in front of him.

'No of course not. But he's been very difficult and we've had to put a lot of pressure on him. We have a powerful lever, but things in the project itself are getting rather out of hand.'

'Out of hand?' said Connor. The other two mandarins looked at him, irritated at the inexperience of the newcomer.

'At first we didn't take the safety warning seriously. Smedley has been neurotic since his accident eighteen months ago. Understandable really. We thought he was just being oversensitive. But recently there have been unmistakable problems, some specific incidents we cannot explain, and the rest of his staff are asking for a shutdown urgently.'

'Now look.' Sir Roger Greaves' tone of authority derived from many years of being in unquestioned charge of all about him. 'Whitehall has stuck its neck out a very long way for I.N.I. A very long way over a good many years. We have not done so because of our untarnished admiration for the simple beauty of your industry. We have done so because you have promised us this project, you have promised us that it will be a major international success and revenue earner, and you have promised to deliver it by this spring. We badly need this kind of success if we are to silence the small-minded people who are calling for closer scrutiny of your troublesome little industry. Why on earth else would we have acquiesced to your request, endorsed I might say by a certain former Secretary of State for Energy, to set up this ghastly village in the first place?'

At the end of the table Roland Dixon looked still more dejected and did not speak. Greaves was glowering across the table, his hands clasped in front of him, when the rumble came. It began long and low in the distance and became louder and nearer, its approach monitored in the widening and terrified eyes of the civil servants.

'What the devil?' The expletive was interrupted by the crash of shattering glass as the wall of windows on one side of the conference room smashed inwards.

'For God's sake!' All six men groped around like drunkards looking for something fixed to the floor for stability. Thornton and Maddox had thrown themselves face downwards and were covering their heads with their hands. As glass splintered around them each caught the fearful look in the other's eye.

'Oh my God,' whispered Maddox, and both men knew.

Moments later the movement stopped and was followed by complete silence. The lights were out and the room was in darkness. There were groans as slowly the six men got to their feet. As they recovered themselves the door burst open and an I.N.I. security guard ran into the room.

'It's Project Nine Hundred sir,' he told Maddox. 'It's reported out of control.'

'Evacuate the plant,' said Maddox without hesitation. 'Order alert A. Maximum alert A.'

All of their natural authority had now evaporated from the Permanent Secretaries and they turned to Maddox and Thornton, their faces expressing their total helplessness.

'Let's get you lot out of here,' said Thornton, and grabbed Connor roughly by the arm, pushing him towards the door. The other men took hold of the jacket of the man in front and stumbled along in procession. Outside in the corridor I.N.I. office staff were running in all directions, barging into each other in their efforts to get out. Some carried bundles of documents which fell off in something like a mad paperchase as they ran. No one stopped to pick them up. Now a siren was wailing, and crackling through it a calm and mechanical voice was being broadcast. 'Green group A collect and report to emergency area eight. Blue group D collect and report to emergency area ten.'

Maddox pushed open an unmarked door and ushered the four men urgently through. Concrete stairs led down three flights to the ground, and outside an emergency exit several large cars were waiting. Maddox practically pushed the four men into the first car and banged the roof twice with the palm of his hand. Instantly it accelerated away in the direction of the gate. As Thornton pulled open the door of the maroon-coloured car another security guard came running towards them.

'Smedley took the journalist and the girl to the village as you ordered, but they're not yet secure. We've also been trying to pick up Jacqueline Smart but we can't find her.'

'Alert the emergency force,' Maddox ordered, then spoke to the driver: 'Get to the village. The explosions will be causing panic and no one must be allowed to escape.'

CHAPTER THIRTY-ONE

'Let's try the phone-box,' said Shilvers, running across the road.

Julia followed him, a few paces behind. Within seconds he had swung open the door and lifted the receiver. He put it to his ear and started clicking the cradle. His brow creased in confusion.

'What is it?' asked Julia.

'Music. Piped bloody music.' He flung down the receiver. Now the caterpillar vehicles were at the bottom of a distant hill and closing all the time.

'Well,' said Shilvers. 'Any ideas?'

At that moment Julia spotted Mrs Penshall crossing the road again, heading towards the little cottage they had earlier seen her leave. They ran across the road towards her, calling her name. She did not respond until they had reached her and Shilvers tapped her on the shoulder. Slowly she turned her head to look at them.

'Mrs Penshall, it's me, Tony Shilvers. Do you remember?' She showed no sign of doing so. Shilvers was aware of the ever growing noise of the approaching convoy. They would be round the corner in a few seconds. Beneath his feet, the earth vibrated.

'I was wondering if we could come in for a cup of tea, Mrs Penshall.' Still she showed no sign of response, no indication that she had even seen him a few moments ago. Any second the military vehicles would appear and it would be too late. Still Shilvers was reluctant to force her. He searched his mind about what to do next. Then Julia spoke.

'Alf told us to call at any time. He said you'd give us a cup of tea any time we were in the area.' Mrs Penshall looked at Julia then back to Shilvers. The words had lit a spark.

'Alf?' Mrs Penshall spoke in a voice which sounded as though she was beginning to stir from a long sleep. 'Oh yes. Do come in.'

Julia and Shilvers bustled through the door at the very moment that the grey-green metal of the first vehicle appeared at the bend. They had not been spotted. They slammed the door. Shilvers pressed his back against it as if to keep out the still growing roar of powerful engines. He was breathing heavily. Julia looked at him and then turned to take Mrs Penshall gently by the arm and guide her towards the kitchen. Shilvers could hear Julia saying what a nice house it was. What to do now? In a few seconds Julia returned.

'She seems perfectly calm. She's making a cup of tea.'

'What do you reckon?' asked Shilvers. By now the vehicles had passed and all was quiet. They must have gone on towards the far end of the village.

'Let's take a look,' said Julia, and they walked into the room which faced the street, cautiously parting the net curtains.

Outside, men in blue air-force style uniforms had alighted from the vehicles and were gathering in groups. An officer was giving them orders. His gestures indicated that they should scatter and search. As the men broke away from the huddle, Shilvers and Julia stepped back. Across the road, two of the uniformed guards were patrolling, looking in shops and alleyways. They carried machine-guns. Both Julia and Shilvers hoped the other had not seen.

'It'll take about ten minutes at the most for them to knock here,' said Shilvers.

Julia looked hard at him. In the street they could hear someone shouting orders. Then Julia spoke.

'Ffitch's car.'

'Don't be crazy,' said Shilvers. 'Even if we get to it we could never drive it out past all these caterpillar trucks.'

'I didn't mean that,' said Julia. 'It has a mobile-phone.'

Shilvers didn't speak for a few seconds. 'Good God, you're right.' He took Julia's face between his hands and kissed her. 'You keep an eye on Mrs Penshall, and I'll go out the back.'

'Forget it,' said Julia. 'I'd have thought you'd have given this rubbish up by now.'

Shilvers knew it was pointless arguing. Seconds later he was looking for the back way out and trying to work out their best route, while Julia was explaining to Mrs Penshall that they would be back for their tea in a few minutes. Mrs Penshall did not seem to mind. The back door of the cottage opened into a yard with a high wall and a wooden door leading out into a back alleyway. Shilvers jumped and pulled himself up to look over the top of the wall. Even as he did so two guards in blue uniforms and carrying machine-guns clattered past on the cobble-stone pavement below. Shilvers kept as still as possible. Below him one of the guards shouted 'Wait!' and the two of them halted. Shilvers held his breath. He was aware that behind him Julia was emerging from the back door of the house, leaving Mrs Penshall calmly drying her hands on an apron. He could not warn her without attracting the attention of the guards. Yet any second she might inadvertently give them away.

'Goodbye, very nice to see you again.' It was Mrs Penshall's voice. The two guards below had heard. Landing on his toes, Shilvers dropped to the ground and as gently as possible he slipped across the bolt on the wooden door leading into the yard. Just on the other side of it, he could hear the shuffling of the two guards. They were waiting for whoever it was to come out. Shilvers turned to Julia and put his finger to his lips. She understood and drew back into the house. Shilvers went back too, and quietly closed the door behind him.

'That's the end of that idea,' he said, 'two I.N.I. guards. We'll have to try the front.' The main road in front of the house was clear except for the distant silhouette of the back end of one of the caterpillar vehicles parked outside the butcher's shop. 'Everything will be all right Mrs Penshall,' said Shilvers, 'Julia and I will be back for that tea in a minute. Tell that to anyone who asks.'

Mrs Penshall smiled amiably as the couple slipped out of the front door and, keeping as close as possible to the walls and ducking underneath windows, they set off towards the spot where they had left Ffitch's car. Once or twice, at corners, they stopped to listen before continuing. It reminded Shilvers of the routine he had seen British soldiers enacting in Belfast. They had gone just a few yards before they heard the sound of running feet approaching at the next corner. Spotting an open door in one of the terraced cottages, Shilvers and Julia darted inside and closed it behind them just as eight or ten uniformed guards double-marched around the corner.

'Spread out. Start searching. Shops first, then houses.'

Shilvers leaned against the door and looked at Julia. She looked behind her, anxious to see whether they had disturbed the occupant of the house. They tiptoed down the passage, past the door into the small front parlour which was firmly closed, towards a door of what seemed to be the kitchen. The door was ajar and they could hear music playing. It's not the radio, thought Shilvers. He listened for a moment. It'was the piped music again.

They edged slowly towards the door. Behind the sound of the music they could hear the occasional clink of someone doing washing-up. Julia turned to look at Shilvers, eyebrows raised in enquiry. As she turned back she gasped involuntarily.

In front of her, standing in the open door, was the shape of a man silhouetted by the light from the kitchen window. As the couple looked at him they saw that he was revoltingly disfigured, his face a bubbling mass of bulges and scars. On one side of his face the skin was drawn tightly across the entire surface, like a sculptor's first effort before carving any features. The other side had gross caricatures of human features, a swollen and distended eye, misshapen nose and a bent slash of a mouth. The man's head was completely bald. With his single eye, the man merely stared at them, silently. Trying hard to compose himself, Shilvers was about to speak when he heard a loud noise behind him.

'Open up. Is anyone at home? Open the door.' It was the guard who had been barking orders, shouting and hammering on the front door. Shilvers turned to look. He could see the door vibrating. He turned again to the man, who continued to look at them, not moving. Julia looked up at him.

'Please?' she said.

There was a pause for a few seconds, then the noisy hammering and shouting began again.

'Coming.' The guttural choke from the man's mouth sent a further shiver down Julia's back. But instead of moving past them towards the door, the man stepped back into his kitchen and beckoned the couple. They looked at each other before stepping forward and into the kitchen. Inside, the man opened the door of a pantry and gestured for the couple to go in. They hesitated, then did so. The man closed the door.

In the darkness Julia and Shilvers held each other but dared not speak. They could just about make out the continued hammering on the front door, which stopped as the man opened it.

'Why have you been so long? Is anyone here? Have you seen any strangers?' The guard's voice was loud and aggressive.

'Strangers?' Julia and Shilvers heard the almost inhuman voice. 'There's been no one here. I've been asleep, but you're making enough noise to wake the dead.' Inside their tiny dark confinement Shilvers held Julia a little tighter.

'Are you sure? Man and a woman. You've seen nothing?'

'Nothing,' they heard the reply. 'Come in and search if you want.' Shilvers and Julia froze.

'That won't be necessary for the moment, but keep alert. Two strangers.' They heard the sound of retreating footsteps on the pavement.

A few seconds later the pantry door was opened, and the man turned away into the kitchen as Julia and Shilvers emerged. Shilvers stepped forward and took his hand. 'Thanks.' Shilvers could feel the grossly distorted fingers. They did not respond to his grip. 'Very many thanks. You're a brave man.'

The man gestured for them to sit at the kitchen table. Julia could make out nothing resembling an expression on his face, but where a few seconds ago she had seen horror, now she saw kindness. She felt grateful.

'You'll be safe for a few minutes now, but not too long mind.' Only the corner of the man's mouth moved as he spoke.

'Can we take a look from an upstairs window?' asked Shilvers. The man nodded and led the way. He was short, perhaps five feet five inches, thought Shilvers, and painfully thin. Shilvers was shocked to see that the small back room of the cottage contained two small beds, and had wallpaper featuring rockets and astronauts. Obviously there were young children here. How was it possible to bring them up in such an environment? The thought made him momentarily nauseous.

From the bedroom window Shilvers could see Ffitch's car. There were guards walking around in groups of two at various points, but none was actually looking after the vehicle. Suddenly Shilvers felt a deep rumble, vibrating through the foundations of the house.

'What's that? Do you feel it?'

Julia held on to his arm. They looked up and saw the light-fitting swinging back and forth. Shilvers looked at the scarred face. The man just shrugged his shoulders, evidently unconcerned. Now the noise had subsided into a low throb, and one which Shilvers seemed to have heard before. He put his head flat against the wall. Yes, once again he could hear that familiar throb of power, like a thousand enormous engines pulsating deep into the earth.

'We're miles from Dounscraig here,' said Julia.

'Which direction is the plant?' Shilvers asked the man.

He gestured with a partly withered hand towards the horizon. Shilvers screwed up his eyes. Was it smoke that he could see? He could not be certain.

'We need to get to that car,' Shilvers told the man. 'Can you help us?'

Again he shrugged his shoulders. 'How?'

'Just divert the guards. You could tell them that we've been spotted in the front, going towards the way out of the village. That'll give us a clear run.' Shilvers saw the man hesitating.

'On the other hand if you're worried, we'll quite understand,' said Julia. 'We wouldn't want you to get into trouble.'

There was a silence, then the man spoke quietly. 'What possible trouble could I be in?' He looked at them with his bulging, horrifying eye. 'What could they do to me that they haven't already done?' He turned and went towards the stairs.

In the back yard the three of them made ready to burst through the wooden door into the alleyway.

'One moment,' said Shilvers. 'We don't even know your name.'

'Penshall,' said the man, 'George Penshall,' and he was gone.

Shilvers and Julia looked at each other for a second, then they heard him shouting outside the gate. 'They're in the street. Making for the west entrance. They're getting away.'

Shilvers jumped and pulled himself up so that he could look over the yard wall. Half a dozen of the guards were rushing around the end of the terrace, leaving a clear run to the car. He jumped down, and as he hit the floor it seemed to move.

'Christ,' said Shilvers, 'it must be a bloody earthquake.' He opened the door and as he did so what seemed like a shock-wave of warm air hit him and knocked him back.

'What the hell?' He looked towards the horizon and now it was for sure, a thick pall of black smoke winding up into the darkening sky.

'Good God. It's Dounscraig.'

Shilvers and Julia leapt forward, past Penshall, towards the car. It was a fifty-yard dash and they made it safely. Once inside, Shilvers reached for the telephone. It was working. He started dialling a familiar number. He paused and looked around him to see that the coast was clear. He completed the number. Next to him Julia was looking around anxiously but there was no one to be seen. In the distance George Penshall was walking awkwardly back into his yard. Now he was closing the wooden door. After what seemed minutes the telephone clicked and Shilvers heard a voice at the other end.

'*Daily Sentinel*.'

'Newsdesk please,' said Shilvers. He heard it ringing and had a momentary image of Frank Chaplin at the newsdesk turning back from the coffee machine to answer the telephone.

'Come on, come on you idle bastard,' said Shilvers helplessly. Just then Julia put her hand on his knee and gripped it.

'Look,' she said calmly.

Around the corner, eighty yards away, a phalanx of a dozen I.N.I. guards was advancing on the car, weapons pointed towards them. They were spreading out as they closed the distance.

'Come on. Come on,' said Shilvers. As he spoke he heard a click and a familiar voice.

'Newsdesk.' It was Chaplin.

The guards were now running. The man in charge had stopped, and Shilvers saw that he was pointing his machine-gun at the car. Another guard reached into the window and grabbed the receiver from Shilvers' hand, jerking the cable loose as he did so. Shilvers had no time to react before there was an enormous flash of blinding white light, followed seconds later by a roar which seemed to enter his body. He looked ahead to see the I.N.I. guards reeling backwards, forearms in front of their eyes. Over to his right he saw a row of running figures dressed in black, spraying machine-gun fire at the patrol of the I.N.I. guards, who fell to the ground as they tried to escape.

Before he could make out who the attackers were, the door was flung open, and someone grabbed him by the arm and started to pull him out of the car. He looked up to see a slight figure dressed from head to foot in black and carrying a sub-machine-gun. This time he recognized the small and beautiful face under the blonde hair. It was Jacqueline Smart.

'Out of the car and follow me.' Her voice allowed no possibility of argument. Immediately Shilvers and Julia got out and ran behind her, back towards the houses. To the right and the left small groups of commandos dressed in black ran across the open ground, firing with sub-machine-guns at the I.N.I. guards. At the road Shilvers could see another group approaching one of the armoured personnel carriers. He watched with growing incredulity as one of them lifted the steel lid on the top and dropped in a grenade. The commandos threw themselves to the ground and seconds later the machine exploded, with flames and smoke belching from every seam. The group in black ran on to approach another of the vehicles from behind. Now the group of three had reached the wall at the back of the row of houses and Jacqueline signalled them to crouch.

'Who the hell are you people?' Shilvers had to shout over the noise.

'There'll be plenty of time for explanations,' said Jacqueline. 'For the moment let's just say that you have walked in and screwed up plans we've been making for two years to blow this little operation open to the world.'

'But I thought you worked for I.N.I.?' asked Julia, shouting to make herself heard against the bursts of gunfire.

'I do, but that's just a day-job.' Jacqueline smiled a fleeting smile and turned to look about her.

Shilvers and Julia were still trying to understand what was happening when the sounds of battle fell away. The momentary calm was broken by the voice of a man in black uniform shouting from the other side of the terrace. The accent was American. It was Gold.

'They're heading out. Direct Action group, gather.'

Jacqueline motioned the couple to follow her as she ran round the buildings to join the rest of the group. When they got there they saw that some thirty commandos were now congregrating, all of them dressed entirely in black. Jacqueline pushed her way through to the centre.

'So you are Anthony Shilvers, the one who has caused us all this trouble?' It was the American voice again, but now it did not sound unfriendly. 'And this will be Julia Somers.' The couple stepped forward.

'I still don't know for sure what's going on, but I'm very glad you people turned up.'

At that moment a distant tremor vibrating through the ground and the buildings around them reminded Shilvers of the earlier rumbles from the direction of Dounscraig. The whole group turned and shielded their eyes from the sky in horror as the plume of smoke belched from the silhouette on the horizon.

'What in the world was that?' Gold articulated the question each of them was thinking.

'I'm afraid I think I know the answer.'

The small voice came from the end of the row of terraces perhaps fifty yards away. Shilvers could see that it was Dr Graham Smedley, now walking slowly towards them. As he approached, Jacqueline Smart broke away from the group and ran to meet him.

'Dad, what in God's name are you doing here?' As father and daughter embraced the man called Gold turned to Shilvers and Julia.

'Jacqueline has been working for us on the inside for five years. Her father is Dr Graham Smedley. He is their top scientist. Until this moment he has known nothing of her real work, for us.'

'It was Smedley who brought us here,' said Julia. 'He told us he was made to do it because I.N.I. were threatening his daughter.' Gold was silent for a moment. Now he knew the answer to something which had been troubling him for several days.

'This explains the recent promotion. They were bringing her close so they would know where to find her if need be.' Now father and daughter were approaching the group, arm in arm.

'That I fear,' said Smedley, 'is Project Nine Hundred.'

'And what, Dr Smedley, is Project Nine Hundred?' asked Gold.

'It's the project that I have been working on for five years. If it had succeeded, it would have made the nuclear industry so safe that even you,' he turned to Jacqueline, 'and even my daughter here, would have approved of it. As it is, in typical fashion, the nuclear industry chose to cut corners and hurry things too fast. The result is what you now see.'

'And what are the consequences?' asked Julia.

'If they are as I think they are, none of us is safe. We need to get as far away as possible.'

'Does that include us?'

The voice had come from the other side of the group of commandos, and they turned to see a huddle of perhaps fifty villagers, clustered together in their fear. The man speaking was George Penshall. Shilvers saw the look of disbelief on the faces of the commandos. The shambling group of men, all of whom had hideously deformed hands and faces, shuffled nearer.

'You bet your life it includes you, and everybody else in the village,' said Smedley from behind them.

'Let's get out of here,' shouted Gold. He pointed to six heavy goods trucks which had brought the Direct Action group and their equipment. Even now commandos were heaving boxes of weapons and ammunition from the backs of the trucks to allow more room for the people of the village. 'You men gather your families and meet back here in five minutes.' The villagers hesitated momentarily, looking at each other as they considered the prospect of leaving. Many had been in the village for several years, and had never faced up to the world in their present state. They had resigned themselves to never having to do so.

'I for one have had all the crap from Dounscraig I'm prepared to have.' It was George Penshall again. 'I say we go.' Without further pause the men headed off towards the houses.

'You go with the others. I'll get Ffitch's car and get hold of Mrs Penshall,' said Shilvers.

'I would have thought you would be tired of that by now. I'm coming with you.' Shilvers smiled. The two hurried back towards the village.

Minutes later they emerged from a small cottage, leading between them the confused and harassed figure of Mrs Penshall. Julia was speaking soothingly to her, and trying to keep her calm as they led her round to where Ffitch's car still stood. As they rounded the last corner Shilvers looked up, and saw the stooping and battered figure of George Ffitch standing to one side and watching them.

'George.'

Julia looked up, and Shilvers let her go on towards the car with Mrs Penshall. Now alone, he stood for a few moments and looked at the pathetic figure before walking the few paces to where Ffitch was standing. When he spoke it was a plea for some understanding or explanation.

'Why couldn't you tell me, George, for Christ's sake? All the years we've known each other, why couldn't you tell me?' Shilvers' voice cracked as he spoke.

Ffitch was looking through him into space. For a moment Shilvers thought he had not heard. When at last he spoke his grainy voice was soft and tired.

'When did it all begin? I don't know. One moment I was an eager beaver sniffing around the best story of my life, the next the nightmare had begun.'

'But why couldn't you tell me, George. It's me, Tony. You could have, should have told me. I might have been able to help.'

'I don't know. I didn't want you to get involved like I was. I didn't want you to have to make the compromises I had to make. I had to watch you to make sure you didn't make the mistake of getting too close as I did. I was doing it for you as much as for them.' Now he turned to look at Shilvers and his voice was more urgent. 'I had no choice. You can see that now can't you? I had no choice.' Shilvers returned his look, and saw his own desperation reflected in the expression on Ffitch's face. He stepped forward.

'Yes,' said Shilvers, putting one hand on Fiftch's shoulder, 'I can see you had no choice.' The two men stood silently for a few seconds. 'Now it's time to get your wife and daughter and come with us.'

Ffitch shook his head. 'No. I will go to them. You get away just now. Make a run for it. I'll go to where they are.'

'But George, Smedley says Dounscraig could blow at any moment. We have to get away.' He pulled at Ffitch's arm, but the older man pushed him away violently. He was shouting.

'No! It's too late for me now. Remember, I helped to do away with that woman's husband. Do you think I could face her, even in the state she's in? You get on your way. Leave me to my own.' With an extravagant wave of his hand he gestured Shilvers roughly aside.

Shilvers waited until a blast from the horn of the car behind him brought him back to the moment. He looked over his shoulder to see Julia in the driving seat and Mrs Penshall installed in the back. In the earlier battle the car had been hit by a small shell, blowing the aerials from the roof and smashing the windows, but it was otherwise undamaged.

'So long George. I hope you make it.'

Ffitch did not reply, but turned and walked slowly back towards the village.

Julia drove along rough dirt-tracks away from Dounscraig in the general direction taken by the convoy of vehicles. In the back seat Mrs Penshall sat silently. Shilvers glanced over his shoulder at her and saw that she was casually looking out of the window, as though on an afternoon outing.

Twenty minutes later, with the convoy of heavy trucks carrying the commandos and villagers making its way across the fields behind them, they approached the nearest village. Julia drove the car directly into the village square.

The scene that greeted them was pandemonium. Everywhere there were people running in all directions, some with suitcases, all trying to pile themselves and their belongings into cars, which blocked every street in every direction. Horns were blasting and in places larger vehicles were literally barging smaller ones out of their way. On the horizon a thick column of black smoke was now rising steadily from the direction of Dounscraig. Shilvers leapt out of the car and ran across the square to a telephone-box. Once again he began to dial the familiar number.

He was interrupted by the sound of an explosion and a dreadful scream from a woman a few yards from him. He looked up to see the last moments before the first of the convoy of trucks careered out of control into the square and, with a jarring crunch of metal, slammed into the side of a tractor which had been abandoned half-way across the road. On impact the back of the truck swung open, and from his vantage point it looked as though a score of bodies were flung out of the vehicle to land in a pile on the side of the road. Some villagers ran towards the scene, and as they did so the other vehicles in the convoy stopped and the passengers began to pile out from every door.

Shilvers looked round urgently for the cause of the impact. He saw it at the far side of the village square. Set close beside a low wall of heavy stone was a small group of I.N.I. guards, gathered around something resembling a mortar. Shilvers saw that the missile they had fired must have travelled just over the heads of dozens of villagers before hitting the truck. Behind the armoured car which had carried the I.N.I. guards Shilvers could see, tucked away around the next corner, the front of a large maroon car. Through the windscreen he could just make out the shapes of two men. One of them was speaking into a microphone. Maddox and Thornton? Yes, he could see them properly now.

Shilvers watched helplessly as the group of local villagers gained their first sight of their neighbours from the village five miles away. Some were trying to extricate themselves from the mass of people who had been thrown from the trucks, others were attempting to get to their feet. Shilvers saw George Penshall gathering some of the men together. Once organized they picked up bricks and pieces of wood from the debris all around them. Then they began to cross the tangled wreckage of cars towards the I.N.I. guards. Gathered together and loping along they looked like a scene from an appalling nightmare. At one moment the locals were in full flight towards the scene of the crash, and a moment later they had stopped in their tracks.

The I.N.I. guards were struggling to reload their mortar, and they managed to fire off a further charge which whistled through the air and hit a wall next to the overturned truck, adding to the mêlée. But by now Penshall's group had arrived at the emplacement, and Shilvers watched as arms lifted high in the air and mercilessly crashed down on the heads of the I.N.I. men.

From the car, Maddox and Thornton saw the danger they were in. In panic Thornton struggled to start the engine and looked about him for a way out. The car was jammed in by other vehicles all around, and now Penshall's group was approaching, the clubs and bricks they carried covered in the blood of the guards. Both men were paralysed with fear, and remained in their seats as the group of their own workers, whose lives had been so hideously scarred, came nearer.

In the midst of the panic and pandemonium there was a moment of total silence. It was broken by a long, chilling scream as George Penshall smashed the car window with a large boulder. In a few grim moments each of the men sought to avenge years of inexpressible misery.

Shilvers' attention was caught by a woman with a pram, who had fallen to the floor and was in a dead faint. All around him Shilvers could see people recoiling in horror at the grisly sight of the villagers from the convoy coming nearer. Each man was like a partially melted wax-work of his former self, and in almost every case the mutilations had left physical disabilities which meant that they shambled along in a grotesque parade.

Now people were falling out of their cars as they tried to run away in their fear. The head of the group of villagers was close by and from the other direction Shilvers saw George Penshall approaching the telephone-box where he stood.

'*Daily Sentinel*.' He could hear the voice in his ear growing in impatience and urgency but could not find a way to speak any words. 'This is the *Daily Sentinel*, can I help you?'

Shilvers' eyes were immovably fixed on the nightmare before him. He saw Penshall a few feet away from him, and at his approach the villagers falling back in horror. Shilvers was watching the dreadfully deformed face as it distorted still further in a mask of agony and appeared to light up as it reflected the shattering flash of light. Then he felt and heard a vast noise apparently coming from every direction at once. He looked at the people running in panic. For a second it almost seemed that they were transparent as they were lifted up in the air and thrown bodily on to their backs. At the same moment Shilvers turned to the car where Julia and Mrs Penshall were still sitting. He watched, quite helpless, as the force of the blast lifted the car into the air, back first, so that it was standing momentarily on its nose.

'Hello. Hello.' Shilvers could still hear the voice coming from the receiver which he was pressing painfully to his ear. The car hung in mid-air for endless moments, as though deciding whether it would roll on to the roof or bounce back. After agonizing seconds the car fell forward with a sickening jolt which smashed the roof flat in one movement. Shilvers was paralysed with horror as he saw, as though in slow motion, Julia's head pushed back over the seat and crack like a plastic doll. He screamed a long long scream that went on inside his head for many seconds after it had subsided into a sob in his throat. 'I'm back to stay you know.' 'I do love you.' Her words echoed in his brain mixing with the cacophony of his own screams and the hell that was all around him.

Shilvers managed to turn his neck to look behind him. There it was, the unmistakable shape, grey and silver against the now deep red sky. Half a mile into the air it went, a thin column like an almighty pillar, and then billowing outwards and on upwards into the heavens. Shilvers just had time to register it before it hit him, a wall of heat smashing its way across the countryside, burning out trees, hedges, cows in the fields and haystacks in its path.

'Hello. Hello. What the hell is going on?' was the distant voice in his ear.

'You'll never know,' said Shilvers.

Gerald Seymour

writes internationally best-selling thrillers

'Not since Le Carré has the emergence of an international suspense writer been as stunning as that of Gerald Seymour.' *Los Angeles Times*

HARRY'S GAME
KINGFISHER
RED FOX
THE CONTRACT
ARCHANGEL
IN HONOUR BOUND
FIELD OF BLOOD

FONTANA PAPERBACKS